Lauren St John

KENTUCKY THRILLER
AND
RENDEZVOUS
IN RUSSIA

Two Laura Marlin Mysteries

Illustrated by David Dean

Orion
Children's Books

This omnibus edition first published in Great Britain in 2015
by Orion Children's Books
Originally published as two separate volumes:
Kentucky Thriller
First published in Great Britain in 2012
by Orion Children's Books
Rendezvous in Russia
First published in Great Britain in 2013
by Orion Children's Books
an imprint of the Hachette Children's Group
and published by Hodder and Stoughton Limited

Orion House
5 Upper St Martin's Lane
London WC2H 9EA
An Hachette UK Company

3 5 7 9 10 8 6 4

Text copyright © Lauren St John 2012, 2013
Illustrations copyright © David Dean 2012, 2013

The paper and board in this paperback are natural recyclable
products made from wood grown in sustainable forests.
The manufacturing processes conform to the
environmental regulations of the country of origin.

A catalogue record for this book is available from the British Library

Printed in Great Britain by Clays Ltd, Elcograf S.p.A.

ISBN 978 1 4440 1413 6

www.orionchildrensbooks.co.uk

KENTUCKY THRILLER
AND
RENDEZVOUS IN RUSSIA

Two Laura Marlin Mysteries

Also by Lauren St John

The White Giraffe Quartet
The White Giraffe
Dolphin Song
The Last Leopard
The Elephant's Tale

The Laura Marlin Mysteries
Dead Man's Cove
Kidnap in the Caribbean

The One Dollar Horse Trilogy
The One Dollar Horse
Race the Wind
Fire Storm

The Glory

CONTENTS

A LAURA MARLIN
MYSTERY

KENTUCKY THRILLER

Lauren St John

Illustrated by David Dean

Orion
Children's Books

*For Thomas Beattie, whose beautiful thoroughbreds
(Troubleshooter especially) so inspired me as a child*

THE HORSEBOX WAS lying on its side when they came over the rise. Afterwards, it occurred to Laura Marlin that if they'd done one thing differently that morning their story would have been someone else's story, only it would have had another ending entirely, and who's to say whether that ending would have been good or bad.

Laura had a theory that life was like a passage and how things turned out depended on which doors you opened or which ones opened for you. For instance, fate could have decreed that she remain forever at Sylvan Meadows Children's Home, where she'd lived since her mum had died giving birth to her. Even now she could have been in her old room overlooking the car park, longing for a life of excitement and adventure like the characters in her books while in reality having nothing to look forward to but another meal of glutinous porridge or bleached vegetables.

Instead, a door in the corridor of Laura's desperately dull existence had blown wide open and who should be waiting on the other side but Calvin Redfern, her mother's brother. He was a fisheries inspector with the handsome but slightly careworn looks of the hero of an old black and white movie. When he'd learned of her existence five months earlier, he'd immediately come forward to claim her. Before Laura knew it, she was living at number 28 Ocean View Terrace in the beautiful seaside town of St Ives, Cornwall, had adopted a three-legged husky named Skye, and was up to her ears in all the adventures she could handle.

That was how she'd met Tariq, a Bengali boy from Bangladesh in South Asia, who'd become her best friend. They were the same age, but where Laura had a cap of pale blonde hair and peaches and cream skin, Tariq was the colour of burnt honey, with glossy black hair shaved short at the back. His brutal childhood as a slave, first in a quarry in his home country and later in St Ives until he was rescued by Laura, had left him thin but very strong, and was responsible for the shadows that sometimes showed in his tiger's eyes before his easy laugh chased them away again.

Tariq and Laura did everything together and for that reason he was the first person she called when her uncle woke up on that sparkling Saturday in April and spontaneously decided they should go to Sennen Cove for a picnic. That should have set the scene for a perfect day, but almost immediately a series of things conspired to delay them.

First, Tariq was twenty minutes late. As he was leaving his foster parents' home near Carbis Bay, a car screeched up and he had to help his foster father, Rob Ashworth, a vet, with a cat emergency.

Next, Skye slipped his lead as Laura was coaxing him into the car. He went racing down the road after a seagull while their eccentric neighbour, Mrs Crabtree, yelled approval. That had held them up for a further eight minutes, and they lost more time still when they drove away without the picnic basket and had to return for it.

All of which meant that they were approximately thirty-six minutes later than they'd intended to be as they twisted through the sunny lanes past fields dotted with sheep. That didn't matter since they weren't on a schedule, but it was the reason Laura's uncle decided to take a shortcut. 'It's such a beautiful day that it seems a shame to waste a second of it,' he'd said. Shortly afterwards, they flew over a blind hill into a shadowed copse and almost crashed into the horsebox.

If it wasn't for the fact that former Chief Inspector Redfern had taken part in numerous high-speed pursuits in years gone by when he was Scotland's most famous detective and thus had lightning reactions, they'd have had a head-on collision. As it was the children were slammed hard against their seatbelts as he braked, swerved and brought the car to a skidding halt beneath a canopy of dark trees. An overnight shower had made the road slicker than an oil spill.

When Laura opened her eyes, he was staring down at her anxiously.

'Laura, are you all right? You've had quite a scare. Thank goodness you and Tariq were strapped in. If something had happened to you both, I'd never have forgiven myself. Skye, are you okay? If you're still capable of washing my face, I guess you are. Well done, Laura, for hanging on to him.'

Laura clambered from the car, bruised, cold and shaky. She leaned on Skye and he whined and licked her hand. Tariq was pale beneath his dark skin. For a good two minutes nobody spoke. Calvin Redfern dug the flask out of the picnic basket and poured them each a cup of hot, sweet coffee 'for the shock'. He gave Skye a couple of dog biscuits. Then the trio stood in the green gloom, regarding the horsebox that could have killed them as if it were a hostile spacecraft that had landed in their path with the sole intention of harming them.

'You can tell from the skid marks what's happened,' Calvin Redfern explained, breaking the silence. 'The driver swerved to avoid something – a rabbit or a deer – and the trailer hitch snapped off, causing the horsebox to overturn. It's an ancient thing, barely roadworthy. I dread to think what sort of injuries the pony or donkey or whatever was in there sustained. Presumably the owner was unhurt because he or she managed to drive away, as you can tell from the muddy tracks.

'I'm surprised your foster father didn't get a call, Tariq.

He's one of the best vets around. Then again, maybe the horsebox was empty. Probably was since I can't see any hoof prints. At any rate, it would have been helpful if the driver had phoned the incident in so that the police could have towed the damaged box out of the road. We need to act fast to prevent a serious accident. Laura, would you mind if I borrowed your red sweatshirt? You can wear my jumper. You're in shock and I don't want you getting a chill.'

As Laura shrugged out of her top, he found a stout stick and stripped it of its leaves. Tying the sweatshirt to one end, he handed it to Tariq. 'Son, I need your help. While I call the police, would you mind standing at the top of the rise and waving this as a red flag warning if any vehicles approach? Make sure you stand safely on the side of the road. There's plenty of visibility coming the other way, so I think the blind hill is our main concern.'

As the boy hurried away, Calvin leaned against his car and took out his mobile phone. 'Laura, would you be good enough to call out the number plate of the horsebox when I get through to the police?'

'No problem.' Yet as Laura walked towards the fallen horsebox with Skye, she felt oddly scared. Overhead, the twisting grey branches of the trees laced together like hands, their dense black foliage muffling the birdsong and shutting out the sunshine. As she circled the horsebox, noting the cracked old tyres, buckled mudguards and caved-in rear, something struck her as strange. There *was* no number plate. In the place where it should have been was an empty slot. Curiously, the area around it was free

5

of dust, almost as if the driver had wiped it clean after the accident. A couple of screws lay on the ground nearby.

'Hold on a minute, Pete,' her uncle was saying into his phone. He put his hand over the mouthpiece. 'What is it, Laura?'

'There is none. No number plate, I mean.'

'What do you mean? Has it fallen off in the crash?' He marched over to her. She saw surprise register on his face. He took in the screws on the ground and the polished bumper. 'Pete, there's something wrong here. The plate's gone and it seems as if someone's gone to a fair amount of effort to erase any fingerprints. I'll take a look and call you back. In the meantime, I'd appreciate it if you could send that tow truck right away.'

The last three words were almost drowned out by a blood-curdling growl from Skye, who was sniffing the horsebox. This was followed almost immediately by a dull thud.

Calvin Redfern went still. 'I don't believe it.'

'I think I saw something move!' cried Laura, crouching down and peering into the darkness of the box. 'Uncle Calvin, there's a pony inside. I think it's still alive.'

Two violent thuds followed, rocking the trailer. 'Alive and kicking by the sound of things.' Calvin Redfern hit the speed dial on his phone. 'I'm calling Rob Ashworth. We need a vet urgently. Laura, take Skye to the car and lock him in. We don't want him frightening the creature any more than it already has been.'

By the time Laura returned, splinters were flying. She bent down and tried talking to the pony in a soothing voice. It worked until two cars drove through the tunnel of trees. Flagged down by Tariq, they drove relatively slowly, but one had music blaring and didn't bother turning it down. The animal started kicking harder than ever.

Calvin Redfern checked his watch. 'It'll be at least ten minutes before Rob gets here. We're going to have to try to help the poor creature before it injures itself any further. Laura, help me try to pull the side back. It's in a wretched state, this horsebox. It wouldn't surprise me if the driver fled the scene because he didn't want to be held responsible. He probably thought the horse was dead.'

'Maybe he was a horse thief,' suggested Laura, pulling with all her strength at the wooden planks that held the box together. She felt one give.

Despite the situation, her uncle laughed as he tackled a screw with his penknife. 'You read too many Matt Walker novels,' he teased, alluding to the fictional detective inspector who was Laura's hero. 'You're always looking for mysteries to solve. It's not that horse thieves don't exist. There are plenty about, make no mistake about that, just not around here. I doubt the Cornish police are overburdened with reports of abandoned stolen ponies on idyllic country lanes.'

'But why else would the driver have gone away and simply left it?' asked Laura, jumping back as a hoof struck the side of the box again, showering her with splinters.

'There could be a million reasons. Maybe he'd been drinking. Perhaps he was uninsured. The pony was silent when we got here, which probably means it was unconscious. The owner might have assumed it was either

7

fatally injured or dead and decided that he or she didn't want to pay the vet bills. There are any number of reasons.'

A pickup truck rattled over the hill, its headlights pushing back the shadows. It squeaked to a halt beside them and a man with the ruddy, weather-beaten face of a fisherman or farmer leaned from the window. 'Need any help, mate?'

Whatever was in the horsebox launched a final assault on the sagging wood. The side exploded, like a boat disintegrating under the onslaught of a hurricane. Tariq came running down the road. 'What's going on? It sounded as if a bomb went off.'

There was a squeal of rage and the creature beneath the wood stirred and gathered itself. Laura caught a glimpse of a chestnut ear and a length of dusty mane before the beast gathered itself and surged to its feet, shaking off debris like a phoenix emerging from the ashes.

She gasped. In the white glow of headlights, the coat of the stallion was all flash and fire, his flaring nostrils scarlet. Every inch of him rippled with muscle. He stood on the wreckage of the horsebox, statuesque in his perfection, gazing at them with a mixture of terror and pride.

Calvin Redfern exhaled. 'I'm not an expert but I will say one thing. That's no pony.'

2

'IF WE CAN'T FIND his owner, can we keep him?'

Laura hung over the fence and gazed adoringly at the red stallion as he tore around the field behind the Carbis Bay Riding Centre. In the week since they'd rescued him, she and Tariq had been to visit him every day after school and now it was Saturday and she still couldn't get over how magnificent he was, or that he was temporarily theirs. When the sunlight danced across his coat, little jets of flame seemed to shoot from it. Catching sight of his audience, he swerved in their direction and came to a prancing halt. Laura offered him an apple. He took it from her delicately.

9

A smile tugged at the corner of Calvin Redfern's mouth. 'No. We absolutely can't keep him.'

Laura wiped her hands on her jeans. In her experience, grown-ups mostly said no without thinking. It was their first response and Laura rarely accepted it without question. 'Why not?'

He laughed. 'How many reasons do you want me to give you? For one thing, I can't afford it on a fisheries investigator's salary. We've been taking care of him for a mere seven days and he's already cost a king's ransom in medicine and food and livery charges. If it weren't for Rob's generosity in treating him for free, I'd be bankrupt. But it's not just that. Who would exercise him? You and Tariq? Me? I'd sooner face down a gang of armed robbers.'

Laura knew what he meant. Over the past week she'd spent many happy hours daydreaming about forming a unique bond with the red stallion, one which would result in her being able to gallop him bareback through the surf on Porthmeor Beach in St Ives, the envy of all. She'd imagined sitting in tandem with Tariq on the horse's high red back as he carried them through poppy-scattered meadows or along the cliff path past Dead Man's Cove, Skye loping by his side.

At the same time, she was quite intimidated by the stallion. He towered over her. Jeanette, the stable girl, said that he was close to 17 hands high. Apart from a few minor cuts and bruises and a slightly swollen fetlock, now healed, he'd suffered remarkably few ill effects from the accident. When he tore across the field, his great hooves seemed to eat up the ground at a furious pace. There was something gloriously wild and almost dangerous about him.

'Are you listening to a word I'm saying?' demanded her uncle, his tone exasperated.

'Of course I am,' said Laura, not altogether truthfully. She caught Tariq's eye as he handed the horse a couple of carrots and grinned. She knew that he too had been fantasising about a summer holiday full of adventures with the red stallion and the husky and that if there was anyone who could turn that fantasy into reality it was her best friend. His foster dad was always saying that Tariq had a way with animals. Something about him seemed to make them happy.

Calvin Redfern sighed. 'Laura, do you really believe that a horse that looks like this, a thoroughbred worthy of a king, has no owner?'

'Well, no, but maybe his owner couldn't afford to keep him, or had no insurance and was worried about the vet bill if he was injured.'

Her uncle rubbed the horse behind his ears. The red stallion tilted his head on one side and looked positively soppy. 'Possibly, but what's much more likely is that he's been kidnapped, possibly for a ransom of some kind.'

Laura stared at him. 'I thought you said that the Cornish police weren't exactly overburdened with cases of abandoned stolen ponies.'

He smiled. 'That's true. I did. But that was before the St Ives police rang me with the results of the forensic tests on the horsebox.'

Laura craned forward so eagerly that she nearly fell off the fence. The red stallion rubbed his head against her and she lost her fight with gravity. She landed on her feet, laughing. 'And . . . ?'

'Well, there are none.'

'You mean they didn't find any evidence?' said Tariq. 'No fingerprints or DNA?'

'Not a thing. It had been wiped completely clean. Tellingly, the serial number on the chassis of the horsebox had been removed – a favourite trick of vehicle thieves. And, judging by that little nick on the horse's neck, the microchip that would have identified him has been removed. But here's what's peculiar. My detective friend, Pete Watson, has trawled the stolen horse database, and I've made a couple of discreet enquiries in the horse racing world via a friend of mine who is head of security at one of the biggest racetracks. No horse matching the red stallion's description has been reported missing.'

The subject of their discussion tossed his head, wheeled and burst into a flat out gallop. Round the field he swept, ears pricked, running for the sheer joy of it.

Tariq was awestruck by his tremendous speed. 'Hard to believe no one would notice if a horse like that vanished.'

'If that beast carries on tearing up my good grass like that, I'll be charging you extra,' warned Vicky Pendleton, a hefty woman with a swinging brown bob and cheerful face. 'Trouble is, I don't have any stables free at the moment. I was going to suggest that you move him to Tip Top Riding Centre over near Penzance, but they had a break-in last night, which doesn't exactly inspire confidence.'

Calvin Redfern, leaning against the fence watching the horse, glanced round. 'Tip Top Riding Centre? You mean the most rundown stables in Cornwall. That place is one stiff breeze away from collapsing in a heap. What were the thieves after? Rusty nails? A bridle held together with string?'

'Hard to say. Nothing was taken. Third in a row, though – well, one was a farm but it was the same story.'

'Third what in a row?' prompted Laura.

Vicky pursed her lips. 'Third break-in in three nights at an equestrian centre. Two riding schools and Hidden Bounty farm, which runs pony trekking holidays. In each case nothing was taken and none of the horses were harmed so the only people who called the police were the owners of Tip Top. The constable who visited told them it was probably teenagers out for a laugh or lazy burglars.'

Laura thought: Or the driver of the horsebox in search of his red stallion. There was a glint in her uncle's eyes and she wondered if he was thinking the same thing. 'What do you think these lazy burglars are after?'

Vicky had her hands on her hips. 'Well, if it's money they want they'll be sorely disappointed if they come looking for it here. The way business is going, they'll be lucky if they can find any loose change down the back of the sofa. Still I'm not going to take any chances with my horses. For the next few nights, my twin nephews are going to guard the place.'

She nodded towards the car park, where a multi-coloured VW van was pulling in. Out climbed two young men with salt-crinkled surfer hair. Their biceps and chests bulged as if they'd been blown up with bicycle pumps.

Calvin Redfern did a double take. 'Good grief, Vicky,

13

what kind of trouble are you expecting? An armed gang? A dozen trained Ninjas.'

'Better safe than sorry,' Vicky told him as she strode away to greet her nephews, Sam and Scott 'They're both black belts in karate. Bruce Lee himself couldn't get past them.'

Laura was of the opinion that the more burly bodyguards the red stallion had the better. She couldn't bear the idea of the horse being stolen again, particularly by the thieves who'd nearly killed him with their reckless driving. She was about to ask her uncle for his opinion on the riding centre break-ins when Tariq said: 'What's that on your T-shirt, Laura?'

'Where?' Laura examined her front, expecting to see a brown stain. To the despair of Rowenna, their housekeeper, she spilled her morning cup of coffee with monotonous regularity.

'Try the back.'

Her uncle turned her round so he could inspect the damage. 'Laura, what on earth have you been doing? You have chestnut stripes across your shoulders. You look like an escaped tiger. Where . . . ? Ohhh . . .'

His eyes met Tariq's and they both turned to gaze at the red stallion sauntering towards them, dark with sweat after his run.

Laura knew what they were thinking. The horse had rubbed his head against her. If he'd left chestnut marks behind, there could be only one explanation. She reached out a hand and rubbed the horse's forehead. A few bright chestnut hairs came loose. The base of the hair was snow white. 'His face has been dyed to disguise his identity,' she cried excitedly. 'He has a star or something.'

'That confirms he's been stolen,' said Tariq.

Calvin Redfern frowned. 'That would seem to be the case. What we have to discover is why and by whom?'

He stopped abruptly. 'Listen to me. I'm talking as if I'm still a detective when all I do these days is arrest fishermen who catch too many fish. And you two are supposed to be having fun and staying out of trouble for once. It's not long since we returned from the Caribbean where you had enough adventures to last you a lifetime. Let's have some peace for a change.'

He held up his hand. 'Don't fret, Laura, I'm going to make a quick call to Detective Watson to tell him that he needs to search for the owner of a red chestnut stallion with a blaze. But then we're going to forget all about it and go on the picnic we missed out on last week. This is a police matter now.'

'But . . . !' Laura protested. She got no further.

Jeanette, the stable girl, came rushing out of the riding centre office, blonde hair streaming behind her. 'Mr Redfern, you'd better come quickly. I think you'll want to see this.'

3

'**OUR RED STALLION!**' Laura cried in wonder after she, Tariq and her uncle had watched the horse sweep to an epic victory in the Kentucky Derby on Vicky's old TV at Carbis Bay Riding Centre. Calvin Redfern had explained that in the US the race was known as the 'Durby' and not the 'Darby' as it was pronounced in England.

Laura peeked out of the window to double check that the horse was still in Vicky's field and not a figment of her imagination. He was there. His ears were pricked and he was gazing into the distance as if straining to see the faraway home from which he'd been snatched.

On television, the red stallion looked quite different. His

fiery coat was offset by a big white blaze, and his muscles rippled with effort as he surged past the other horses. His name, it turned out, was Gold Rush. Fans called him Goldie.

'And a gold rush he has proved to be for his owners, Americans Blake and Christine Wainright,' the newsreader enthused on the BBC lunchtime news. 'After breaking several track records as a two-year-old, he went on to win the coveted Triple Crown at three, achieving legendary status. Ten days ago, Goldie, as he is known to his fans, now retired at the grand old age of seven and worth $75 million . . .'

Tariq gasped.

Laura's mouth dropped open. *'Seventy-five million!* For a *horse . . .'*

'Shhh,' scolded Vicky. 'We're trying to listen.'

'. . . was stolen when the lorry in which he was travelling to his Kentucky home in the US was ambushed by masked raiders. Two stable employees were seriously injured trying to stop them. The theft was kept a secret from the media and public while the Wainwrights attempted to negotiate with the kidnappers. On the advice of detectives, the family refused to pay a ransom demand. A week ago, the kidnappers disappeared into thin air. Now Kentucky police are appealing . . .'

A breaking news headline scrolled along the bottom of the screen: REWARD OFFERED FOR SAFE RETURN OF $75 MILLION KENTUCKY DERBY STAR.

The newsreader turned her attention to a factory fire drama in Scotland and Vicky switched off the TV. Everyone in the office rushed outside to see the red stallion, including the beefy nephews, Sam and Scott.

'Doesn't seem such a silly idea now, getting in reinforcements,' Vicky remarked to Calvin Redfern.

'No,' he agreed. 'It doesn't. And we might need even more. I'll speak to the police about it. We have to try to keep this quiet until Detective Watson can get in touch with Goldie's owners, the Wainwrights, but I doubt we'll be successful. Before you know it, you'll be swamped with reporters. Dozens of cranks will be claiming they own the horse, or trying to collect the reward. But that's not what's worrying me. My concern is that any gang professional enough, and determined enough, to snatch a multi-million dollar racehorse and whisk it across the Atlantic, is likely to try again.'

A chill went through Laura as it occurred to her that the infamous Straight A's were just such a gang. They were professional enough and determined enough to kidnap a famous horse and spirit it across the sea. But she put the thought firmly from her head. The Straight A gang were criminal masterminds. Their cunning schemes usually involved millions or billions of pounds. Twice she and Tariq had got in the way of the Straight A's' wicked plans and twice they'd almost paid with their lives. But it was hard to imagine the gang going to the effort and expense of stealing a horse from America, only to abandon it by the roadside in some battered horsebox.

'Should we hide Goldie in a stable to keep him safe?' Vicky asked.

Laura looked round. 'Wouldn't that make it too easy for

the gang to get him into a corner and catch him if they do slip past your nephews?'

'Plus he might injure himself if he panicked in a confined space,' Tariq put in.

'Mmm, I think Tariq and Laura have a point,' Calvin Redfern told Vicky. 'The field might be the safest place for him, especially if you put a few others horses in with him. He'll have the space to run away if the worst comes to the worst. They'll have a heck of a job to catch him. But hopefully it won't come to that.'

'Would you like me to leave Skye here for added security?' Laura offered, but Vicky drew the line at that. Her aged fox terrier was, she claimed, the best burglar alarm in Cornwall and she refused to have his nose put out of joint by a husky, even if it was one with three legs and a history of spotting villains.

It was a decision she'd soon regret.

The phone call that changed everything had come later that day as they'd walked through the door of number 28 Ocean View Terrace. The picnic had been postponed yet again after they'd discovered the red stallion's true identity, because Calvin Redfern needed to speak to the police and there was Goldie's security to organise. By the time they'd driven back to St Ives, a late afternoon breeze was crinkling the sea around Porthminster Beach. The slowly sinking sun illuminated the shallows

19

and turned them a Greek Island turquoise.

Skye bounded noisily up the steps to greet Rowenna, their housekeeper. He was making such a racket that Laura almost didn't hear the phone ring, but at the last second she managed to grab the receiver.

'Quiet, Skye. Shhh! I'm sorry. Hello?'

'Evenin', ma'am,' drawled a rich, mellow voice. 'My apologies for disturbin' you. It sure sounds as if you have your hands full.'

'Oh, that's just Skye, my husky. He loves life.'

A laugh boomed from the receiver. 'A philosophy of which I heartily approve. Now young lady, I believe you have something that belongs to me. Something very precious. Thanks to your kindness in rescuing him, I'm told you are in possession of my horse, Gold Rush. We call him Goldie. We think of him as family, the same way you probably do about your husky.'

Laura had warmed to Blake Wainright on the phone and she'd done so again when he walked through the door twenty-four hours later, and not just because he made a big fuss of Skye. He was a tall, sinewy man dressed in the type of black suit and flowing white shirt a country singer might wear. As she showed him into the living room, she'd noticed that he had a long, range-walking stride, and that his eyes were the colour of faded jeans with deep smile lines around the corners. He had silver-white hair rippling over his collar, and a perfectly curled moustache. At the end of his long legs, now stretched out in front of him, was a pair of steel-tipped black cowboy boots with red stitching.

'You've heard of Shergar, I presume?'

Laura cupped her chin with her palm and leant forward so she wouldn't miss a single word of Blake's slow, musical drawl. It was an accent that conjured up images from a film she'd seen about America's Deep South. Of treacle-dark bayous overhung with oaks draped in Spanish moss, of alligators blinking in their depths, of white-whiskered black men playing the blues, of plates piled high with pink crawfish, of horse-drawn carts festooned in roses and steamboats on the Mississippi.

But Blake Wainright was not from New Orleans, the subject of the movie. He was from Lexington, Kentucky, a very different corner of the South if the photos on his mobile were anything to go by. They showed fields of lush green grass lined with white fences, behind which dozens of shining thoroughbreds grazed. Lexington was, he'd told them, the heart of the racing industry in the US; birthplace of some of the fastest horses ever to scorch the track.

Among the greatest of these was the red stallion.

'You've heard of Shergar, I presume?' Blake Wainright asked again. Calvin Redfern had gone into his study to call Vicky at the stables, so Laura and Tariq were drinking coffee with the visitor.

Tariq said shyly: 'My foster dad, Rob Ashworth – he's the vet who treated Goldie after the accident – mentioned him last night. When I told him that Gold Rush had been stolen by a gang demanding a ransom, he said: "Shades of Shergar".'

Blake Wainright's moustache twitched. 'Shades of

Shergar indeed. Did he explain further?'

'He said that Shergar was one of the greatest horses in the history of Irish racing – a horse to make your heart sing. He described him as a big bay with four white socks and a blaze and a loving, bombproof personality, and said that some of his wins were so effortless he barely seemed to break out of a canter. He said that to the people of Ireland, Shergar was a national hero.'

'I couldn't have put it better myself.' Blake Wainright's voice was so gravelly that it resonated in Laura's chest. 'Unfortunately for that wonderful horse, fate took a cruel twist. On a foggy winter's night in 1983, masked men in balaclavas drove into Ballymany Stud in County Kildare with a trailer. They tied up the family of his groom, James Fitzgerald, and forced James at gunpoint to load Shergar. The horse was driven away and that was the last anyone ever saw of him.'

Laura was on the edge of her seat. 'He vanished without trace?'

'Without trace. To this day, no one knows what became of him, although there are many theories and some of those involved have confessed anonymously.'

'My uncle would have found Shergar if they'd thought of calling him,' Laura told him loyally. 'He's a fisheries inspector now, but he used to be one of the best detectives in the country – as good as Matt Walker. Matt's a fictional detective but he's a genius.'

Blake Wainright raised an amused eyebrow. 'Is that right? Sounds as if both of them should have been on the case. There was a lot of police bungling – not helped by the fact that eight long hours elapsed before the cops were told that the horse was missing, so vital time and evidence was lost. The gang issued a series of ransom demands, but it soon became clear they'd made a critical error. They believed that the horse was owned by the Aga Khan, one of the richest men in the world. In fact, he was owned by thirty-five shareholders – what's known as a syndicate. Quite correctly, the shareholders refused to pay the ransom and the horse was never seen alive again. To this day, nobody involved in the crime has ever been caught or brought to justice.'

'That's one of the saddest stories I've ever heard,' said Laura. 'Poor Shergar. Can you imagine how terrified and alone he must have felt. When Goldie was stolen, weren't you afraid that the same thing would happen to him?'

Blake Wainright stared hard into his coffee cup. He cleared his throat, his faded blue eyes suddenly moist. 'Like I said, Goldie is family to us. People keep going on about the money, but that's the last thing on my mind. I've hardly slept since the horse was taken. When the police called to say that he'd been found, it was like being handed fifty Christmas presents all at once. I jumped on the first plane from Kentucky to Newquay via London, and caught a taxi to St Ives. So here I am, a bit jet-lagged, but over the moon that my beloved Goldie is safe and well.'

He smiled. 'Speaking of which, as nice as it is to chat to you both, I can't wait to see my horse. When your uncle returns, I'd be very grateful to be taken to him.'

Calvin Redfern strode into the room. Always an imposing figure, his handsome face now looked like the sky over Porthmeor Beach when a sea storm was sweeping in.

'I'm afraid that won't be possible.'

The American leapt to his feet. 'But why not?'

'Because,' Calvin Redfern said, 'the horse is gone.'

~ 4 ~

'GONE?'

Blake Wainright's face was as white as his hair. He said faintly: 'How could he possibly be gone? You told me that two cops, a couple of musclemen and the fox terrier reputed to be the best burglar alarm in Cornwall were guarding him. Are you telling me that the kidnappers slipped past them?'

Calvin Redfern looked grim. 'It would appear so. When Vicky arrived at the stables this morning she found her nephews, the two police constables and the dog, sound asleep. It was some time before she could rouse anyone and now she says they're all stumbling around, groggy and with splitting headaches. That would suggest they'd been drugged, although how it was managed no one can think.'

'What happened to the third constable?' asked Laura.

Her uncle stared at her. 'There were only two men on duty last night. I know that because I was with Detective Watson when he assigned them.'

'Laura's right,' confirmed Tariq. 'A third one came later. He held the paddock gate open for us when we went to say a final goodbye to Goldie before leaving yesterday. He had a stone in his shoe so he was bending down and we didn't really see his face, but I noticed that he was youngish – in his early twenties or so. He had blue-black stubble and black hair cut quite short at the back.'

'An inside job?' demanded Blake Wainright. 'Is that what you're telling me? One of the policemen supposedly protecting Goldie has stolen him?'

'Not a real policeman,' Laura said, trying to sound soothing. 'A fake one. He probably volunteered to make coffee or a meal for everyone and slipped sleeping powder into it.'

Calvin Redfern raked his fingers through his greying dark hair. 'I can't tell you how sorry I am, Blake. This is immensely embarrassing for the police. I've left a message for Detective Watson.'

The American had the look of someone who wanted to bang his head against the wall in despair, but he said with spirit, 'No cops! I mean no disrespect, sir, but those morons were no use at all when it came to finding Shergar and now the Cornish police have blown it with Gold Rush.

What I would appreciate, Mr Redfern, is if you could drive me to the stables yourself. I understand that you were once the best detective around. If there's a clue to be found, I'd like you to locate it.'

Calvin Redfern gave Laura and Tariq a hard look. His detective past was something he didn't usually advertise. He opened his mouth as if to refuse, but was conscious that someone had to try to make amends for the policing disaster. 'We'll do our best,' he promised at last.

The field was empty apart from a couple of Shetland ponies. They alone seemed cheerful. Everybody else at the riding school was in a fog of gloom, no one more so than Vicky and her twin nephews, who were nursing sore heads and feeling sorry for themselves. Their bulging muscles and martial arts skills had been no use at all.

'It's as if someone's put my brain through a tumble dryer,' grumbled Sam. 'Last thing I remember is sitting down to eat the pizza that nice constable ordered. After that, I have total amnesia.'

'They'd never have got away with it if I'd been awake,' Scott moaned in frustration. 'A couple of roundhouse kicks and they'd have been begging for mercy.'

'Yes, but you weren't awake, were you,' retorted his brother. 'You were snoring like a dragon with sinusitis. They might have begged you to shut up, but that's about it.'

Scott was indignant. 'Ever heard *yourself*? You sound

like a hippo with flu. Your whole bed shakes. They could measure the vibrations on the Richter scale . . .'

Laura and Tariq left them squabbling and took the husky down to the field. In spite of his objections, Calvin Redfern had persuaded Blake Wainright to speak to Detective Watson, who'd screeched into the riding centre a short time ago, full of apologies.

Laura was determined to find the clue the American so desperately wanted before the police did. She could relate to the anguish he'd clearly felt when her uncle told him that Goldie had gone missing again. If someone stole Skye, she'd be devastated. And yet so far the only clue was a few tyre tracks, which, Calvin Redfern said, had been made by the most commonly used tyres in the United Kingdom, so were not much use as a clue at all.

She stood by the gate and did her best to think like her hero, Detective Inspector Matt Walker. Laura's dream was to be a great detective when she was older and when she wasn't pestering her uncle about the methods he'd used to solve cases, she spent hours combing the pages of her Matt Walker novels for tips.

In *The Case of the Missing Heiress*, Matt had observed that quite often in kidnappings the solution was in front of investigators' eyes, but they spent so much time working on complicated theories that they missed the blindingly obvious. Laura unclipped Skye's leash. He was straining to explore the field. She tried to decide where to start searching for clues. Matt believed that every crime scene told a story. It was simply a matter of knowing how to read it.

While Tariq searched the field with Skye, Laura studied

the tyre tracks. They led to the five-barred gate, where the thieves appeared to have parked to make the loading of the horse as easy as possible. There were distinct tracks on the approach to the field and a flurry of hoofprints and boot marks just inside it.

'Wellingtons,' Calvin Redfern had said ruefully of the bootprints, prodding one with a stick. 'Only about ten million sold every year.'

If the footprints and tyre treads told no story, maybe the pattern of them – what Matt Walker called 'tracking psychology' – would. The vehicle had driven directly to the gate, but departed erratically, turning in a wide loop and zooming away in a zigzag. Even if they were in a hurry, it didn't make sense that the thieves would transport a multi-million dollar horse in such a dangerous manner.

Unless . . .

Laura stared at the chaos of prints and churned up earth. Unless the horse wasn't on board when they sped away.

She considered the circumstances. Rob Ashworth had once commented that horses lived by their memories. A stallion with the strength and speed of Gold Rush, a highly strung horse who found himself approached or seized in the dead of night by men he associated with a series of negative or painful events, would not willingly allow himself to be led into another horsebox, particularly when his experience in the last one had been so traumatic.

Across the field, Tariq was with Skye. The husky was sniffing at a fence post.

'Tariq,' called Laura, breaking into a run. 'Check for hoofprints, deep ones, on the other side of the fence.'

Even before she reached him, he was giving her the thumbs up. Goldie might have vanished again, but this time at least he was free.

~ 5 ~

'I DON'T WANT to rain on your parade, but I'm telling you now, there's more to this kidnapped stallion business than meets the eye,' Mrs Crabtree told Laura. 'Always is in the racing game. It's a magnet for chancers, gamblers, criminals and dreamers. The pretty horses, the rainbow jockey silks, the fancy hats of the ladies who go to watch, they're just the window dressing. Behind the scenes, there are tricks going on that would be the envy of any conjurer. Big money involved, you see. Wherever there are millions at stake, there'll be men trying to make even more and they'll do whatever it takes. Sleight of hand, smoke and mirrors, rabbits out of hats, you name it, they'll have it up their sleeves.'

Laura sat on her neighbour's stone wall trying to keep a big grin off her face and only half-listening. She was watching Skye who in turn was watching the surfers bob like seals on the heaving blue-grey surf a few hundred metres below. The horizon was peach-pink with the setting sun. Usually by this time she'd be ravenous and in the kitchen pestering their housekeeper, Rowenna, to hurry up with dinner, but tonight she wanted to linger in the sea air and savour the excitement of the day.

It had been harder than expected to convince Detective Watson and the other grown-ups that the red stallion had escaped from the Carbis Bay riding centre rather than been stolen.

'Nonsense,' barked Vicky, unwilling to admit that a $75 million horse might have got out of her field. 'That fence is a metre and a half high. He would have to have the leaping power of a champion show jumper to get over it.'

'Or be very afraid,' Tariq pointed out.

Vicky ignored him. 'Besides, any thief cunning enough to trick four men and a dog into eating a pizza loaded with sleeping powder would have thought to bring tranquilisers to sedate the horse if he was giving trouble.'

Laura shrugged. 'Maybe the gang never managed to get close enough to inject him or knock him out with chloroform or whatever else they were planning. Goldie probably took one look at them, remembered what happened the last time they grabbed him, and bolted for his life.'

And so it had proved. Thanks to Skye, the search party

had been out on the moors for barely twenty minutes when they found the red stallion grazing happily on a hillock. Blake Wainright was beside himself with joy. Only problem was, no one could get close to the horse. Every time they drew near enough to see the whites of his eyes, he raced away, tail held high – though whether through fright or because he was revelling in his newfound freedom, it was hard to tell. Laura suspected the latter.

'He always did have a mind of his own,' admitted the American, his elation at finding Goldie subsiding as the day wore on and the search party pursued the stallion up and down gullies, across a stream and through a thicket of gorse. They'd attempted to send two riders after him, but the barrel-bellied trekking cobs had no hope of matching his effortless blasts of speed.

'It's a game to him,' panted Vicky, crossly plucking thorns out of her jodhpurs. It had started to drizzle and everyone in the group was hot, wet, scratched and exhausted. She turned to Tariq's foster father, who'd joined them for the search. 'Rob, you must have a way of tranquillising a horse from a distance? Can't you use a blowpipe or something?'

Blake Wainright was horrified. 'As if Goldie hasn't been through enough. There's no way I'm going to allow him to be sedated.'

'And neither will I,' objected Brian Meek, the man from the insurance company set to lose millions if Gold Rush couldn't be recovered. He was unsuitably attired in a suit and slippery street shoes. He'd already fallen twice and broken the handle off his briefcase. For reasons unknown, he'd insisted on bringing it.

'Well, the horse can't stay on the moors for much longer,' Calvin Redfern curtly informed him. 'He'll be snatched again or end up injuring himself. If you have a better suggestion, I'd be glad to hear it.'

There was a stony silence as the grown-ups looked to each other for answers and found none. Meanwhile, on the horizon, the object of their frustration guzzled grass contentedly.

'None of this would be happening if his groom was here,' lamented Blake Wainright. 'Ryan Carter, his name is. He's the boy who takes care of Goldie. Been with him since the horse was born. They're inseparable. Unfortunately, he risked his life to stop the thieves stealing Goldie and they put him in the hospital. Looked like an Egyptian mummy when I left, bandages and splints all over the place. It's been a double disaster because Ryan also takes care of Noble Warrior, Goldie's first-born son, who's set to run in the Kentucky Derby in a few weeks' time. It could cost us the race and a lot more. Horses are real sensitive that way. They run best for the people they trust.'

'Tariq could do it,' Laura said suddenly.

There were ten astonished faces, including Tariq's.

The American was taken aback. 'Excuse me?'

'What I mean is, if anyone can catch Goldie it's Tariq. He has a way with animals and Goldie already adores him.'

'She's right,' agreed Rob Ashworth. 'If I'm dealing with a nervous or difficult animal in my surgery I always call Tariq. They seem to trust him on sight.'

34

'Can't hurt,' said Wainright, who was beginning to despair of ever being reunited with his $75 million dollar stallion.

Tariq, who was shy and not at all convinced that he had a special talent with animals or anything else, took a bit of persuading but at last he agreed to try.

What happened next would stay in the minds of all who saw it for years to come. After picking his way towards the red stallion through the heather and gorse, Tariq was met by the same response the search party had encountered all day. Goldie wheeled and galloped away. The difference was that the Bengali boy kept his eyes locked on those of the stallion.

The horse began galloping in circles around him, watching Tariq warily. After a while, Tariq moved his gaze to Goldie's shoulder. The effect was instantaneous. The stallion slowed to a walk. Instead of going up to him, Tariq turned from the horse and stood motionless. After some hesitation, Goldie's curiosity got the better of him. He walked up behind Tariq and did something that caused even the insurance man to blink back a tear. He rested his head on the boy's shoulder.

Blake Wainright drew in an uneven breath. 'Not much surprises me these days, but I have to confess to being stunned. That's an old horse whisperer's trick, but rarely have I seen it done so well. Who knew that it would take a theft and a journey to the wildest reaches of Cornwall, England for me to find the one boy in ten million capable of helping Noble Warrior win the Derby.'

'You're not paying attention to a word I'm saying,' scolded Mrs Crabtree.

'Am,' said Laura as her neighbour's fuschia-pink tracksuit and blonde curls came back into focus. Mrs Crabtree was in her sixties, but she dyed her hair and still dressed to stop traffic. 'Well, okay, I was briefly distracted but I'm all ears now.'

'What I was *saying* is that something about this stolen racehorse business smells bad to me and if you had a mind to listen to your elders and betters, you'd walk away now.'

'Nothing to walk away from,' Laura assured her, reaching down to rub Skye's downy ears. 'Goldie's safe and sound and within forty-eight hours he'll be on his way back to Kentucky with Mr Wainright. I doubt we'll set eyes on either of them ever again. Of course the horse thieves are still at large, but that's a police matter now. It's none of my business.'

Mrs Crabtree put one hand on her hip and pointed a garden trowel at Laura with the other. 'Thousands would believe you. *I* don't. When you scent a mystery, you're like that husky with a bone. You'll not let go until it's solved. Well, take some advice from a friend . . .'

'It's really not necessary,' said Laura, gathering Skye's lead, 'but tell me if you must.'

'Don't trust anyone you meet or believe anything you see.'

~ 6 ~

LAURA WAS NOT afraid of flying, but the journey from Charlotte, North Carolina to Lexington, Kentucky tested her nerve. Ten minutes after take-off, the rain shower forecast by air traffic controllers turned into a violent storm. The flight attendant rushed to stow the drinks trolley and issued stern warnings about seatbelts. Almost immediately gale force winds began tossing the little plane around the skies as if it were made of paper. Black raindrops streamed down the windows. Beyond them, the swollen clouds were purple and the late afternoon sky as dark as night.

'Be careful what you wish for . . .'

37

In the short space of time she had been living with her uncle, Laura had had frequent cause to remember the warning given to her by Matron at the Sylvan Meadows Children's Home, but never once had she wanted to change her new, adrenalin-filled life. Not until this minute at any rate. Now, not even the prospect of spending ten days with her best friend on a Kentucky horse farm, watching some of the most glorious thoroughbreds in racing prepare for the Derby, was of any comfort, especially since it was by no means guaranteed that they'd reach Lexington at all. Not unscathed, at any rate. The sixteen-seater plane was bucking like a furious bronco. Laura wondered how much more it could take. In films, light aircraft seemed to have a nasty habit of disintegrating in storms and going down in flames. She hoped very much that this particular one was sturdier than it appeared.

She glanced at Tariq. He was frightened too, she could tell, but unlike a couple of their fellow passengers, including an unseen woman further up the aisle who was sobbing hysterically, he was doing his best not to show it. He turned from the diamond droplets that splattered the window and saw Laura looking at him. Smiling, he reached for her hand. She squeezed back gratefully.

'Can you believe we're here?' There was real excitement in his voice and she realised that being flung about in mid-air like a leaf in a hurricane hadn't dampened his enthusiasm for the holiday ahead in the least. 'I don't mean on this plane, which is the last place in the world I'd like to be right now, but in the United States? For ten whole days? With *horses!*'

In spite of her fears, Laura couldn't help giggling. Tariq's love of animals was one of the things she liked best about him and his ability to bond with them was the reason for their impromptu trip to Kentucky.

'No,' she told him. 'I can't.'

And she couldn't. It didn't seem real that just two days ago they'd been following Goldie's tracks across the moors, explaining their theory that the horse had escaped rather than been stolen to an incredulous Blake Wainright, Detective Watson and Calvin Redfern, and a disbelieving Vicky.

From the moment Tariq had handed him Goldie's lead rope, Blake Wainright had become obsessed with the notion that he was the only boy on earth who could help Noble Warrior win the Derby. At a dinner to thank Goldie's rescuers, he'd attempted to persuade Calvin Redfern and Rob and Rina Ashworth to pull the children out of school and jump on the next plane to the US to enjoy an all expenses paid trip on his farm in Lexington, Kentucky.

'My wife Christina and I are indebted to you and your kids,' he'd told them. 'Allow us to treat you to the holiday of your dreams. I'm biased, I know, but Fleet Farm is close to heaven in my book. You'll love every minute. Gleaming thoroughbreds everywhere you turn and eighty acres on which Laura and Tariq can ride or play. They'd be great company for my teenage granddaughter, Kit, too. She's not been . . . Well, put it this way, it would do her the world of good to have some young friends around the place. As for the Kentucky Derby itself, it's an unforgettable spectacle.'

Laura and Tariq, who'd overheard the conversation as they helped Rowenna dish up dessert, had started doing little hops of joy. But their celebrations were premature.

'We'd love to take you up on your offer,' Calvin Redfern said, 'but speaking for myself and Laura, it's likely to be next year. I can't take the time off work.'

'Same here,' Rob had agreed. 'I have a busy veterinary practice. I can't just drop everything.'

'And the children have two more weeks of school before the holidays,' Rina pointed out.

But Blake Wainright had refused to take no for an answer. He gave an impassioned speech about how staying on Fleet Farm and seeing close-up what it took to prepare a horse for the biggest race in America would be the experience of a lifetime for the children if they were allowed to come on their own. Calvin Redfern burst out laughing.

'Look, I'm a big believer in travel as education, and I'm sure Rob and Rina feel the same way, but schools have rules and they're not going to break them purely because you feel that nobody but Tariq can help your horse win his race.'

'If the school could be persuaded to let Laura and the boy go, and if my wife homeschooled them for a couple of hours a day while they're there – as she does with Kit – would you consider allowing them to return with me to the US the day after tomorrow?' persisted the American.

'You have no chance of talking the school into it,' Rina assured him. 'The head teacher, Mrs Letchworth, is immoveable on these things.'

'But if she were to say yes, would you let them come?'

Rob smiled. 'I don't see why not. Tariq would be in his element on a horse farm, especially if Laura was with him.'

Calvin Redfern saw no harm in agreeing. As a former Chief Inspector, it had been easy for him to check the Wainrights' background. He'd already established beyond doubt that they were one of the most popular couples in racing, with a reputation for honesty in their business dealings and kindness to their horses. Not that it was likely to matter. Like Rina, he was certain that the school would never allow the children to leave before the end of term.

He'd reckoned without the power of Wainright's chequebook. Next morning, the American had approached the school with a donation generous enough to enable them to build a new library. Hours later Mr Gillbert, Laura's teacher, had informed her in a hushed voice that she and Tariq had been given special permission to travel to Kentucky on a matter of national importance. They'd be leaving within twenty-four hours. He'd then spoiled the surprise by handing them a giant pile of homework to pack in their suitcase.

It had been decided that Blake Wainright would fly with them as far as Charlotte, North Carolina before departing to await the arrival of Gold Rush on a following flight. There were veterinary inspections to be done when the horse entered the US and these could take hours. Wainright would travel the rest of the way to Kentucky in the lorry with Goldie. While it was highly unlikely that the masked raiders would make a further attempt to steal the horse, everyone agreed that it would be safer and more pleasant for the children to complete their journey to Lexington by plane. A flight attendant would take care of them and they'd be met at the airport by Blake's wife, Christina.

Safer and more pleasant? Thirty thousand feet up in a thunderstorm?

Thieves or no thieves, Laura wished that she and Tariq had travelled with Goldie and Blake Wainright in the lorry. The storm was getting worse by the minute.

To take her mind off it, she tried to picture Kit, the Wainwrights' fifteen-year-old granddaughter. Would she be friendly or stuck up? All her life Laura had wished she could have an older sister and when Kit had first been mentioned she'd briefly entertained fantasies that she and the American girl might hang out and have fun together like sisters do. But the realist in Laura knew that was unlikely.

She imagined Kit as pretty and sophisticated – the opposite of Laura who was generally in tatty jeans and an old sweatshirt. She'd practically have been born in the saddle and own a fancy white pony with a long, silky mane. Her bedroom wall would be plastered with rosettes. She'd be grateful that Tariq and Laura had helped rescue Goldie, but she'd find the idea that they could help Noble Warrior win the Derby a joke.

As the plane bounced and swayed in the gale, Laura shook herself mentally. She had to stay positive. 'Just think, Tariq, tomorrow morning when our classmates are sitting down to lessons in St Ives and Mr Gillbert is droning on about algebra, we'll be waking up on a Kentucky horse farm and it's all thanks to you.'

There was a blast of thunder so loud that it sounded as if the plane was about to break in half. Everyone jumped and the woman down the aisle sobbed louder than ever. Tariq gripped Laura's hand. 'Don't thank me until we land in Lexington. We still have to get there in one piece.'

'Oh, we'll get there,' Laura said determinedly. 'We *have* to. Ever since we almost collided with the horsebox, I've had an odd feeling that somehow all of this is meant to be. It's as if nobody but us could have found Gold Rush and nobody but us could have rescued him. As if we were always meant to come here. To America. To Kentucky.'

'As if it were predestined?'

'Yes. As if it were fate.'

Tariq gripped the armrest as the plane dipped and swayed. 'I know exactly what you mean. It's that which makes me wonder . . .'

A fresh wave of adrenalin rippled through Laura. 'Wonder what?'

'What fate has in store for us . . .'

~ 7 ~

'**WELCOME TO BLUEGRASS** country,' cried Christine Wainright, rushing to greet them as they wandered dazed and trembling into the arrivals hall at Lexington airport. A tall, elegant woman in a navy blue suit, she shook Laura and Tariq's hands very formally before spontaneously giving each of them a hug.

'It doesn't seem right to stand on ceremony when I feel as if I already know you,' she said. 'My husband has spoken so highly of you both that I'm afraid I already consider you friends. We are so deeply in your debt. If you and Mr Redfern hadn't saved Goldie . . . well, it just doesn't bear thinking about. I expect Blake told you, we love that horse

44

like a child. All our horses are like family to us, but Goldie and Noble Warrior – he's our Derby baby – they'll always have a special place in our hearts.'

Mrs Wainright had an accent as slow and melodic as that of her husband and silver-blonde hair swept up into a bun. Her smile was warm and outlined in mulberry. There was no sign of her granddaughter, Kit. She said worriedly: 'Your journey was bearable, I trust? The storm didn't make it too bumpy?'

Laura didn't have the heart to tell her that they'd spent most of the flight fearing for their lives, were nervous wrecks and more than a little queasy. 'It was great,' she lied. 'A bit bumpy but nothing we couldn't handle.'

Tariq mustered a grin. 'No problem at all.'

Christine laughed. 'From what my husband tells me, the pair of you can handle quite a lot. My granddaughter, Kit, is looking forward to meeting you, but she had to stay behind and finish some schoolwork. Now you must be shattered. How about I whisk you home to Fleet Farm?'

It was not until she sank into the springy backseat of the Cadillac that Laura realised how exhausted she was, or how cold. She was relieved when Christine put on the car heater. The drive to the farm passed in a haze. The departing storm had smudged the sky with violet and yellow bruises. It hung low over the parallel lines of the white fences that framed the picture-perfect homes of America's finest racehorses.

'Double fences to keep the stallions in and the mares and foals out or vice versa,' Christine explained.

Tariq had his nose pressed to the window, not wanting to miss a thing. 'Why here?' he asked, as they began to pass farm after farm where sleek, shining bays, chestnuts and greys grazed in emerald-green pastures. Fluffy foals with impossibly long legs experimented with wobbly bursts of speed. 'Why did Kentucky become one of the best places in the world to raise a racehorse?'

'The secret lies in the Kentucky Bluegrass. And before you ask why it isn't blue, it has that name because it has tiny cornflower-blue flowers if it's allowed to grow to full height. Which it rarely is. The reason it's so good for racehorses is that the soil is rich in limestone and calcium. As they eat they take in nutrients that build strong bones and legs of iron.'

'Is that what Noble Warrior has?' Laura wanted to know. 'Legs of iron?'

Christine smiled. 'That and his sire's big heart. Like Goldie, he'll give you everything he has and then he'll reach inside and find something more. He's a sweetheart too, though people who see him race find that hard to believe. On the track he's all fire and fury. Off it, he's as soppy and loveable as a Labrador. But he's nervy. That's the reason Blake was so keen to bring you over, Tariq. If Warrior's routine is upset, he's like a scared little boy. Since Ryan's been in hospital, Warrior has been out of sorts and running poorly in training. My husband is hoping that you'll be able to work your magic and have him racing at full strength by the Derby.'

There was a pause as she slowed the car, turned and stopped in front of high iron gates. Overhead a scrolling sign announced Fleet Farm. The gates purred open. Beyond them was a paved driveway lined with white fences.

Laura had noticed that what made the farms unique were their colourful painted barns. Fleet had two. The mares' and foals' barn was cream with a green roof and red shutters. The stallion barn, a black one trimmed with white shutters and a red bell tower, stood proudly on a hill against the stormy sky. As they drew nearer, a young man in a baseball cap emerged from it and began hosing down a bay horse. Christine waved and called to him, but his only response was to touch the brim of his hat. Face sullen, he resumed what he was doing. When Laura glanced back, he was watching them go. His body language reminded her of a hostile terrier.

'Was that one of the grooms?' she asked.

Christine shook her head. 'That's Ken, Noble Warrior's exercise rider. He's helping out with a couple of the horses while Ryan is in hospital. They're best friends, you see. Ken took it very hard when the horsebox was hijacked and Ryan and the driver, Jason, were attacked. Blames himself. He was supposed to have gone with them on what was meant to be a routine outing to take Goldie to the Equine Hospital for a checkup. Instead he slipped off to watch a football game. When Ryan was beaten half to death and Goldie stolen, he was devastated.'

Her mouth tightened. 'He can be a bit moody sometimes, Ken. Don't take anything he says to heart. Underneath it all he's a good boy – one of our best.'

The Cadillac glided over the hill and came to a halt in a storm-darkened yard ablaze with pink, purple and yellow rhododendrons and azaleas. Towering over them was a white mansion flanked by the largest oak trees the children had ever seen. The front door was at least twice as tall as that at number 28 Ocean View Terrace and had a stained glass image of the winged horse Pegasus inset into the heavy wood. White pillars lent a Colonial air to the grey-tiled porch.

Laura climbed stiffly out of the car and looked up at the house. 'It's beautiful,' she said in awe. 'I think it's the most lovely place I've ever seen.'

For an instant Christina's eyes seemed to sparkle with tears, but they were gone in blink. 'I feel the same way. That's what makes it so hard that . . . that we have to . . . Let's put it this way: whether or not we get to keep Fleet Farm has a lot to do with how Noble Warrior performs in the Derby.'

She turned to Tariq, who was lifting the luggage from the boot of the car. 'My husband was rather vague on your background, my dear. How did you become such an expert on horses at such a young age?'

The Bengali boy set the suitcase down and smiled. 'I'm not.'

Christina paled beneath her tan, but she said brightly. 'You're being modest, I assume. Laura, is he always so self-effacing? Presumably, Tariq, you've had quite a bit of experience grooming them, riding them or healing them? Blake seemed to feel that you were England's answer to the horse whisperer.'

Tariq regarded her with clear amber eyes. 'I've learned a little about horses in the last few months while I've been living with my foster father – he's a vet, but I've never ridden a horse and Goldie is the first I've ever touched. I'm definitely not a horse, dog or any other kind of whisperer. Animals seem to like me, that's all.'

'They *like* you?' All of a sudden Christine looked every day of her sixty-eight years. 'How about you, Laura? Please tell me that you're a great rider or have spent hundreds of hours watching racing or hanging out at your local stables. Please tell me that you at least are an accomplished horsewoman?'

'I'm not,' admitted Laura, hating to disappoint her. In her short acquaintance with Mrs Wainright, she'd grown to like the woman as much as she did her husband. 'I know even less about horses than Tariq does, and I've never in my life been riding. The only thing I'm quite good at is solving mysteries and finding clues. Your husband seemed to think that might be quite useful around here.'

'Mysteries? Clues? Dear God, it sounds like something out of a detective novel.' Christine leaned on a column for support. 'Just when I thought things couldn't get any worse, my husband has put the future of Fleet Farm into the hands of two youngsters who barely know one end of a horse from another.'

49

~ 8 ~

LAURA AWOKE WITH a start thinking she was in her bed at number 28 Ocean View Terrace. The room was so dark that she panicked and reached for Skye. Usually he slept at the foot of her mattress, taking up more than his fair share of space. When she recalled that she was in Kentucky, far from her husky and the uncle she adored, she felt a pang so sharp it brought tears to her eyes.

Lightning shivered across the room, briefly illuminating the oak corners of the four-poster bed, the rocking chair and assorted Kentucky Derby memorabilia. On the wall opposite a photograph showed the beaming Wainrights posing with Gold Rush after his Derby win. The famous garland – four hundred red roses sewn onto green silk – adorned his powerful chestnut neck. The garland was the reason that the race was nicknamed the 'Run for the Roses'.

Above the dresser was a framed newspaper article about Goldie's victory, headlined: "**KENTUCKY THRILLER: Gold Rush Proves his Worth in Derby Triumph**.' In the accompanying grainy photo, the red stallion was at full stretch, every sinew straining. All four hooves were off the ground and he looked as if he were flying. The reporter described the race as the 'most exciting two minutes in sport'.

The rain pitter-pattered against the window. Laura groped for her watch on the bedside table. It wasn't there and she didn't have the energy to hunt for it, nor did she want to put on the light. Was it midnight? Two a.m.? Three-thirty? She hadn't the faintest.

She wondered if Tariq, sleeping in the adjoining room, was awake, and, if not, whether he'd mind if she disturbed him and said that she was homesick and wanted a chat. She doubted it. Despite his horrific background in a Bangladesh quarry, a dusty hell that had led to the deaths of his mum and dad, Tariq was the most easygoing and kind-hearted boy she knew.

She was poised to knock on his door when she heard a car engine. Tiptoeing to the window in her pyjamas, she peered out into the rainy dark. It was Goldie and Blake Wainright arriving home after their long journey from North Carolina. Her bedroom was on the second floor and she had an unrestricted, if blurry, view of the barn and the lorry. Three black-cloaked figures were milling around in the white triangle of headlights. The distance and slanting rain made it impossible for Laura to make out their faces and their hoods disguised them further.

One of the men lowered the ramp of the lorry and another untied the horse. As the stallion stepped carefully down the slope, the light fell on his chestnut hide. He disappeared into the barn with the cloaked figures. Moments later, the lorry started up and rumbled away down the drive.

The tallest of the three men emerged from the barn and strode up the hill towards the house. Laura caught a glimpse of Blake Wainright's snowy hair beneath his hood and was glad that he and his horse were safely home.

A wave of tiredness came over her and she returned to bed. Sinking into the mattress was like being swallowed by a cloud. Almost before her head touched the pillow, she was unconscious again.

Hours or maybe minutes later she woke again. Her eyes opened to the lightning's ghostly flicker. It was still pitch dark. She reached for Skye and felt a painful wrench as she remembered that she was in Kentucky, far from home. She wondered what time it was and reached for her watch. It was only then that she recalled that she'd already been through this exact routine. She'd been awake earlier in the night and seen Goldie and Blake Wainright return.

Rain was falling softly. Over its musical tinkle she caught the faint rumble of an engine. Jumping out of bed, she ran to the window. A lorry was backing up to the barn. Three hooded, black-cloaked figures were fussing around it. They lowered the ramp. One climbed into the lorry and emerged leading a chestnut horse.

Laura was confused. Had she or hadn't she seen Goldie being unloaded earlier that night? Had she dreamed it, or was she dreaming now?

She pinched herself hard. No, she was definitely awake. Since it was unlikely that the Wainrights were having two chestnut horses delivered in the dead of night, that could only mean she'd dreamed Goldie's arrival earlier. How weird that the dream had been so accurate – a virtual premonition. It wasn't hard to believe that her imagination could conjure up the red stallion, given the time she'd spent with him in Cornwall, but how could she have known that the men would be wearing black cloaks? The lorry too was identical.

The men disappeared into the barn. Then something strange happened. The chestnut horse was led back out of the barn and loaded onto the lorry. The ramp was raised, the red brake lights pulsed and the lorry drove quietly away.

Laura stared out at the barn. Aside from the soft hiss of rain, all was silent and still. She felt dizzy with tiredness. What had just happened? Why had Mr Wainwright brought Goldie home only to send him away again? Or was the outgoing chestnut another horse altogether? If so, what did that mean? Had she dreamed some of it or none of it? How much time had passed between delivery and departure?

Laura returned to the cloud bed, head spinning. Sleep hovered. She gave up trying to keep her eyelids from drooping and surrendered to the mattress's snug embrace.

There was a faint sound. Tariq's slim shadow was at the door. 'Laura, are you awake?'

Laura sat bolt upright. It suddenly occurred to her that what she'd witnessed must have been a theft. Why else would the hooded figures have driven off with a chestnut stallion? She hadn't seen the blaze on the horse's face so she couldn't positively identify him as Gold Rush, but they'd definitely been the same colour, the russet hue of leaves at the height of autumn.

'Tariq, did you see the lorry that just drove away?'

He perched on the edge of the bed. His voice was husky with tiredness. 'What lorry? Is that what woke me? I thought it was thunder.'

Quickly Laura told him what had happened. But even as she attempted to explain what she'd seen, she could hear how ridiculous it sounded. A horse that may or may not have been Goldie had arrived at an indeterminate time in the night. Some while later another horse or perhaps the same one had been taken away again. A robbery might have taken place, or Laura might simply have been dreaming.

Tariq looked doubtful. 'Is there any part of the story you're absolutely sure about?'

Laura thought about it. 'I definitely saw Mr Wainright walking towards the house after the first horse had been delivered, and I definitely saw the second horse, or the same horse, being taken away again. I think I did anyway.'

'But you're not a hundred per cent convinced that you didn't imagine part of it?'

Laura was indignant. 'I was wide awake when the

second horse was driven away. You know I was because I sat up as soon as you came in.'

'No, you didn't. I spoke to you three times before you answered.'

Laura slumped back into the pillows. 'You don't believe me.'

He tugged at her pyjama sleeve. 'I do believe you. I do. It's just that . . . well, you're not certain what happened either.'

The outline of his face had grown clearer. Through the crack in the curtains, dawn was approaching. Outside the window, a cheerful bird was celebrating the end of a long, wet night.

'What if everything I saw was real?' Laura said. 'Goldie arrived and the lorry left, then later the same lorry or an identical one returned with another chestnut horse. Shortly afterwards, it drove off carrying a chestnut that might have been Goldie or might not. What would that mean?'

'It probably means you're right – Goldie or one of the other stallions has been stolen.'

Laura sat up again. 'So what do we do about it?'

But she already knew what they had to do. Beside the bed was a red panic button. Christine had pointed it out when she'd shown her and Tariq to their rooms, explaining in great detail that it was only to be used in the most extreme emergency since it not only woke up the household and brought Fleet Farm's security manager running, it also roused the local police.

With a nervous glance at Tariq, she reached out a hand and pressed it.

9

'TELL ME AGAIN why you thought Goldie had been kidnapped?'

Laura knew that Blake Wainright was being as understanding as could be expected under the circumstances, especially since he'd only had two hours sleep and was exhausted after his epic journey across the Atlantic. All the same she wanted to crawl under the breakfast table and hide. For the twentieth time that morning she began a halting account of the night's events.

Christine, who felt sorry for her, said encouragingly: 'Blake arrived home with Goldie at about two-fifteen a.m., so you definitely witnessed that. I'm afraid you must have

56

dreamed the rest. You've had quite an exciting time of it recently, what with rescuing a champion racehorse twice and flying halfway round the world. It's hardly surprising if some things get scrambled in sleep.'

She smiled. 'Don't give it another thought. Now why don't you have one of Anita's famous waffles? You've hardly eaten a thing.'

The sun was spilling in through the French doors, forming droplets of gold on the starched white tablecloth, and the scent of jasmine mingled with the aromas of coffee and maple syrup. The events of the night seemed more surreal than ever. Laura nibbled miserably at one of the waffles conjured up by the Wainrights' Hispanic cook, Anita. It was indeed delicious, but after a couple of bites she laid down her knife and fork. Her stomach was in knots. She and Tariq had been in Kentucky for a matter of hours. How could everything have gone so wrong?

Pushing the panic button had, as expected, caused instant pandemonium. First, Christine and Blake came tearing into the room in their dressing gowns, hair awry. In their wake was what resembled a slim, pale boy wearing blue-spotted pyjamas. It was only when the lights blazed that Laura saw that the 'boy' was in fact a teenage girl with short, mousy hair that stuck out in every direction. In the chaos, no one remembered that Laura and Tariq had not yet been introduced to Kit, the Wainrights' elusive granddaughter. She hadn't been at dinner and there had been no explanations as to her whereabouts.

Throughout the drama, and there had been plenty of it, Kit had hung back and never once uttered a word.

Not even when the cops had come blasting up the drive, blue lights twirling. Plump with doughnuts and bristling with weaponry, they'd rushed about barking orders and directing a machine-gun volley of questions at Laura and Tariq. At one point, Laura had been quite sure that she was about to be arrested.

The most intimidating man on the scene by far, however, had been Fleet Farm's head of security, Garth Longbrook, a former commando in the US Navy. He was balding, super fit and not amused at being dragged from his bed less than two hours after he'd climbed into it.

'Save me from amateur detectives,' he'd said sarcastically in a voice loud enough for Laura to hear after he'd searched the barn and found all eight stallions, including Goldie, standing happily in their stalls. Not so much as a wisp of hay was out of place. Noble Warrior had been a little agitated, but Garth Longbrook claimed that this was to only to be expected given the number of strangers invading the barn.

'What time did you see this *supposed* second lorry?' he'd demanded of Laura, even though she'd already stated five or six times that she had no idea. She bitterly regretted that she hadn't summoned up the energy to turn on the light and find a clock. She'd eventually located her watch under the bed.

'If only I'd made the effort to get it, I'd know for certain whether there was another lorry or if it was a dream after all,' she'd whispered to Tariq.

Not that she'd said that to Garth Longbrook. When she'd asked if there was CCTV footage of the barn that could be checked, he'd regarded her with barely concealed dislike before marching off, muttering to himself, to do just that. Thirty minutes later, he'd triumphantly led Laura, Tariq and Blake Wainright into his office and scrolled through the black and white footage of the night to demonstrate that there was no evidence of any vehicle, apart from the one that had brought Goldie and Blake Wainright, loading or offloading a chestnut horse in the dead of night.

The more people tried to prove to Laura that she was mistaken, the more convinced she became that she was right. She *had* seen something. Something *had* happened. The only question was what.

'How often does the camera scan the barn?' she'd asked as they gathered in Garth's office, a meticulously ordered space in the office building adjacent to the main house.

He'd swivelled in his chair and regarded her with a look that could have fossilised a tree. 'Every ten minutes.'

'So in theory the lorry could have come and gone in that time?'

Out of the corner of her eye, Laura noticed Kit glance up sharply. A small smile seemed to play around her mouth, but it was gone before Laura could be sure.

'It's possible but not probable, isn't that right, Garth?' said Blake Wainright. 'The men in the lorry would have had to know exactly when each ten-minute cycle started and stopped, and even then it would have been a challenge for them to enter the farm through a locked and alarmed gate, offload one horse and reload a different horse in such a short time. That would suggest that it was an inside job, which I refuse to accept.'

His head of security did not bother to disguise the impatience in his voice. 'With respect, sir, might I remind you that NO crime has been committed. Nothing has been taken. The horses are safely in their stalls. There *was* no second lorry.'

Blake Wainright gave a deep chuckle, lightening the mood. 'Quite right, Garth, no crime has been committed. However, I'm grateful to Laura for alerting us when she thought one had been. Better safe than sorry is my motto. Now I don't know about anyone else but I'm starving. Who wants breakfast?'

The morning sun had chased away the storm's gloom, but it failed to lift Laura's mood. Tariq kept trying to catch her eye and pull funny faces to make her laugh, but it didn't work. Part of her felt embarrassed and guilty for waking up the whole household and creating so much chaos. The other half was determined to find out the truth about what had happened.

She looked up to find the silent Kit watching her. The girl glanced away quickly, letting her fringe flop over her eyes like a curtain. She was dressed like a cowboy, in a blue-checked flannel shirt, jeans and worn range-rider boots. 'May I be excused, Grandma?' she said.

Christine smiled at her, but the smile, Laura thought, contained a warning. 'You may be excused, honey, but only from the table. Your grandfather and I have some business to attend to. I'd very much appreciate it if you could show Laura and Tariq around Fleet Farm. I'm sure they'd love to say hello to Goldie and meet Noble Warrior.'

Kit scowled. 'Can't Ken do it? I'm not a babysitter. I want to finish my book.'

Laura was shocked by the girl's rudeness. She said quickly: 'I'm sure Tariq and I can find our own way around the farm.'

Christine continued as if she hadn't spoken. 'Kit, sweetie, you'll have plenty of time to read your book later and Ken is very busy. It's wonderful for you to have some youngsters to hang out with for a change rather than us old folk. I hope you'll make the most of it.'

The look on Kit's face said she'd rather drink a toad smoothie than hang out with Laura and Tariq, but she mumbled, 'Yes, Grandma.'

Her grandfather reached out a large tanned hand and squeezed her shoulder. His eyes crinkled at the corners. 'Hey Possum, don't forget that we owe Laura and Tariq a big debt of gratitude for saving Goldie. They'll always be heroes in my eyes. A few hours of lost sleep is not going to change that.'

Kit murmured obediently, 'Yes, Gramps,' and was out of the door before he could say anything else.

Blake gave Laura and Tariq an apologetic smile and lifted his hands. 'Girls will be girls,' he said lightly, but Laura thought he looked sad.

They'd caught up with Kit and were halfway down the garden when the American girl stopped abruptly. She had the same denim blue eyes as her grandfather, but without the twinkle that made his so appealing.

'Let's be clear,' she snapped, 'I'm not the one who owes you anything. I don't care about stupid Goldie. He could have stayed kidnapped for all I care. If it weren't that Grandma and Gramps would be broken-hearted, I wouldn't care if a hundred thieves stole every one of our horses. I hate them. All they do is cause trouble. And you're not heroes to me. You're just a couple of strangers who are going to get in the way of my reading and guitar playing. Books and music are the only friends I want. The sooner you go back to where you came from, the better.'

Laura and Tariq stared at her in open-mouthed disbelief, but it turned out that she wasn't finished.

'Oh, and by the way the idea that some boy who doesn't know the first thing about horses can help Noble Warrior win the Derby is the most idiotic thing I've ever heard.'

Tariq recovered first. 'First, we would never in a million years think of ourselves as heroes. Lots of people helped rescue Goldie. We just happened to be two of them. Secondly, we love animals – especially horses and dogs – so *we're* glad that Goldie's safe even if you're not. As to whether or not I can help Noble Warrior win the Derby, I agree that it's a pretty crazy idea. After last night, your grandfather probably does too. But Laura and I like Mr and Mrs Wainright a lot and we're honoured that they've invited us to their beautiful farm. If we can help them with Noble Warrior, even in a small way, we're going to do our best.'

Now it was Kit's turn to look shocked. 'Umm, look, I didn't mean . . .' Her voice tailed away.

Laura was bristling with indignation. She could not believe that this odd girl with the sticking up hair and tomboy clothes had just told them to their faces that the sooner they left, the better she'd like it.

She lifted her chin and stared Kit in the eye. 'I agree with Tariq. We think your Grandma and Gramps are wonderful and we're going to do what we can to help them, whether you think that's idiotic or not. Oh, and you don't have to worry about us getting in the way of your reading. Tariq and I have each other. We don't need another friend.'

Before Kit could respond, Anita called: 'Miss Laura! Miss Laura, hurry. Your uncle is on the phone. He say they catch 'um. They catch the wicked men who stole Goldie.'

10

LAURA TOOK THE call in the airy living room beneath an immense oil painting of a jockey holding the reins of a bay stallion. It was so nice to hear her uncle's kind, calm voice and Skye barking in the background that Laura felt emotional again, but she forgot her own troubles as soon as she heard Calvin Redfern's news.

'Detective Watson has just called,' he told her. 'I thought you'd like to know that he's made two arrests in the Goldie case – a father and his twenty-five-year-old son. They run an international horse transportation business, which made it relatively easy for them to get the stallion across the Atlantic with forged paperwork.'

'So the Straight A gang weren't involved?' was Laura's first question.

Her uncle laughed. 'You sound almost disappointed. No, the Straight A's were not involved. As far as the police can tell, the two men acted alone. Their family business was about to go bankrupt and they thought that kidnapping a multi-million dollar racehorse and sending ransom notes would be the quickest way to make themselves a small fortune. They weren't planning to take the horse out of America, but when the ransom wasn't paid and it looked as if the police were hot on their trail, they panicked and put him on a flight to the UK. They were on their way to deliver him to a potential buyer when a deer leapt out in front of them and the horsebox overturned. Thinking the stallion was dead, they abandoned him.'

'Oh,' Laura said, feeling strangely dissatisfied. She should have been happy that the mystery of Goldie's abduction had been solved and the thieves were behind bars, but she wasn't. The events of the past few hours haunted her.

'That means the case is now closed, Laura,' her uncle was saying firmly. 'No more investigating. Blake Wainright has just told me what happened at Fleet Farm last night. You did the right thing to raise the alarm when you thought a theft had taken place, but it's obvious that it's greatly inconvenienced everyone concerned. From this moment on, you and Tariq are to remember that you're in Kentucky on holiday. You're forbidden to poke your nose into other people's business. No looking for mysteries where there are none, or seeing criminals where there are only decent men and women trying to do their jobs.'

'Yes, Uncle Calvin.'

'Don't say yes if you don't mean it.'

'Yes, Uncle Calvin. I mean, no, Uncle Calvin. Of course, Uncle Calvin.'

He sighed. 'It's at times such as this that I wish you and I weren't quite so alike. Oh, well, I guess I'll have to trust you. Now how about saying hello to Skye.'

When Laura went outside, Tariq and Kit were standing a couple of metres apart and in silence. The American girl was wearing a scowl. She stalked off towards the stallion barn without a word. Ignoring her, Laura relayed the news about the capture of Goldie's kidnappers to Tariq. Kit pretended she couldn't care less, but as soon as Laura had finished she turned and said: 'Thank goodness for that. Now everyone will stop going on and on about Goldie until I could scream, and life can get back to normal around here.'

They were almost at the barn when Laura noticed sunlight glinting from a metallic object close to where the lorries had parked the previous night. Unnoticed by the others, she bent down and picked it up. It was a piece of something silver. What remained resembled a lopsided tick or part of a letter of the alphabet – the top of an A or the fork of a V or Y. Laura popped it into her pocket. In all probability it was nothing, but one never knew. The most unlikely things could turn out to be clues.

Recalling her promise to her uncle, she felt guilty. Then she remembered that, according to all the grown-ups there *was* no mystery about the previous night. 'NO crime has been committed,' Garth Longbrook had declared. If that were true, there would be no harm whatsoever in taking a closer look at what went on behind the scenes at Fleet Farm. If there were no illegal goings on, a little poking around could hardly be considered an investigation. There was nothing wrong with healthy curiosity.

Inside the light, airy barn were a dozen beautifully clean stables. Four were empty, but the sculpted heads of some of America's finest thoroughbreds hung over the rest. They turned dark, interested eyes as the children approached. Kit introduced each one, but stood as far from them as possible. While Laura and Tariq stroked their velvet muzzles and went into raptures about their sleek, muscled forms, she hung back, looking strangely wistful.

Goldie was in the eighth stable. He remembered them at once and whickered with pleasure. Incredibly, he looked no worse for wear for his ordeal.

'If he has jet lag, he's hiding it well,' joked Tariq.

Ken emerged from the office beside the stable, looking even surlier that he had the previous day. When he saw Kit his eyebrows rose slightly, but he made no comment.

'This is Laura and Tariq,' Kit told him. 'They want to meet Noble Warrior. Gramps says that, unless Ryan gets out of hospital sooner than expected, Tariq is to be Warrior's groom between now and the Derby.'

Ken ignored Laura but gave the Bengali boy a slightly contemptuous look. 'Does he now? Had much experience grooming champion racehorses, kid?'

'No,' admitted Tariq, feeling foolish. 'But I'm a hard worker and a quick learner.'

Ken shrugged. 'In that case, you can start at once.'

'Great,' said Kit. 'I'll leave you to it.' Before anyone could object, she was gone.

Ken pushed open the office door, revealing a small, homely space that had the aroma of fresh coffee. A black and white cat was curled up in the sunshine on the windowsill. Racing photographs papered the walls. A young man with tangled blonde hair that hung almost to his shoulders was sitting at the table juggling rainbow-coloured skittles. A foreign language newspaper was spread out beside him.

'Don't let Mitch Raydon catch you doing that,' warned Ken.

The young man bounced to his feet with a cheeky grin. 'I am doing what?'

Laura blinked. The skittles had gone.

He came forward with his hand outstretched. 'My name is Ivan and I hear already that you are Miss Laura and Mr Tariq. We have you to sank many times for finding Goldie for us. We owe you. Anysing you need while you are here, ask Ivan.' He winked at Laura. 'If you ask Ken, don't hold your breath.'

'Very funny,' said Ken with a scowl. 'That's rich coming from the most work-shy man on the farm. And you wonder why Mitch gives you such a hard time. Now, where is that spare jacket? I left it hanging over the back of a chair.'

'Perhaps Mitch put it in locker. He's neat freak – zat's what zey say in your country, is it not?' Ivan pulled open a few lockers and drawers. When he discovered it, he presented it to Tariq with a flourish. 'Zis is very big but you can push up the sleeves, I sink.'

The jacket had the words 'FLEET FARM' and a galloping horse sketched in white on the back. Laura was as sure as she could be that the men in both lorries had worn cloaks with the identical logo. She'd been some distance away and looking down on the scene through a blur of rain, but she recognised the shape.

The jacket almost swamped Tariq, but he put it on with a smile and Ivan rolled up the sleeves for him.

'Don't you have work to do, Ivan?' demanded Ken.

The young man gave a mock salute. 'Aye, aye, captain.' He flashed the children another grin. 'Remember what I tell you. Anysing you need, ask for Ivan.' Then he was gone.

Ken escorted them to the last stable in the row. Noble Warrior was standing in the rear of the stable with his ears back, resting one foot. Christine had described him as a sweetheart, but to Laura he looked bored and out of sorts.

'You'll notice that he's much smaller than Goldie, his sire,' Ken told them. 'Tiny but perfectly formed. That's because he's a twin – something almost unheard of in racing. He has an identical brother named Valiant, who belongs to Nathan Perry, owner of the farm next door. When they're standing still, the only person who can tell them apart is Ryan. But there's a big difference in their speed. Valiant is an okay horse, but Warrior is dynamite. We call him the Pocket Rocket.'

Laura noticed that while he was talking about the horses that were his passion, Ken's face came alive and his eyes sparkled with enthusiasm. When he stopped, his sullen look returned. He unbolted the stable door and nodded at Tariq. 'You think you can help Warrior win the Kentucky Derby? Here he is. Introduce yourself to him.'

With an anxious glance at Laura, Tariq walked into the stable. Laura, who was annoyed with Ken for testing her friend – and she had no doubt that that's what this was, a test – followed him in.

Noble Warrior snorted uneasily and showed the whites of his eyes. Tariq hesitated.

'You're not afraid, are you?' jeered Ken. 'That wouldn't be a good start. A groom who's afraid of horses.'

'No, I'm not. But I'm worried that something is bothering him.'

'Most racehorses are like human athletes,' Ken told him. 'They're pampered and indulged and that tends to make them moody. You need to be able to handle that. But you don't need to fret about Warrior. He's a pussy cat.'

Tariq took a step further and Noble Warrior's chestnut ears pinned flat against his head. Again the boy hesitated. Ken made another jibe. It was on the tip of Laura's tongue to say, 'Something's wrong. I don't think we should be in here,' when the horse exploded.

With a squeal of fury, he reared, striking out with his hooves. Tariq and Laura barely had time to leap for the stable door before he came after them, teeth bared. Laura felt the rush of air as his jaws snapped shut just millimeters from her arm. He wheeled and tried to kick

Tariq. Ken grabbed the boy and wrenched the stable door closed in the nick of time. The horse's hooves clattered against it. Noble Warrior let out another scream of rage.

'What the heck is going on here?' demanded Blake Wainright. Kit was beside him, eyes wide with terror, and behind her was a short, wiry man with a leathery brown face and glittery black eyes. Laura wondered if he was the trainer, Mitch Raydon. Blake Wainright advanced on Ken. 'If Warrior is injured and can't run in the Derby, we're finished. Do you understand that? Finished.'

Ken looked shaken himself. 'I'm so sorry, sir. I don't know what to say. As soon as Tariq and Laura entered the stable, Warrior went berserk. He seemed to be trying to kill them.'

Mitch Raydon moved nearer. 'Obviously, this means that the boy can't be his groom. If Ken hasn't the time, I'll get Ivan to do it.'

'It means nothing of the kind,' Blake Wainright responded irritably. 'Warrior must have got some sort of fright, that's all. Now Tariq, you and I will go into the stable together. Take that silly jacket off. It's much too large for you and it'll simply get in your way if you're working with him. Christine is going to order some Fleet Farm clothing for you and Laura. You'll be much more comfortable in something your own size. Now I know you've had a fright, but trust me when I say that Noble Warrior is as gentle as a kitten. Let me introduce you to him.'

Tariq handed the jacket to Laura and their eyes met. She could see that he wasn't looking forward to another encounter with the stallion.

Blake opened the stable door. 'All you have to do is approach him with the same calm confidence you had when you were dealing with Goldie.'

The boy stepped into the stall, talking all the time in a low, calm voice. The horse was sweating and trembling but he made no move to attack. Tariq crept forward until he was near enough to touch the horse. Cautiously, he put a hand on the stallion's neck. Noble Warrior tensed. He turned his head, snorting with fear. His muzzle touched Tariq's chest. Tariq stroked his graceful head with kind hands. Warrior began to relax. At length, he gave a great shuddering sigh and all the tension left his body.

The tautness drained from Blake Wainright's body too. He chuckled. 'There you go! What did I tell you? They're made for each other.'

For the next half hour, Ken gave Tariq an advanced grooming lesson under Blake's watchful eye. Kit had disappeared again and Mitch had excused himself to supervise the arrival of a new mare. Leaning over the stable door, Laura felt immensely proud of her friend. Few boys would have had the courage to return to the stable after what had happened, but he'd done so without hesitation.

At the same time, she couldn't help wondering about the transformation in the stallion. He'd changed from savage mustang to angel in seconds for no obvious reason. What had set him off? The only thing Tariq had done differently was to remove the jacket.

Blake, Tariq and Ken were absorbed with the horse. Laura moved out of view. She studied the jacket. It looked new and clean. Ken had put on one just like it and Noble

Warrior hadn't batted an ear. On impulse, she lifted it to her nose and almost gagged. The right sleeve smelled strongly of – of what?

Laura tried to work it out. It reminded her of something. She wracked her brains. Then, it came to her. It was reminiscent of the big cat enclosure at the zoo near Sylvan Meadows. A foster family had taken her there when she was nine. She'd stood outside the lion cage, breathing in their wild smell, a smell she was sure would be natural and even wonderful on the plains of Africa but which was rancid and overpowering in the confined space. To Laura, who'd wept at the sight of the forlorn lions shivering in the British winter, it was the smell of unhappiness.

But how could such a smell get onto a supposedly clean jacket at a horse farm in Kentucky? More importantly, why?

Instinctively, horses are petrified of big cats, their main predator in ancient times. If someone had deliberately daubed the scent of a lion or something similar on the jacket, there could be only one explanation, that he or she had wanted to terrify a horse and, presumably, the wearer. But which horse and who was the intended victim? The jacket had apparently been a random one found in a locker. Was it too much of a leap to think that it was always intended for Tariq and meant to scare him so much that he'd refuse to help Noble Warrior?

Laura wondered if she could sneak the jacket up to her room and keep it in a safe place until an opportunity arose to examine it more closely, but before she could think of how to conceal it Ken emerged from the stable. 'You done with that?' he asked grouchily and practically snatched the jacket away.

She couldn't protest without causing a scene. Watching him disappear into the office, a frown creased Laura's brow. She'd been at Fleet Farm for less than twenty-four hours but one thing was crystal clear. There were many more questions than answers.

11

'I WOULDN'T TAKE them riding for all the tea in China,' declared Kit.

Outside the breakfast room, Laura and Tariq exchanged glances. It didn't take a rocket scientist to guess who she was talking about. The previous night, she'd stayed completely silent at dinner when Blake was telling his wife about the visitors' dramatic meeting with Noble Warrior. Recalling the girl's stricken face and sudden exit from the barn, it had occurred to Laura then that there might be more to her behaviour than met the eye.

'I wouldn't care if a hundred thieves stole every one of our

horses,' she'd ranted earlier in the day. *'I hate them. All they do is cause trouble.'*

What trouble, Laura wondered. Was it something to do with the finances of the farm? And why did the girl detest horses so much? Christine had told them that Kit's parents were divorced. Her mum was a busy professional who spent much of her time travelling, and Kit rarely saw her father. She'd been all but brought up by the grandparents she adored. To Laura, that made it more curious still that Kit hadn't inherited their love of horses. She could hardly bear to touch them.

Kit showed no sign of embarrassment when they entered the dining room, although she must have known they'd overheard her.

Christine, however, looked mortified. 'Come in, come in,' she said, mustering an over-bright smile. 'I hope you slept well. Help yourself to a couple of Anita's fluffy pecan pancakes. There's farm butter, cream and strawberries to go on top, and maple syrup in the jug.'

They were tucking into mountainous heaps of syrupy pancakes when she brought up the subject of riding again. 'I was just saying to Kit that I'd like her to take you both horseback riding this morning. If that's something you'd enjoy, that is.'

Kit's mouth set in a mutinous line.

With a pleading glance at her, Christine continued: 'Kit prefers not to ride herself, but I was about to suggest that she escort you on her bicycle. Would that be okay with everyone?'

Before any of the children could agree or disagree, she

said: 'Good, then that's settled. Kit will meet you both at the mares' and foals' barn, which is where we keep our working horses, at ten a.m. Your horses will be saddled and waiting, and she'll be ready with her bike. Now, can I interest anyone in some coffee?'

U

'My wife says it is a crying shame,' said Roberto, Anita's husband, whose job it was to take care of the mares, foals and working horses. He tightened the girth on Laura's horse, a pretty palomino.

Laura followed his gaze and saw Kit cycling slowly up from the house. She dismounted and began examining a tyre as if inspecting it for a puncture.

'What's a crying shame?' asked Tariq, leading his own pony, a brown and white paint horse, in their direction. He'd been up since the crack of dawn taking care of Noble Warrior, but he was positively glowing. Nothing made him happier than being around animals.

Roberto handed the palomino's reins to Laura. 'Is it not a shame when the best young horsewoman in Kentucky choose two wheels over a horse?'

Laura stared at him. 'Kit's a good rider?'

He snorted. 'She ain't good, she fantastic. The best. Eighteen months ago, she Rising Star of the Year at Kentucky Horse Park's Annual Show. The other youngsters, they go green with envy. She took home all trophies for her age group. Jumped like a superstar. But her heart, always it has been in racing. She dream of being jockey since she knee high to grasshopper. But not any more. Not since accident. Now . . .'

He lifted his hands in a helpless gesture. 'Now, no one can get through to her. The Wainrights, they feel they are responsible. Their hearts are broken. She like daughter to them, you know. I tell them, no one can see inside the mind of a horse. It was accident, end a story.'

'What happened?' asked Laura. In the distance, Kit was kneeling beside the bike. She stood up and began pushing it back to the house.

Roberto leaned against the paddock rails. He lowered his voice. 'She was exercising horse for Mr Wainright and the trainer, Mitch. But this horse was special one. She ride Red Bishop, favourite for Kentucky Derby one year ago. Plenty people, including me, warn Mr Wainright against putting young girl on these fast, powerful horses, but he always say Kit had best instincts of any exercise rider he knew. It is true. Difficult horse, they go like dream for her. They love her and she love them. Not any more, a course, but in them days.'

Tariq moved closer. 'So what went wrong?'

Roberto opened his big, dry hands. 'Only God knows. Kit and Bishop were on last furlong of the gallops, easing up like Mitch tol' them, when all of a sudden that horse went crazy.'

Into Laura's mind came an image of Noble Warrior exploding into fury the previous morning. 'Did something startle him?'

Roberto shook his head. 'No one saw nothing. Maybe

he lose his mind. He threw Kit and bolted for boundary fence' – he nodded towards the horizon – 'way down the end of farm. Beyond is old limestone quarry. Very dangerous. Giant cliffs. Nobody go there but that fool boy, Ivan. The gate between has chain and lock. That day it was open. Red Bishop he slip and break leg. Terrible business. *Terrible.*

'Kit, she was just bruised, not hurt, but for three weeks she not speak one word. When she finally talk she tell her Grandpa it all her fault that Red Bishop die and she never want to ride again. She say she hate every horse. We tell her it's not true till we blue in face, but she not listen to anyone.'

He looked quite bereft. 'She and I, we good friends once. She always under my feet, wanting to play with foals, wanting me teach her training tricks. Now I don't see her no more. She always in the house, always sad.'

Laura stroked the nose of the palomino. Her heart went out to Roberto as much as to the silent girl. Who could blame Kit for not wanting to be around horses? An event like that would traumatise anyone. 'Kit said something about the horses being the cause of all the trouble around here.'

Roberto stared at her broodingly. 'She did? She right, I s'pose. See, Red Bishop, he belong to our neighbour, Nathan Perry. He Mr Wainright's best friend. When Bishop broke leg, he sue Mr and Mrs Wainright for many millions of dollars. He say Blake and Mitch very negligent putting a child on his champion horse. Before that, the Wainrights own farm outright. Now the bank are every day calling to scream for money. Blake and Nathan, they don't speak no more.'

'But what about Gold Rush?' Tariq wanted to know. 'If he's worth $75 million, couldn't they sell him?'

Roberto shook his head. 'Goldie not owned by Wainwright family. He belongs to syndicate of lotsa businessmen. The Wainrights love him like their own precious child, but they have only one tiny piece of him. We had many promising mares and foals here, but all were sold to raise money for lawsuit. The ones you see here are only boarding at Fleet Farm. But it wasn't enough. Lawyers, you know, these people eat money. The Wainrights' only hope is Noble Warrior. He the one racehorse that belongs just to them. If he doesn't win Derby, they lose farm for sure.'

Tariq thought of the money Blake had donated to their St Ives' school. If he was short of cash, he must have parted with the money only because he was expecting a miracle in return. Tariq's stomach gave a nervous heave. No pressure then.

The faint squeak of brakes warned of Kit's approach. Perhaps realising that he'd said more than he should have, Roberto gave a guilty start.

'Thanks, Roberto,' Laura said loudly. 'You've been a huge help.'

He smiled gratefully. 'No problem, Miss Laura. You have fun riding Honey. She a honey. Most gentle horse on farm. Your horse is call Braveheart, Tariq. Brave his name, brave his nature. Enjoy!'

Kit propped her bike against the mounting block. Her hair was sticking up in every direction and she was wearing ripped jeans, a checked shirt and a cowboy hat. She made no attempt to approach the horses. 'Sorry I'm late. Flat tyre.'

Her voice was gruff and it was obvious it took effort for her to apologise to them. 'You ready?'

'Yes, we are,' responded Laura, feeling very much warmer towards the girl than she had done only ten minutes earlier. 'We're looking forward to it.'

~ 12 ~

WHATEVER KIT'S FEELINGS about horses or annoying visitors who got in the way of her reading and guitar playing, she was a superb teacher. In no time at all, Tariq and Laura had been taught how to mount and hold the reins properly, Western-style, and had mastered the basics of the rising trot. Kit managed to give most instructions from her bike, but she did have to dismount to adjust their stirrup length.

The day had dawned cold and misty, but as they rode across the farm the clouds cleared to reveal a peacock blue sky. The sun beat down pleasantly on Laura's fair skin. Her palomino mare, Honey, was a dream to ride. Sweet and willing. Beside her, Tariq couldn't stop grinning. He'd

82

taken to horse riding like a dolphin to the waves. His skewbald pony stepped out keenly, ears pricked.

Kit cycled ahead, leading them past emerald pastures and along a sandy road to the training track – an all-weather surface made of sand, carpet, wax and shredded tyres on which the horses were put through their paces every morning. As they neared it, Ivan emerged from behind a stone wall leading a black colt. He was wearing a Fleet Farm jacket and a billowing pair of yellow and blue polka-dotted pants. A disembodied voice shouted after him. 'Lazy good for nothing! You're wearing out my last nerve Ivan. One more mess up and you're out.'

'Greetings, my friends!' he cried cheerfully. He touched his forelock. 'Hey, Kit, zat is a good horse you are riding. More reliable than zis one and no sweat!'

Kit gave a weak smile, but it was obvious that she didn't appreciate his attempt at humour. 'Hi Ivan. What have you been doing to upset Mitch this time?'

He grinned and shrugged. 'I never do nothing. He get out the bed on the wrong side. Working wiz Mitch is like knowing a tiger wiz a sorn in his paw. Okay, kids, see you. Must keep zis baby moving.'

'Is Ivan an exercise rider?' Laura asked when he'd gone. She couldn't imagine that his billowing pants were very suitable for racing across the farm on the back of a one-ton animal. They'd have a parachute effect.

Kit gave a rude laugh. 'Ivan ride? He couldn't stay on a rocking horse. No, he's what's known as a hotwalker. When the exercise riders are done, the hotwalker cools the horses down by walking 'em and hosing 'em down.

The reason Mitch is always on his case is 'cos Ivan spends any spare moment he gets juggling, turning somersaults or working on his fitness in the old quarry. He takes a stopwatch. He's obsessed with improving his running times.'

At the mention of the quarry, a shadow passed across her face. As if suddenly remembering that she wasn't supposed to be enjoying herself, she said huffily: 'Stop dawdling. I haven't got all day. I'll show you the track and then we're returning to the barn. I'm not a tour guide, you know.'

Beneath Laura, Honey had begun to fuss and fret. Laura wondered if the black colt had upset her. She stroked the mare's satiny gold neck. It worked momentarily, but as they passed through the gate and saw the circular track, Honey became increasingly distressed, especially when Mitch's red truck roared to life. With a wave of his hand, the trainer drove off in the direction of the house and barns. He'd finished work for the morning.

Honey threw up her head, showing the whites of her eyes. 'What do I do, Kit?' called Laura, alarmed.

Kit, who'd ridden her bike to the track's edge, braked with a grimace. But when she saw how Honey was playing up, her expression changed to concern. 'Keep calm, Laura. Try not to let her know you're nervous. Keep your hands down and still. Don't jab her in the mouth. You'll be fine.'

But Laura was not fine. Something was seriously wrong with Honey. Lather was collecting like foam on the mare's flanks. Her ears were back and she was snorting and threatening to rear.

Tariq tried to manouevre his horse alongside her so that he could grab Honey's reins, but Braveheart refused to cooperate.

Kit laid down her bike carefully so as not to frighten the mare further. 'Hold on, Laura,' she said in a calm, authoritative voice, sounding much older than her years. 'Don't worry. I'm not going to allow anything to happen to you, I promise.'

It was easier said than done. Hardly had the words left her mouth than Honey wheeled on the spot, almost sending Laura flying. Then she bolted.

Laura caught a glimpse of Tariq's frightened face as she hurtled by, clinging to Honey's mane. She hauled desperately on the reins, but to no avail. Honey had the bit between her teeth and was galloping along the dirt road beside the track as if the hounds of hell were on her trail. Faster and faster they flew. Laura tried to follow Kit's advice and pretend she wasn't scared, but it was no use. She was terrified.

Ahead lay the quarry. Roberto had said that the gate was always kept locked, but what if it had been left open as it had been on the day of Kit's accident? Would Honey sense danger and stop? Or would she race on until she reached the giant cliffs Roberto had described, carrying them both to their doom? The beloved faces of her uncle, Tariq and Skye came into Laura's head. What if she ended up in hospital with multiple fractures? Worse still, what if something happened and she never saw them again?

The thunder of the mare's hooves roared in Laura's head. It seemed to be getting louder. As they tore towards the boundary fence, Laura tried once more to stop her. Honey responded by speeding up. As they drew nearer, Laura saw that her worst fears were realised. The gate was ajar.

'No!' she cried as Honey swerved through. Already half out of the saddle, she only narrowly avoided being catapulted into a thorn bush by the mare's corkscrew turn. Before them lay the gaping expanse of the quarry, its sheer cliffs dropping away to reveal a white valley in which rainwater had formed deep blue pools. As Honey raced blindly towards the edge of the void, shale spat like sparks from her flying feet.

Laura's life flashed before her eyes. They were going to die and there was not a thing she could do about it. A kind of numb acceptance stole into her veins. Then the faces of Skye, Tariq and her uncle flashed through her mind and she rallied once more. She had to fight until her last breath to save herself – and Honey. Weakly, she gathered the reins.

Over the clatter of hooves came an echo, a staccato rhythm that grew louder and louder. Braveheart's head came into view, alongside Laura's hip. His eyes were wide with fear but he galloped at full stretch towards the abyss. Laura risked a glance sideways. Kit was on his back, driving him on. As Braveheart drew level, the American girl reached out and grabbed Honey's bridle.

'Hold tight, Laura,' she yelled. Pulling with all her strength, she steered the horses away from the crumbling edge, turning them in a tight circle until Honey's wild flight slowed and the sweating palomino came to a shaky-legged halt.

Kit was on the ground and at Laura's side in a second. Laura toppled from the saddle, collapsing into the American girl's arms. As she did so, there was a low rumble and the section of cliff across which they'd just galloped broke off and plunged into the valley. The rocks pelted the limestone basin far below. The girls stared at each other in shock. Before they could react, Tariq, whose horse had been commandeered by Kit, came flying up to them on the bike.

'Laura, Kit, thank God you're okay.' There was a catch in his voice. He flung the bike down. There was a split second of awkwardness and then the three of them were hugging and sobbing with relief.

The man who watched from the trees saw the trio clinging together in an unbroken circle.

~ 13 ~

'I GUESS INSTINCT just took over.'

Hours after her heroic rescue of Laura, Kit was still stunned at what had happened – not because she'd done the impossible and snatched Laura and Honey from the extreme edge of a disintegrating cliff, but rather because she'd found the courage to ride a horse again.

Tariq had described her recruitment of Braveheart with laughing admiration. 'One minute I was watching Honey streak away into the distance at a million miles an hour and feeling totally helpless, and the next Kit was virtually pulling me out of the saddle. She told me not to worry because she was going to save you if it killed her.'

'And it almost did,' Laura said with a shudder. 'I'll never be able to thank you enough for saving my life, Kit, but I feel very guilty when I think how close you came to going over the edge yourself.'

Kit giggled. 'Don't feel guilty. It wasn't that close. There were at least six centimetres between us and the abyss!'

The teenager was sitting cross-legged on her bed in her rather untidy room with her newfound friends. And they *were* friends. How could they not be after what they'd been through together? Across her lap lay an acoustic guitar, on which she absent-mindedly strummed a country song as they talked, and all around the room were piles of mystery and adventure books. The transformation in her was quite extraordinary. It was as if someone had reached inside her and switched a light on.

Her grandparents had been quite awestruck by the change. A groundsman had spotted Honey bolt and had radioed the house to alert them. They'd come racing to the quarry expecting to find three children in various states of injury or anguish and instead found them falling about laughing. What had set them off was a comment by Tariq. He'd been describing Kit's impressive mounting technique to Laura.

'She was on Braveheart's back in a single bound, and boy did he understand that the situation was urgent. He couldn't have galloped any faster if his tail was on fire.'

Perhaps because they'd been so close to disaster and had survived, they were euphoric. Everything seemed funny to them. But the reaction of the Wainrights and Garth Longbrook, who'd come tearing up to them in the

Fleet Farm truck and leapt out anticipating the worst was sobering. Christine had flung her arms around each of them in turn. Her eyes were red and she was shaking. 'Thank goodness you're all right,' she kept saying. 'Thank goodness you're all right.'

Blake had apologised to Laura at least a hundred times about the behaviour of Honey, supposedly the safest horse on the farm. 'I can't understand it,' he said over and over. 'I'm mystified. I can only imagine that a bee stung her. I'm so sorry, Laura. What you and Tariq must think of us. We've invited you to Fleet Farm for a relaxing holiday and so far you've had a couple of sleepless nights, narrowly avoided being trampled by Noble Warrior and almost been catapulted over a cliff by Honey. It wasn't how I planned to thank you for rescuing Goldie.'

Garth Longbrook's main concern was that the quarry gate had been left open. He'd glared at Laura as if she were somehow responsible. 'Three times I've bought a lock for it and three times it's been broken and removed,' he said angrily. 'If I catch the person who's doing it, they'll be banned from Fleet Farm for life. As soon as I get back to my office, I'm calling the security company and getting them to put a CCTV camera and an alarm on this section of fence.'

Christine had wanted to radio Roberto and ask him to lead the horses back to the barn, but Kit insisted that she, Laura and Tariq were perfectly capable of doing it themselves. That was how Laura came to find the cause of the palomino's frenzied flight. She was unbuckling Honey's bridle when a small plastic phial dropped out of the hollow of the mare's browband. Kit had turned away to undo the mare's girth so she didn't notice Laura pick it up and, acting on instinct, sniff it. The phial was nearly empty but the few drops of orange liquid that remained smelled the same as the sleeve of the jacket that had so enraged Noble Warrior. It smelled of wildcat. It smelled like a predator.

As she put it in her pocket and covered it with her hand, Laura noticed something interesting. The plastic softened as it warmed. It was then that it hit her that the whole thing had been planned. Someone had put the phial in Honey's browband knowing that as the horse got hotter the plastic would pop, dribble down the palomino's nose and release the wildcat odour guaranteed to drive even the most docile horse out of its mind. The fact that the quarry gate had been left open was too much of a coincidence. Someone had meant to harm Laura. But why?

The only possible conclusion was that she, like Tariq, was a threat. Tariq because he potentially had the special touch that could help Noble Warrior win the Derby, and Laura because . . . well, because she had a reputation as an ace investigator. Those were Blake's words, not hers.

'I've told everyone at Fleet Farm that Britain's best girl detective is coming to stay,' he'd said with a grin on the night before they flew to the US. 'Not that there'll be any mysteries for you to solve now that Goldie has been found – well, apart from the matter of who abducted him, but it never hurts to have an extra pair of eyes around the place. There are still a lot of unanswered questions about why the horse was stolen in the first place.'

Laura had followed Kit into the house with that thought weighing heavily on her mind. Goldie's thieves might be behind bars, but they may not have acted alone. Clearly there was someone, or several people, at Fleet Farm who didn't want anyone – not even a couple of kids – nosing around.

When Kit nipped into the kitchen to fetch three glasses of iced lemonade, Laura took the opportunity to update Tariq on the phial hidden in Honey's bridle. She'd already told him about the wildcat scent she'd found on the jacket.

Now, sitting on Kit's bed, she realised that in order to get at the truth she had to test their fragile new friendship. Picking nervously at a thread on her jeans, she said: 'Kit, would you mind if I asked you about your accident?'

The American girl flinched as if she'd been struck. She drew in an uneven breath. 'What would you like to know?'

'What exactly happened?'

Kit put aside her guitar and hugged her knees. 'It was a year ago today. That's what makes it so weird. It's almost as if some twist of fate meant you to have an accident on the anniversary of mine.'

Laura looked at Tariq but made no comment. 'Go on.'

Kit gave a sweet smile that softened her face. Her hair was still sticking up all over the place, but she'd put on a pink T-shirt and cropped khaki pants. Laura noticed for the first time that she was actually very pretty.

'I was helping Gramps prepare Nathan Perry's stallion, Red Bishop, for the Derby. It was sort of our tradition. I'd wanted to be a jockey since before I could walk and I'd always dreamed of riding at Churchill Downs – that's the home of the Derby. No one encouraged me more than Gramps. Even when I was a little kid, he'd discuss training methods with me and talk about form – how a horse is performing. That's important, but even when they're running poorly no horse is ever just a number to Gramps. Each of them is special in their own way.

'As I grew older and stronger, Gramps would let me exercise some of the racehorses. He used to say that there was no creature on earth that responded to honesty and kindness like a thoroughbred.

'On that particular day, Mitch, the trainer, was having a lot of trouble with Red Bishop. Bishop's usual exercise rider had been fired and he hadn't taken to the new man at all. I'd ridden him a few times and he'd always been an angel with me so Gramps decided on the spur of the moment that I should take him out that morning. Mitch was really adamant I shouldn't, particularly with the Derby so close. They almost came to blows over it. Mitch said it was the worst idea he'd ever heard. He wanted to check with Nathan – he's our neighbour and he used to be Gramps' best friend – but Gramps can be pretty stubborn and he said that what Nathan knew about training wouldn't fit on a postage stamp.

'Mitch stormed off but he came back about five minutes later in a really good mood. Gramps told him that he wanted me to ride Bishop and if Mitch didn't like it he could put it in his pipe and smoke it. The strange thing was that Mitch told him he thought it was a great idea if I took Bishop out and there was no need for Gramps to get so stroppy about it.'

'When did you first realise that something was wrong?' asked Tariq.

'Around the second furlong. Bishop was a big horse but he'd always been a gentle giant. It's a cliché, but in his case it was true. I'd always loved to watch him run. It was as if he went into this happy place in his head.'

She smiled at the memory, but her face quickly clouded. 'He galloped like a dream for the first part of his workout, but then he began to fidget. I could tell that something was upsetting him, I just couldn't figure out what. Come to think of it, he was behaving a bit like Honey did before she bolted. I kept thinking that he'd relax once he got into his stride. Instead he began to gallop as though he was being pursued by a hungry mountain lion. I tried to pull him up on the last furlong and he seemed to be slowing. Then all of sudden he went berserk.'

Tears filled her eyes. 'That's all I remember. When I came round, Gramps told me that Red Bishop had broken a leg in the quarry and they'd had to put him to sleep.'

She said passionately: 'I'll never forgive myself. I made up my mind that I'd never ride again, never so much as touch a horse. And I haven't. Until today.'

Laura said: 'Maybe it wasn't your fault – what happened with Bishop, I mean.'

'You sound like Grandma and Gramps. That's what they're always telling me.'

'Well, perhaps they're right.'

Kit shook her head violently. 'No. No, they're not. I

94

shouldn't have been riding him. I'm responsible for kill
. . . for killing—'

'Was there anything unusual about Red Bishop when
he was found?' Tariq interrupted. 'I know he was badly
injured, but did the vet or anyone else mention anything
peculiar? Did they notice a funny smell on his bridle or
saddlecloth, for instance?'

Kit went rigid. She stared at Tariq as if he'd suddenly
grown two heads. 'How could you know that?' she
demanded. 'Who have you been talking to?'

'Just tell us,' Laura said gently. 'It's important.'

Kit was pale. 'All I know is that the veterinarian told Ken
that Red Bishop's bridle had a really strange odour when
they removed it. He said it smelled like a bear's lair or a
cougar, like some wild creature. He questioned how the
smell had got there, but I don't think anyone paid much
attention at the time. They were too preoccupied by the
loss of the Derby favourite.'

The blood roared in Laura's ears. She'd been expecting
to hear something of the kind, but having it confirmed
made her feel ill. 'Kit, what would you say if I told you that
you're not responsible for Red Bishop's death? That I'm
pretty sure that what happened to you wasn't an accident.'

Kit snorted. 'I'd assume you were making a really
bad joke. What are you trying to tell me? That someone
wanted to hurt me or destroy Bishop? That his bridle was
sabotaged in some way?'

'That's exactly what I'm saying,' Laura told her. 'And I
can prove it.'

~ 14 ~

'WHERE DO WE BEGIN?' Kit wanted to know.

The three were sitting on a rise behind the mares' and foals' barn, shaded by an old oak hung with Spanish moss. Laura could not decide whether the effect was gorgeous or ghostly. Scattered on the rug before them were the remains of a picnic lunch of po-boys – delicious crusty rolls stuffed with fried green tomatoes, cheese and spicy mayonnaise. They were accompanied by root beer, a drink that tasted like bubblegum and wasn't beer at all. For dessert, there were homemade red velvet cupcakes with vanilla icing.

Before coming outside Laura had shown Kit the little plastic container she'd found in Honey's bridle.

Unfortunately, the remaining drops of orange liquid had leaked out and it no longer smelled of wildcat. Even more unfortunately, the jacket Tariq had been wearing when Noble Warrior attacked him had been washed. Once again Kit and Tariq had to take Laura's word for what she'd seen and smelled.

Nevertheless, Kit had helped Laura hide the phial, carefully wrapped in an 'evidence' bag, in the back of the Wainrights' vast refrigerator in order to preserve it for possible testing.

Much to Laura's relief, Kit hadn't dismissed the sabotage theory out of hand. In fact, she'd taken it very seriously.

'It sounds far-fetched. I mean, what kind of monster would do such a thing?' was her initial reaction. But she admitted that three accidents taking place on one farm, all apparently caused by a wild animal smell, was too much of a coincidence. Especially when one took into account the theft of Goldie.

Laura couldn't help thinking that this was the second time she'd been promised a dream holiday which had rapidly turned into a nightmare. Her Caribbean adventure had begun the same way. One minute she and Tariq were looking forward to a blissful couple of weeks on a snowy white island surrounded by turquoise waters and the next they were at risk of being devoured by sharks or incinerated by a flaming volcano. This vacation was showing every sign of going the same way. Each time Laura relived the moment when Honey accelerated towards the cliff edge, she shivered. Beneath its pristine, lovely surface, there were dark forces at work at Fleet Farm.

'According to Gramps, you've both had plenty of experience with investigations,' Kit was saying between bites of cupcake. 'You know about this stuff. With the Derby coming up in four days, my grandparents have way too many worries already. If you don't mind, I'd rather that we kept this a secret between us for the moment. With any luck, there's a simple explanation and we can clear it up on our own. Is that a deal?'

'You have our word,' Tariq said.

'Deal,' agreed Laura, feeling a pang of guilt when she recalled again her promise to her uncle. But as Kit said, there was probably a simple explanation for the odd goings on at Fleet Farm. There was no sense in causing unnecessary stress to the Wainwrights or her uncle when they could clear the mystery up on their own.

Kit wiped her mouth with a napkin. For a girl who'd just been told that somebody had tried to do grievous bodily harm to either her or Red Bishop, she looked strangely excited. 'Right, where do we begin?'

Tariq put down his root beer and took a notebook from his pocket. He was wearing a black Fleet Farm polo shirt and olive-green cargo shorts. His feet were bare. 'We need a who, why and how list. Who are our main suspects for each incident? What motive could they have? How did they plan it so that each event looked like an accident?'

'Exactly,' agreed Laura. 'Kit, who stood to gain last year if you or Red Bishop were harmed?'

Kit lay back on the grass with her hands behind her head. 'Me? Nobody. Red Bishop is a different story. He was hot favourite for the Derby. Any time a dead cert doesn't win a major race, lots of people benefit. A gambler or a bookmaker who stood to lose a lot of money on him might have wanted him stopped. So might a trainer who wanted a different horse to win.'

'What about your neighbour, Nathan Perry?' Laura asked.

Kit sat up. 'Don't be nutty. Nathan was Bishop's owner. There wouldn't have been a prouder man in the whole of Kentucky if his stallion had won the Derby. Especially because of what happened with Noble Warrior and Valiant.'

Tariq put down his pen. 'What do you mean?'

'Haven't you heard? You see, Gramps and Nathan were joint owners of Noble's dam. That's what we call a horse's mother – the dam. When they discovered she was expecting twins, they agreed to toss a coin to decide who took which foal. Nathan got Valiant, a good horse but not a great one. He could barely outrun Honey. Gramps got Noble Warrior, who's grown up to be one of the best racehorses in America. He's odds-on favourite for the Derby.'

The word 'revenge' came into Laura's head, but she didn't say it out loud. 'Let's put a question mark after Nathan's name. He could well have been nursing a grudge for years.'

Kit's eyes widened as a thought occurred to her. 'What if someone is trying to destroy my grandfather? Someone besides Nathan, I mean. Before the lawsuit, Fleet Farm was one of the most successful racing operations in the country. Whoever hurt Bishop must have known that

99

Gramps' reputation would be damaged and he'd end up with loads of debts.'

Laura was impressed. 'That's the kind of deduction Matt Walker would make. He's a fictional detective, but he's always coming up with super-smart theories. But don't be too quick to dismiss Nathan. It's hard to imagine that anyone could be wicked enough to injure their own horse, but remember that Red Bishop wasn't guaranteed to win the Derby. He could have finished last. On the other hand, by suing your grandfather Nathan could end up owning Fleet Farm.'

Kit bit her lip and said nothing.

Tariq wrote Nathan's name on his pad below 'gamblers' and 'bookmakers.' He also wrote, 'Somebody may be out to get Fleet Farm at all costs,' and tucked the pen behind his ear. 'Okay, let's turn to the events of the last couple of days – Noble Warrior attacking us and Honey going berserk? We're strangers here and we're just kids. Why would anyone want us out of the way?'

'Because there's something they don't want found,' Kit answered. 'But who or what it might be, I haven't a clue. I like everyone who works on Fleet Farm.'

Tariq's pen was poised over his notebook. His skin looked like burnt honey in the dappled sunlight and his amber eyes were serious. *'Everyone?'*

'Well, nearly everyone. Mitch is all right, but it annoys me that he's always being mean to Ivan, who's fun and cool. He's also always complaining about being short of money. Ryan once told me he has a brother who's forever in trouble or out of work and borrowing cash from him.

But Gramps won't hear a word against Mitch. Says there's no better trainer.

'Ken has been like a bear with a sore head ever since Ryan was beaten up by Goldie's abductors, but he loves horses more than anything in the world. I can't imagine him laying a finger on one. You saw how upset he was about what happened with you and Honey today.'

And they had. He'd come rushing out to greet them as they'd led the horses back to the stables, looking as if he was about to burst into tears. 'I'm so sorry you've had to go through this, Laura,' he said. 'I'm so sorry, Tariq. Kit, if something had happened to you I . . . I . . . If something . . . This is bad. This is so bad.'

He'd offered to untack their horses and rub them down. When Kit had told him that they'd prefer do it themselves, he'd stumbled away looking more downcast than ever.

Lost in thought, Laura took a swig of her root beer.

'Garth Longbrook is hardly likely to be involved,' Kit was telling Tariq. 'He's our head of security.'

Laura had her own opinion of Garth Longbrook, but she decided to keep it to herself. She gazed out at the yearlings that dotted the green pasture nearest them. Any one of them could grow into a legend like Eclipse, or Seabiscuit, or Secretariat. Across the globe, owners, trainers and jockeys competed to spot that special horse using science, psychics or any other means available in a race as intense as any on track. Over the centuries, it had driven many men mad.

She shielded her eyes from the sun. On the horizon, a lone figure was running in the direction of the quarry. It was Ivan, on his way to do his sprint training, despite the heat of the day. Odd that a young man with a reputation for idleness should be so obsessed with physical fitness.

'What about Roberto?' Tariq suggested. 'He saddled Honey. It's unlikely to be him because it's so obvious, but I have to ask.'

Kit laughed. 'Never. Not in a million years. Roberto has worked for Gramps for about twenty years. He's the gentlest soul I've ever met.'

She looked at Laura. 'I'm not sure that you'll ever solve this mystery. Dozens of people come and go every single day at Fleet Farm. Owners, exercise riders, grooms and trainers. It could be any one of them.'

Laura smiled. There was a point in every Matt Walker novel where the list of potential suspects seemed infinite and the riddle insoluble. 'It could be any of them, but it isn't. The truth is staring us in the face. We only have to know how to look for it. Try not to worry. If we're patient, we'll get to the bottom of this. What I'd really like to know is how the culprit got hold of the wildcat scent.'

'If that's what it is,' pointed out Kit, who had yet to be convinced about the cause of the accidents or the origin of the odour.

'A zoo,' suggested Tariq, writing it down.

'How about a pet tiger?' Kit volunteered. 'Thousands of Americans keep tigers in their apartments or backyards. There are bound to be a few in Kentucky.'

Laura was aghast. 'But that's cruel. Wild tigers are almost extinct. They are meant to be free and living in jungles, far from humans. They are meant to hunt and roam and raise their cubs. They don't belong in living rooms.'

'I agree, but lots of people think differently. Okay, what else?'

'I don't suppose there are any circuses in town?' asked Tariq.

Kit knocked her root beer over. It gushed onto the rug and soaked the last bite of her cupcake but she didn't appear to notice. 'There was a European circus in Lexington for Derby week last year, right around the time of my accident. The same circus is on again this week. The billboard advertising it has a photo of a tiger leaping through a hoop of fire. They call themselves Rock The Big Top.'

Laura's pulse quickened. She'd learned the hard way that coincidences often turned out to be nothing of the kind. Ordinarily, she loathed circuses that used animals and would have walked across flaming coals to avoid them, but she'd be failing Kit if she didn't pursue such a strong lead. 'How difficult would it be for us to get to this circus? Somehow we have to find a way to go.'

Kit went red. 'We're already going. Grandma told me that she'd bought tickets as a surprise for us when I was setting out to the stables this morning, only I didn't say anything because I was still furious with you and Tariq for coming here and ruining my vacation. I was planning to wriggle out of it if I possibly could.'

Laura glanced sideways. 'And you don't feel like that now.'

'Of course not,' said Kit, dabbing inadequately at the rug with a paper napkin. 'Now I think that you're pretty amazing and that I've been the world's biggest moron. I only hope you can forgive me. We're going to the circus tomorrow night. If there are any villains there, I plan to help you track them down.'

~ 15 ~

THE ROCK THE BIG TOP circus had a candy-striped tent and an old-fashioned merry-go-round with quaint plumed horses, but in every other way it was a cutting-edge show. In the first half alone they saw sky-walking acrobats, trapeze artists flying without wings, or indeed harnesses, and a magician who made a peacock disappear. Some eye-popping feats seemed more suited to science fiction than real life.

They were dazzled by a swarthy man in a billowing white shirt, who encased himself in swirling twists of flaming rope; by a juggler who tossed fizzing fireworks; and by a beautiful dancer who flowed like mercury over, under and through the legs of two shimmering white unicorns. For her final trick, she did a backflip off one and landed lightly on the rump of the other.

'They're not real unicorns, of course, they're Andalucian stallions from Spain by the look of them,' Blake Wainwright told Laura as they filed out into the darkness for the interval. 'But they look like the real thing and how superbly they performed. What exquisite creatures.'

He looked at his watch. 'Now if you'll excuse me, I need to find somewhere quiet so I can phone the farm. With only days to go until the Derby, we're on tenterhooks in case some fool takes it into his head to steal Noble Warrior or get at him in some way. Garth's pulling out every stop to make the stallion barn as secure as a bank vault.'

Christine waved him off vaguely and beamed at the children. She was so overjoyed that her withdrawn, taciturn granddaughter was once again laughing and communicative that she wouldn't have minded if the show had featured eight decrepit mules. That it had been quite breathtaking was a bonus. 'I don't know about you, but I need to powder my nose. Would anyone else—?'

'We're fine,' Kit said quickly. She, Laura and Tariq were determined to do as much snooping around as possible during the short interval. 'Why don't you give us our tickets and we'll meet you back in the tent? We thought we might check out the Haunted House.'

Christine's smiled faded. They'd passed the gothic mansion while exploring the amusement park earlier and it had looked quite horrible – like some sort of ghostly, ghastly stage set. 'Are you sure that's a good idea, sweetie?'

'Only briefly,' Kit assured her, 'and then we'll be going for candy floss.'

Christine glanced at the queue forming outside the ladies' bathroom and decided that the sooner she joined it the better. She rummaged in her purse for some dollars and handed them to Kit. 'All right, dear, but please don't do anything that gives our guests nightmares. Remember that Laura's already had to cope with a runaway horse. I'm sure she and Tariq have had quite enough drama for one trip.'

As soon as she'd turned her back, they slipped into the lively crowd. Fairground rides twisted and spun overhead, creating a kaleidoscope of colour against the night sky. White and blue strobe lights raked the darkness. The noise was deafening. Pop music competed with shrieking rollercoaster passengers and the music box blare of the merry-go-round. Laura was entranced, if a little dizzy. The swirling lights and general cacophony made the ground beneath her feet feel curiously unstable. She inhaled a lungful of burger smoke and the burnt sugar scent of candyfloss and caramelised nuts.

Towards the rear of the grounds it was quieter, apart from the screams emanating from the Haunted House. As they neared it, a couple of white-faced boys burst from a side door, followed by two girls bent double with laughter. Much teasing of the boys ensued. Laura didn't blame them for being scared. The exterior of the fake mansion was spooky enough. Spiders lurked in the cobwebs dangling from the porch and the yellow attic windows seemed to stare down at her like watching eyes.

She dreaded to think what the interior was like.

Contrary to what Kit had told her grandmother, the children had no intention of visiting the Haunted House. They were more interested in the caravans and animal trailers that lay behind it, partially concealed by a wall of white sheeting. There was no obvious security. After a short search, Tariq found a flap hanging loose. Judging by the number of cigarette butts on the ground, they were not the first to use it as an access route.

Kit went first, followed by Tariq. Laura brought up the rear. She was pulling the flap closed behind her when she caught a glimpse of Ivan. Fleet Farm's hotwalker had as much right to visit the circus as anyone else, but for some reason Laura's internal radar began to beep. Ivan rounded the front of the Haunted House and vanished from view.

She said hurriedly: 'I think we should split up. We've only got twenty minutes and we'll cover more ground. I'll meet you back in the main tent.'

Before Kit or Tariq could object, she'd ducked under the flap and was gone.

Kit shook her head in wonder. 'Is she always like this?'

'Like what?' asked Tariq.

'Like a beagle on the scent when she has a mystery to solve?'

Tariq grinned. 'She has a nose for trouble if that's what you mean. Her uncle was once one of the best detectives in Britain and Laura takes after him. Now, we don't have much time. Let's try to find the tiger trailer.'

In the thirty seconds it took Laura to reach the Haunted House, Ivan had disappeared. She scanned the nearby crowds but there was no sign of him. The front door of the gothic mansion was squeaking on its hinges. Could he have gone in there? The thought of entering the spider-plagued house made every hair on Laura's body stand on end, but she didn't see any alternative. Ivan had been striding along like a man on a mission. He didn't have the look of someone who was merely enjoying a night out at the circus.

She wished now that she hadn't been so hasty in sending Kit and Tariq away, but she also knew that she had more chance of remaining undetected if she tracked Ivan on her own. She glanced around in the hope of seeing other children and/or parents on their way to the Haunted House. It would be easier to cope with if there were. Unfortunately, families tended to veer away as they approached it. Perhaps the screams of previous victims had put them off.

She hurried to the ticket booth and handed over five dollars. The old crone at the counter, made up to look like a witch, did not inspire confidence. She fixed a glass eye on Laura and croaked: 'Without yer Mum 'n' Dad? Yer a brave one.' When Laura nodded, she cackled.

It's just part of the act, Laura decided. Nothing to do with me. Nothing to worry about.

She took her ticket and crossed the gravel path to the

house. Turning a blind eye to a pair of very realistic looking tarantulas, she walked determinedly up the porch steps and pushed open the front door. All she had to do was tell herself that nothing she saw or heard was real. Everything was for show. The ghosts would be projected lights or out-of-work actors wrapped in sheets.

Once inside, it became much harder to keep a grip on reality. It was pitch black for starters. She literally couldn't see her hand in front of her face. She'd hoped that a couple of previous visitors would be lingering there, providing a modicum of comfort, but she was alone with only the piped whine of a mournful wind for company. Mad laughter suddenly boomed in her ear and she almost jumped out of her skin.

Picking cobwebs out of her hair, Laura moved on jelly legs towards the outline of a door. As she passed through it, cold fingers brushed the back of her neck. She thought she heard a whisper: 'Laura, Laura, Laura . . .'

Her heartbeat accelerated and a small scream escaped her, but she managed to force herself on. She found herself in an old living room, spookily lit. A rocking chair began to swing crazily, as if occupied by some unseen person. The wind howled in the chimney. Above the sofa were a series of portraits in gilded frames. Their malevolent gazes followed her across the room. A floorboard creaked behind her. She swung to see a ghostly figure dart across the room before vaporising. Laura consoled herself with her out-of-work actor theory. It was all theatre.

She strained her ears to hear if Ivan was in an upstairs

room, but a very realistic thunderstorm had started up and it was impossible. How she wished she'd brought Tariq with her. Tariq was much stronger than most boys his age, and although he claimed to be ignorant of martial arts and was often painfully shy and quite gentle, she was convinced that he had some Far Eastern self-defence skill up his sleeve and would use it if ever called upon to do so. At any rate, she always felt safe around him.

As she made her way up the stairs, lightning shuddered and thunder crashed. At the top was a hall of mirrors, lit by a flickering gas lamp. The wavering light added to the disorienting effect. The room was full of Lauras, reflected from every angle. Every movement caused her multiple selves to fracture.

There was a scraping noise. A dark figure passed briefly across one of the mirrors, causing a ripple effect, like a stone dropped into a still pond.

'Ivan?' Laura called hopefully, turning in a circle, but no one answered. There was a rustle and a woman's face loomed at her left shoulder. The light flickered out. When it flicked on again, she was alone.

For the first time, real terror seized Laura, because the woman's face was one she knew. The face of someone she'd thought was dead; the face of a monster. 'Where are you?' she shouted. 'Show yourself.' There was mocking laughter and fragments of her tormenter danced from mirror to mirror, too quick for Laura to focus on. Here an eye, here a corner of a black silk skirt, the pocket of a dark red blouse, the tip of a shoe.

'We warned you, Laura Marlin . . .' The voice was barely

audible yet it had the effect on Laura of nails scraping a blackboard.

Just when Laura thought she might faint from fright, the room was flooded with light. A man on a crackling speaker system boomed: 'Ladies and gentlemen, please return to the Big Top and take your seats. This evening's performance will resume in three minutes.'

Laura could have wept with relief. She glanced around the room. She was entirely alone. There was no woman. It must have been her imagination, like everything else. She was about to make a thorough search of the mirrored room when the lights snapped off and she was marooned once more in the dark. It was the final straw. Her nerves could not take another second in the house.

She rushed out onto the landing and clattered down the steps, and that's when she heard Ivan's voice. It was coming from outside. Fear momentarily forgotten, she tried the nearest window. It was sealed shut. At the foot of the stairs was a wooden chest. By standing on it, she was able to peer out through a vent.

She was gazing directly into the performers' car park. More particularly, she was staring straight into the open door of a caravan. It was warmly lit with a golden light and three men were visible. One was dressed in black and had his back to Laura, but she had no difficulty recognizing the others. Arms slung across one another's shoulders, they were laughing in a way that would have persuaded any onlooker that they were not only the best of friends, but held each other in the highest esteem.

They raised their glasses.

'Zis time next week, everysing will be different,' Ivan said, his face alight. 'We will be bright shining stars.'

Mitch laughed. 'I'm not sure if the newspapers will see it that way, but who cares about them. I'm counting on you, mate. Don't you forget it.'

'Shame about za dry run wiz Noble Warrior. Zat was a waste of time.'

'Never you mind about that. I have a plan. A genius one. Will tell you about it later. Foolproof it is.'

Laura suddenly became aware that the speaker system in the Haunted House had been turned off. If anything, the silence was spookier than the thunderstorm or ghostly moans. Footsteps clattered up the porch and a muffled voice called: 'Anyone in here?' Before Laura could move a muscle or cry out, a door slammed shut and keys turned in the lock. She leapt off the trunk and rushed through the darkness, cobwebs coating her face with sticky threads. 'I'm in here,' she yelled. 'Don't leave me. Please don't leave me. Help!'

There was no response. She wrenched at the door and jiggled the handle, but it was immovable. There was a whisper of cloth brushing wood, followed by the flare of a match. Laura felt someone touch her hand and she swung in terror. Before her was the ghoulish face of her nightmares, flickering in the candlelight.

We warned you, Laura Marlin . . .

The edges of Laura's vision wavered then everything went black.

~ 16 ~

'**IMAGINE THE ATTENDANT** being so irresponsible as to lock the Haunted House while you were still inside it, Laura!' Christine said incredulously as they drove home. 'She must be senile. If Ivan hadn't heard you scream and hadn't run into Tariq, who was searching for you, you might have been stuck in there for the night with the spiders and bats and heaven knows what. It beggars belief. The Rock The Big Top people are lucky we're not planning to sue them.'

'Please,' her husband said wearily, massaging his temples as they stopped at a traffic light. 'I appreciate the distress that this unfortunate incident has caused, but surely we've had enough of lawyers to last a lifetime. I'm only sorry that Laura didn't get to see the second half of the show. It was quite spectacular.'

Sandwiched in the back of the car between her best friend and Kit, who kept giving her protective hugs, Laura was only half listening. Her head still ached. She kept going over and over the sequence of events in her mind, trying to understand what had been real in the Haunted House and what hadn't.

It had been a shock to see Ivan's cheeky face peering down at her when she came round from a dead faint. She'd been expecting to see the woman she dreaded. When she saw Fleet Farm's hotwalker instead, she was confused. She'd suspected him of being up to no good and yet here he was rescuing her. It was a relief when Tariq came rushing up and hugged her so hard that she squeaked.

'What are you doing in locked house?' demanded Ivan. 'Who do zis to you?'

'Don't know, I didn't see them,' mumbled Laura, still slightly dazed. 'Please don't mention it to the Wainwrights.'

Ivan frowned. 'We must call cops and find who do zis wicked sing.'

'Why are *you* here?' Laura interrupted before she could stop herself. 'I mean, what are you doing at the circus?'

He was surprised. 'I come to see za show, like you, but also to see my cousin, Mikhail, from Crimea. He is magician and juggler.' He flashed a grin. 'He teach me many tricks. One day I want my own circus, better than zis one. No more walking sweaty horses.'

'Did you come alone?'

Ivan laughed and put a hand on her shoulder. 'You ask

too many questions, Laura, girl. We must go before za Wainwrights get too worried. But, yes, I come by myself. Who else will come wiz me to circus? Mitch? Give me break. Unless he's come here to check up on me. Zat would be more likely.'

Back at Fleet Farm, Laura and Tariq met in Kit's bedroom for an agreed progress report by torchlight. They were each armed with a mug of hot chocolate topped with marshmallows.

Kit and Tariq had little to tell. They'd got as far as the cage of a poor, depressed tiger before being nabbed by a security guard and escorted like criminals back to the embarrassed Wainrights. When Tariq discovered that Laura had not been seen, he'd waited only until the guard departed before racing out of the tent to find her before anyone could stop him.

For now, however, Tariq was more interested in what Laura had learned in the Haunted House.

'But why would Ivan lie about meeting Mitch?' asked Kit. 'Are you *sure* it was Mitch? You know how much they loathe each other.'

'Yes, I do and yes, I'm certain. But maybe it's an act. Maybe they're friends and they only pretend to hate each other.'

Kit was puzzled. 'For what reason?'

'Right now, I don't have a clue.'

She looked up at their expectant faces. 'There's something I need to tell you both. When I was in the hall of mirrors I saw . . . I *thought* I saw . . . someone I knew. A woman. I hoped it was my imagination playing tricks on me . . .'

116

'But it wasn't?' guessed Kit.

'No. I knew that when I heard her voice and felt her touch my arm. If I live to be a thousand, I'd never forget the coldness of her hands, like some lizard, or the grating way she speaks, as if she has a clothes peg over her nose.'

There was a catch in her voice. 'But Tariq, I thought she was . . . I thought she was dead.'

Tariq froze. 'J-Janet Rain?'

Kit glanced from one to the other in growing alarm. 'Who is this Janet Rain? You make her sound like a monster.'

'It's worse than that,' Tariq told her, 'because she's just one of many. Janet Rain is the woman who helped kidnap Laura and I in the Caribbean, and would have tortured Laura's uncle to death if she'd had her way. She's a member of a gang of evil masterminds known as the Straight A's. They're responsible for some of the worst crimes on earth. Calvin Redfern calls them a Brotherhood of Monsters. The last time we saw Janet we were escaping from a volcano and I guess we thought – *hoped* – that she was gone forever. The newspapers reported her missing, presumed dead.'

'Well, she's not,' said Laura, pulling herself together. 'She's very much alive and at large. The question is, are the Straight A's in town because they're after us, or are they here to cause havoc during the Kentucky Derby?'

'Or both?' added Tariq, which was of no comfort whatsoever.

~ 17 ~

'I AM QUITE determined that nothing will go wrong today and you will finally start to have the vacation you deserve,' declared Christine at breakfast next morning, a Friday. 'I'm afraid that, at this rate, you'll leave the South with the wrong impression of us entirely. We pride ourselves on our culture, our hospitality and our gentility and you don't appear to have experienced any of those things.'

'That's not true at all,' Laura said warmly. 'You and Mr Wainwright and Kit have been lovely. And Anita's food is utterly delicious.'

Tariq, his mouth full of waffle, nodded enthusiastic

agreement. They'd started with eggs and hash browns and moved on to Anita's speciality.

Christine looked pleased and relieved. 'Well, that's good to hear.' She smiled at her granddaughter. 'I gather you took Tariq and Laura to see Noble Warrior's final workout this morning?'

Kit was positively glowing, but she played down the reason for her happiness like a typical teenager, not wanting to seem uncool. 'It was good. He went pretty well. Yeah, it was all right. And then afterwards we stopped by to give a few carrots to Goldie.'

'That's nice, sweetie. And how was he?'

'Yeah, he was all right.'

Laura turned away to hide a smile. At the track that day, she'd seen a very different side to the American girl. It was the first time Kit had been to watch the horses train since her accident the previous year and she'd been unable to contain her excitement. Laura and Tariq had been treated to a running commentary.

'You guys know about exercise riders, right? They're the unsung heroes of the racing world. The jockeys get all the glory. That's okay because they pilot the greatest horses in the biggest races, they're responsible for the split second decisions that can make or break a career, and they're fire-tested in battle. You get jockeys who've broken every bone in their body, but their guts are forged in steel and they keep going back for more. They're fearless because they have to be, but also because they're addicted to the thrill of it. They need speed!'

She'd nodded towards Ken, emerging from the dawn

mist on Noble Warrior. His reins were loose and he swayed with the stallion in one supple motion.

'We have a couple of full-time exercise riders – Ken and Eddie. The rest are freelance. They get paid per horse. They'll ride six or seven horses a day for maybe five hours. A good exercise rider can make or break a horse, but on Derby Day, when the jockey's being praised to the skies, they hardly ever get a mention. That's okay too. Most exercise riders would do it for free. They gallop for the love of it.'

For Laura and Tariq, crouched by the side of the track, what followed was a revelation. For several magical hours, they watched these passionate horsemen put through their paces awkward two-year-old 'babies', some eager, some naughty, as well as strapping stallions and bucking mares – 'broncing' was Kit's word for it, all with the same calm professionalism.

'If I'm not smart enough to become a vet, I want to be an exercise rider,' Tariq whispered to Laura.

Every horse that flew by was gleaming, sinewy and fast, but even Laura's inexperienced eyes could tell that there was something special about Noble Warrior. The red stallion was one of the smallest horses on the track, and yet he lived up to his reputation for being a pocket rocket. Ken jogged him half a mile up the track before turning back. For a further half mile he held the horse in a slow gallop. Then it was as if he'd flipped a switch. Warrior streaked down the track like a flame across oil.

'The average racehorse can cover around six metres in a single stride,' Kit told them in a hushed tone. 'The legendary stallion, Man o' War covered eight and a half. We think Noble Warrior could get close to that. When all four of his feet are off the ground, he flies like Pegasus.'

It was so awe-inspiring to see Noble Warrior thunder past them, his muscles straining beneath his fiery coat, that Laura felt quite emotional. 'I can see why you love racing so much,' she told Kit. 'It's an adrenalin rush, but it's also something more. The horses have so much power and grace and such big hearts, it sort of touches your soul.'

'I guess it's what people mean by poetry in motion,' said Tariq, equally moved.

Kit nodded fiercely, unable to speak. At last she said huskily: 'And I do. Love it, I mean. All that rubbish I talked about hating the horses and not caring if Goldie was gone for good, it was only because I was hurting so much. I blamed myself for what happened to Red Bishop and the thought that I could never again touch a horse or follow my dream of riding in the Derby, was agony. It made me lash out at everything and everyone, including you and Tariq. I'm so sorry.'

Laura gave her an affectionate punch. 'If you apologise one more time, you really are going to be sorry.'

Ken, standing in his short stirrups, had pulled Warrior up. The horse's nostrils flared red. Dragon-like, he breathed smoke into the chilly morning air. Ken patted him, swung off his back and handed the reins to Ivan, who led the stallion away to cool him down.

'How did he feel?' Kit called as Ken passed them, on his way to collect his next mount. 'Is he ready to take on the best horses in the country?'

Ken's serious face lit up briefly. 'Ready as he'll ever be.'

'What happens if he doesn't win the Kentucky Derby this time around?' Tariq wanted to know. 'Can he try again next year?'

Kit laughed. 'Only three-year-olds can enter the Kentucky Derby, so this is his one chance to claim his place in history. If he doesn't do it now, there won't be a next year because he'll have to be sold, along with every other horse we own. Goldie will have to go too. The bank is hounding Gramps for their money. When Warrior races on Sunday, he won't just be running for the roses or for the glory. He'll be running to save Fleet Farm.'

After breakfast, Tariq went to the stallion barn to help prepare Noble Warrior for his journey later that day to Churchill Downs, the famous home of the Kentucky Derby. Laura excused herself to call her uncle. He was thrilled to hear from her.

'How's it going?'

He sounded so near that Laura felt as if she could reach out and touch him. She wished she could. She'd had an unforgettable morning at the track, but the memory of Janet Rain's cold, clutching hands and her whispered threat, 'We warned you, Laura Marlin,' had haunted her sleep. She'd have done anything for one of her uncle's bone-crushing bear hugs and a lick or two from her beloved husky.

'Great,' responded Laura, 'except that I miss you and Skye terribly.'

His laugh boomed down the line. 'Not as much as we miss you.'

Before he could ask any probing questions, Laura launched into an edited account of the wonders of the circus and described her morning at the track.

'What an amazing experience,' he said. 'I'm sorely tempted to hop on the next plane and fly out for the Derby, but I doubt my boss would agree to it.'

'Oh, why don't you try?' pleaded Laura, her spirits suddenly lifted by the prospect of her uncle flying out to deal with the Straight A's and solve the mysteries at Fleet Farm that had so far eluded her.

'Any other news?' Calvin asked, deftly avoiding the question. 'Staying out of trouble?'

'Doing my best,' Laura said, which was perfectly true. It wasn't her fault if trouble kept finding her. 'Only . . .'

'Yes?'

'Uncle Calvin, do you know what the Straight A gang are up to these days? Have you heard any news?'

'There was a long silence. When he spoke, Calvin Redfern's voice was no longer teasing and warm, but stony and focused, the way it went when he was in work mode. 'Laura, what do you know?'

'Nothing. I thought I saw Janet Rain at the circus, that's all.'

'Let me get this right. You thought you saw one of the world's most wanted women at the circus. Was she a lion tamer? A trapeze artist? Seriously, did you definitely see her or is there some doubt about it?'

'I think I saw her, but I'm not sure.'

There was another silence. 'Do you have any reason to think the Straight A gang are targeting Fleet Farm?'

'No.'

'Well, then put them out of your mind. I'll make some enquiries, but you are to stay as far as possible from anything that might even remotely interest the Straight A gang. I've a good mind to ban you from going to the Kentucky Derby.'

Laura gasped. 'You can't.'

He sighed. 'I wouldn't be so cruel. But Laura, promise me that you and Tariq will stick close to Kit and the Wainrights at all times. Promise me that you'll take great care.'

Laura's shoulders sagged with relief. She smiled into the phone. 'Now that I can definitely do.'

As soon as she'd hung up the phone, Laura walked down to the stables. Kit and Tariq were absorbed with preparing Noble Warrior for his journey to Churchill Downs. They looked up distractedly when she put her head over the stable door before resuming their grooming and feet checking. Laura didn't mind in the least. She wanted to cuddle Goldie, who always seemed pleased to see her, and do a little investigating. Her uncle had warned her to stay away from the Straight A's. There was no law against her helping her friends.

As she'd hoped, the stable office was empty. Lying on the table was the daily logbook. With a quick glance over her shoulder, she opened it. On every page were detailed daily notes on feeding and training written in several hands. On impulse, she turned to the page that dealt with the day after their arrival, in the early hours of which she'd seen the mysterious second lorry and chestnut horse.

Apart from a careful account of Noble Warrior's performance in training that morning and a note that he'd run poorly – in the margin was the comment, 'Hardly surprising, given the disturbance in the night' – but otherwise it contained nothing untoward.

Remembering the conversation she'd overheard at the circus, Laura flicked through the diary to see if there was any reference to the 'dry run' that she'd overheard Ivan talking about, but could see nothing. Ivan was a puzzle. On the one hand, his actions and words at the circus had been extremely suspicious. On the other, he'd rescued her from the Haunted House and been concerned for her welfare afterwards. So now she was confused. Was he an angel or a villain? It was hard to know.

On the walls of the office were dozens of photos of racehorses. Racehorses in the winner's circle, racehorses in photo finishes and in training. One caught her eye. It was a picture of Noble Warrior and his twin, Valiant, standing side by side. They were identical, peas in a pod. Laura could never have told one from the other except that Noble Warrior was wearing a halter with a brass Fleet Farm identification tag, and Valiant's halter had a silver V on the side. It was the silver V that made Laura's breath catch in her throat. She had a piece of it in an evidence bag in her room. It was the fragment she'd found the morning after they'd arrived.

Laura unpinned the photo and sat down to examine it closer.

The door opened and Mitch strode in. When he saw her with the logbook, he snatched it away. 'That, Miss, is private property. For the eyes of Fleet Farm staff only.'

Laura jumped up guiltily. 'I'm so sorry. I was just interested, that's all.'

'That's okay,' said Mitch, softening. 'But I'd appreciate it if you don't come in here unless you're with Kit or a staff member.'

Laura apologised profusely and gave him her word it wouldn't happen again.

'Think nothing of it,' Mitch said more kindly.

'Umm, I wondered if I could ask you a question?'

He checked his watch. 'Sure, fire away.'

'What is a dry run? Is it some kind of training term?'

He laughed. 'A training term? No, it's just an expression. Haven't you ever heard it? It means a rehearsal of some kind. A sort of trial run.'

The gears shifted in Laura's brain. A thought hovered but she couldn't quite grasp it.

The trainer picked up the photo on the table. 'Poor Warrior. No matter what he does in his life, no matter what he wins, he'll never escape the shadow of his twin.'

It was an odd comment, given that Noble Warrior was far more successful than Valiant and was hardly in danger of being overshadowed by him, but before Laura could ask anything else a dark look came over Mitch's face. Abruptly he tucked the book under his arm and jingled his keys to indicate that it was time for her to leave.

It was then that Laura saw her chance. 'How was the circus last night?' she asked casually. 'Did you enjoy it?'

He snorted. 'Circus? You couldn't get me to the circus if you paid me. No time for that kind of silliness at all. No, I spent the whole evening with Garth Longbrook, planning security arrangements for the Derby. Now, was that all?'

And with that he was gone, leaving Laura wondering yet again if her eyes had deceived her.

18

AT NOON, the lorry carrying Noble Warrior left Fleet Farm for Louisville, a journey of around an hour and a half, depending on traffic. Ken was in the driver's seat, accompanied by Kit and Tariq, who would keep an eye on the stallion throughout the journey, and Ivan, whose role was to watch for potential horse thieves.

Since there was barely room for four in the cab, Laura had to ride in convoy with security chief Garth Longbrook. He sported a fresh crew cut and was dressed in black commando-style clothing as if he was expecting a war. Prior to leaving the farm, she'd seen him tucking a gun into the glove compartment of his blue truck.

'Expecting an ambush?' Laura asked, tongue firmly in her cheek. She found it amusing how over-the-top the man was being.

He glowered at her. 'The mark of a true professional, kid, is always be prepared. Those criminals got past me once. It won't happen again. Not on my watch. Of course, it helps that Noble Warrior is travelling in an unmarked, rented lorry. The Fleet Farm lorry is still in the repair shop. The thieves smashed it up pretty badly.'

Laura tried to pluck up the courage to say something about the eureka moment she'd had in the night. Before she went to sleep, she'd been thinking about Mitch's reply to her question about the dry run. He'd said it referred to a rehearsal or a test run of some kind. Matt Walker frequently went to bed with a riddle in his head, because he claimed that the unconscious mind had an uncanny knack of solving it. Laura had done the same and the answer had astonished her.

She was now convinced that what she'd seen from her window on the first night had been a rehearsal for a crime. The thieves had practised stealing either Goldie or Noble Warrior. That had got her thinking about the whole subject of identical twins and another bit of the jigsaw had fallen into place.

What she didn't know was who to tell. She'd wanted to discuss it with Tariq but they hadn't known until the last second that they'd be travelling separately. She could risk ridicule and tell the security manager, but after the panic button fiasco of the first night she was nervous of incurring the wrath of the Wainwrights with another false alarm, and anyway what would it achieve? Garth had already torn a strip off her once for interfering. 'Spare me from amateur detectives,' he'd ranted. She didn't fancy going through it again.

For the first twenty-five minutes of the journey to Louisville, everything went smoothly. Garth tuned in to a country music station on the radio and unbent enough to ask Laura a little about St Ives. In turn he told her a couple of anecdotes from his years in the Navy. She warmed to him as he spoke and began to think she'd misjudged him.

'Mitch mentioned that he had dinner with you last night while you were going over the security arrangements,' she said, wondering if she'd catch him out in a lie.

However, Garth confirmed the story straight away. 'That's right, he did. I cooked him pepper steak, my speciality.' He braked suddenly. 'Hello, what's going on here?'

Ahead of them the lorry's exhaust was billowing black smoke. Its hazard lights came on and it spluttered slowly to a halt, only just managing to crawl into the car park of a roadside diner.

Garth sprang out of his truck and strode over to the lorry. Ken hopped down from the cab, followed by Ivan, Kit and then Tariq.

'Disaster, boss. The engine's packed up,' said Ken. 'I thought we could get a bit further if I nursed it along, but it quit on me.'

The security manager was livid. 'Of all the cursed luck. This is the last thing Noble Warrior needs.'

'You sink I should give Mitch a call?' Ivan suggested

worriedly. 'He can call rental company and maybe get us another lorry quick quick.'

'Good idea, Ivan,' Garth Longbrook said. 'Mitch will give them a blast and convey the urgency of the situation. Morons. That's the last time we use their firm.'

Ivan had to walk almost to the other end of the car park in order to get a phone signal. They watched him striding up and down, gesturing passionately. Finally, he returned. 'Mitch is bringing new lorry, but zere will be small delay. Maybe one hour.'

Garth made a noise that sounded like a dog growling, but a resigned shrug followed. 'Not a whole lot we can do about it, so let's make the best of it. You kids go with Ivan and Ken and have a bite to eat in the diner. I'll stay here and guard the lorry.'

Everyone turned to go except Laura. As soon as they were out of earshot, she said urgently to Garth: 'Please ask Ken to stay with you. This is how they're going to do it. This is how they're going to swap the horses.'

He was bewildered. 'Who? What horses? What are you talking about?'

'Noble Warrior and Valiant,' Laura said, her voice rising in agitation. 'They're going to exchange them. I'm not sure who's behind it, but I'm pretty sure they had a kind of dress rehearsal the night we got to Kentucky. The second lorry wasn't my imagination. Everything was real, including the chestnut horse they brought to replace Goldie or Noble Warrior. I'm not sure why they decided to change the venue. Maybe because you beefed up security.'

The security manager's head had started to sweat. He

ran a palm across his bristles. 'Miss Marlin, I'm a patient man, but you are trying my nerves severely. Since you and your friend arrived at Fleet Farm, there's been one catastrophe after another. Detectives are supposed to solve problems, not cause them. Now I'd strongly suggest that you join Tariq and Kit for lunch and keep your half-baked notions to yourself. I have a racehorse to protect.'

Ivan came trotting down the path from the diner. 'Everysing all right? I bring you burger and soda, Mr Longbrook.' He grinned at Laura. 'Come, Lapushka, leave the security to zee expert. Zere is no one better zan zis man.'

Ears burning, Laura followed him without another word. In the diner, a cheerful place with red-checked tablecloths, pine furniture and more country music, she exchanged glances with Tariq. He nudged her under the table. He was worried, too, she could tell. Neither of them believed that the breakdown was coincidental and both kept sneaking looks at the lorry, partially visible through the restaurant blinds. Garth Longbrook was leaning against it, smoking. Turning away, Laura scanned the menu and ordered a veggie burger, although the last thing she felt like doing was eating. Humiliation has a tendency to ruin the appetite.

Kit smiled kindly at her and offered her a taste of her malted shake. 'Don't pay any attention to Garth,' she said under her breath. 'Gramps didn't hire him for his personality.'

Before long, Laura was laughing in spite of herself. Ivan performed a couple of card tricks with the flourish of a born showman, and made dollar bills appear behind their ears and cents turn up under milkshakes. Ken's watch reappeared in the middle of his Caesar salad. He glared at Ivan as he fished it out and tried vainly to extract bits of Parmesan from the links of the silver strap.

'Remind me why we brought you along.'

Ivan winked at Laura and Kit, who were sitting side by side. 'Because Warrior is not going to win zee Derby without me,' he teased.

Laura joined the general laughter, but she felt uneasy. The warning given to her by her St Ives' neighbour, Mrs Crabtree, now seemed astonishingly insightful. The racing game was '*a magnet for chancers, gamblers, criminals and dreamers,*' she'd said. '*The pretty horses, the rainbow jockey silks, the fancy hats of the ladies who go to watch, they're just the window dressing. Behind the scenes, there are tricks going on that would be the envy of any conjurer. Big money involved, you see. Wherever there are millions at stake, there'll be men trying to make even more and they'll do whatever it takes. Sleight of hand, smoke and mirrors, rabbits out of hats, you name it, they have it up their sleeves.*'

Laura looked over at Ivan, who was pulling a red silk bandana from his mouth. Was he the joker he made himself out to be, always smiling, always friendly, always ready to be helpful? There was plenty of evidence to support this. He had, after all, rescued her from the Haunted House. Or was he a chameleon? A man who hid a ruthless cunning beneath his carefree exterior? A man who pretended to be idle and useless, but was in fact honed to Superman fitness by his gruelling workouts in the quarry?

'Is everything all right, Laura?' Kit asked. 'You looked quite fierce for a moment.'

Laura forced a smile. 'Oh, I was just thinking about how I'm going to punish Tariq if he steals another one of my sweet potato fries.'

She glanced out of the window and was startled to see Garth Longbrook dashing across the lawn to the diner, clutching his stomach.

He burst through the door, eyes streaming and unfocused. His normally swarthy skin was blue-white. 'Something in the burger didn't agree me. Sorry folks. Lorry is arriving. Ken, can you deal—?' was all he managed to croak before bolting to the bathroom.

'Jeepers creepers,' said Ken, looking down at the remnants of his own burger. 'I hope we don't all get food poisoning.'

Before they could debate the matter further the replacement lorry pulled into the car park. Garth was forgotten as they rushed out to supervise the transfer of Noble Warrior in the face of an approaching storm. The wind had picked up and fat drops of rain were darkening the asphalt.

Mitch, the driver, jumped down from the lorry's cab and pressed a button to lower the back. 'Unbelievable,' he said. 'Last time we'll ever use Equine Hire. Know what their slogan is? Hire us! You can rely on us! I've threatened to sue if Noble Warrior doesn't win the Derby.

'Now Ken, I have an idea. Both of these lorries have rear doors that slide open as well as lower. Instead of dropping the ramps, we can open them on their hinges. If you get into the driver's seat and reverse so that the backs of the lorries are almost flush against one another, I'll press the buttons to slide both doors back. It'll be a breeze to then walk Warrior from one to the other. Save him going down one ramp and up the other, getting wet and being unnerved by all these cars zooming around. What do you think? How about it?'

'Genius,' said Ken. 'The less we stress the boy, the better. Let's get to it.'

'Need any help, Mitch?' Kit offered hopefully.

'Thanks, Kit, but I think we should keep this simple. I can manage on my own.'

With that, he swung onto the back of the lorry containing Noble Warrior, while Ken edged the empty van nearer. He turned off the engine. There were a few anxious moments as hooves thudded and the lorries rocked beneath the weight of one ton of horse. Finally, Mitch called: 'All done.'

Ken started the engine again and moved forward cautiously. Laura joined the others at the rear of the vehicle. The chestnut stallion was safely installed. They could see his quarters and the tips of his ears. He was resting one foot.

'Would it be okay if I get in the lorry with him for a few minutes?' Tariq asked. 'I might be able to talk to him and relax him a bit.'

Mitch shook his head. He pressed the button that closed the door. 'No more delays. The best thing we can do for the horse is get him to the track ASAP and get him bedded down and comfortable.'

He clapped his hands together. 'Let's get the show on

the road, people. I'll wait here with the other lorry until the breakdown truck arrives. You head on to Louisville.' He glanced around. 'Wait a second, where's Longbrook?'

There was a croak and a green-gilled Garth limped around the side of the lorry. He raised a weak paw. 'Sorry again, folks. Glad you managed without me. I'm better but not yet firing on all cylinders. Ivan, would you mind driving me to Churchill Downs? I don't think I can be trusted to take the wheel. Laura, you go with Ken, Kit and Tariq in the main lorry. I'll need you all to help me keep an eye out for horse thieves. My guarding skills are somewhat compromised.'

As the lorry pulled out onto the rain-darkened highway, wipers swishing, an hour and twelve minutes behind schedule, Kit said anxiously: 'I hope this isn't a bad omen. Gramps is counting on us to get Noble Warrior to the track in one piece and in the best shape of his life. He's counting on us to help Warrior win the Derby.'

Laura said nothing. She had a sick feeling in her stomach and it had nothing to do with the burger she'd eaten.

19

'**THAT'S NOT** Noble Warrior!'

It was six a.m. on Saturday morning and the first time any of the children had seen the chestnut stallion since leaving Fleet Farm. The previous afternoon the hire company mechanic had called Blake Wainwright from his workshop to report that the lorry's engine had been sabotaged. Blake, who was already in Louisville with Christine, immediately rang Ken and instructed him to bring Kit, Laura and Tariq directly to the hotel before the lorry went on to Churchill Downs. All Kit's protests had been in vain.

'Sweetheart, do you know what this means?' her

137

grandfather had asked patiently. 'It means that somebody out there doesn't want Noble Warrior to run in the Derby. Until we know how serious the threat is, I don't want you kids anywhere near the stables. Calvin Redfern and the Ashworths will never forgive me if anything happens to Laura and Tariq. It's a great shame because I really wanted Tariq to spend some time with Noble Warrior after his journey. It's uncanny how the horse has taken to the boy. Loves him to bits.'

That evening, he and Christine took the children to a Mexican restaurant in atmospheric downtown Louisville. Against a backdrop of blooming desert cacti and sun-drenched markets, they ate tortillas and cheese enchiladas and sizzling fajitas served in skillets, washed down with an ice-cold sour cherry drink. It was fun, but for Laura and Tariq it didn't lessen the disappointment of not being allowed to help the chestnut stallion settle in for his first night at the historic track.

In the hotel room that she shared with Kit and Tariq, Laura slept badly. The luxurious surroundings couldn't erase Garth Longbrook's harsh words, which played over and over in her head. 'Detectives are supposed to *solve* problems, not cause them.'

He was right. She couldn't deny it. In the five days that she'd been in Kentucky, she hadn't come up with a solitary solution to the many mysteries that simmered below Fleet Farm's tranquil surface. Well, she had but they'd all fizzled away to nothing. She still didn't know where the wildcat phial had come from, or who'd planted it. The circus had been a dead end. She'd pinned nothing on Ivan. Even her encounter with Janet Rain now seemed remote, like a half forgotten nightmare.

Her only comfort was that Matt Walker had once or twice found himself in the same situation – all at sea and criticised for his supposedly far-fetched theories. Each time his gut instincts had proved as true as any compass.

Dawn was breaking before Laura fell into a coma-like sleep. Kit had woken her barely an hour later. As a result, she'd been groggy and uncommunicative over a breakfast of coffee and bagels.

It was not until they pulled off the highway and Laura saw the famed twin towers of Churchill Downs that she suddenly came to life. When she stepped out of the car and inhaled the misty morning air with its heady mix of horse and cut grass, some inexpressible emotion – part excitement, part terror – surged through her veins.

Five minutes later, she, like Blake Wainwright and Ken, was staring in mute astonishment at Tariq as he gestured towards the shining chestnut leaning over the stable door. The stallion's ears flickered back and forth, like little radio aerials. He wanted his breakfast and was trying to decide who was most likely to get it for him.

The Bengali boy was outwardly calm but his tone carried a note of urgency. 'This horse is not Noble Warrior,' he said again.

Ken gave a short laugh. 'You're kidding, right? Of course, it's Noble Warrior.'

Blake ruffled Tariq's hair. 'He's just fooling with us, aren't you son?'

Tariq regarded him with clear tiger's eyes. 'I wish I was,

sir, but I'm not. Believe me, this isn't Warrior. Look, usually he loves his left ear being rubbed. He goes all soppy. But this horse doesn't like his head being touched at all. He's nervous of us because he doesn't know us.'

Kit studied the stallion from several angles. 'Are you sure, Tariq? He might simply be a bit stressed from the journey.'

Laura said: 'Tariq is right, I know he is. Oh, it's not that I can tell the difference between the two horses. Obviously, I can't. But everything points to that. That's been their plan all along. They must have switched the horses when the lorry broke down. It didn't occur to me that it would have a false compartment. Mitch didn't move Noble Warrior at all. He simply shut the back of the old lorry and left the stallion in there. Then he opened the false compartment of the new lorry and let Warrior's replacement in, knowing that we'd believe he was Noble Warrior because it would never occur to anyone it wasn't. He also knew that there was only one person in the world who could tell that the new horse was actually Warrior's twin and that person wasn't in hospital. If I'm not mistaken, this horse is Valiant.'

Kit started to speak, but before she could get a word out Garth Longbrook rounded the corner with a smiling Mitch.

'Morning, folks,' said the security manager brightly, looking a great deal healthier than he had the previous day. 'Sorry we're a bit late, but we've been trying to track down Ivan who's not been seen since last night. How's our champion this morning?'

Blake ran his fingers through his white hair. 'Garth,

we have a bit of a dilemma. It's preposterous, I know, but Tariq has a theory that Noble Warrior has somehow been substituted and Laura here believes this stallion is actually Nathan Perry's horse, Valiant—'

'Rubbish!' Mitch said furiously, his mood changing from sunny to stormy in an instant. 'That's absolute baloney. I'd know Noble Warrior anywhere. This is insane. Churchill Downs has acres of CCTV and some of the best security anywhere in the world. As if anyone could steal Noble Warrior from here, much less substitute his twin. Who are you going to believe, me or some idiot children who've known the horse for less than five days?'

Blake Wainright's faded blue eyes flashed a warning. 'As I was saying, Laura has this hypothesis that the switch happened during the breakdown, but of course that can't possibly be true because you, Garth, were there throughout, as was Mitch who I'd trust with my life.'

Garth looked as if he might blow a gasket. Laura feared that if his gaze alighted on her, she might be incinerated. 'If I might speak frankly, sir,' he growled, 'these children have done nothing but cause chaos since the day you clapped eyes on them . . .'

'That's a total lie!' Kit burst out. 'First off, Gold Rush was stolen on *your* watch and we'd never have got him back had it not been for Laura, her uncle and Tariq. Second, I was almost killed and poor Red Bishop lost his life – also on your watch. I blamed myself and was devastated and utterly miserable for an entire year until Laura figured out that it wasn't an accident. Someone wanted Bishop out of the picture. This horse looks like Warrior to me, but if

Laura and Tariq believe he's been exchanged we should listen to them.'

'Garth, are you hearing this?' cried Blake. 'Could foul play have been involved in Bishop's demise? Did you have any idea of this?'

The security manager was apoplectic, but he took a deep breath and tried to get his temper under control. 'With the greatest of respect, sir, Laura Marlin fancies herself as an amateur detective and has an overactive imagination, and as Mitch pointed out this young boy knows next to nothing about horses.'

'That may be true,' said a voice from behind them, 'but he sure knows enough to tell identical stallions apart.'

They turned to see a slender, wiry youth with a mop of untidy brown hair and an open, friendly face. He was very pale. One of his legs was in plaster, his right wrist was bandaged and he was leaning on crutches.

'Ryan!' gasped Ken.

'Ryan, what the heck are you doing here?' demanded Blake. 'You should be in hospital.'

'Tariq is one hundred per cent correct,' Ryan told the assembled group. 'This is Valiant, not Noble Warrior. If you doubt my word, let's take him out onto the track. Valiant is barely fast enough to win a local handicap race. He couldn't match Noble Warrior's worst practice time. You need to face the fact that the horses have been exchanged.'

'Impossible,' Garth Longbrook said faintly, but his bluster had gone. His stricken expression reflected his inner turmoil. Despite his best preparations, another monumental disaster had taken place.

Blake Wainright looked defeated. 'Can you prove it? I mean, we can call the veterinarian and check his microchip – as you all know Nathan and I refuse to allow any of our horses to have the lip tattoos that are standard in racing – but in the meanwhile it would be helpful to know.'

'Yes, I can,' said Ryan. 'When Noble Warrior was a yearling, he got a fright one day when I was cleaning his feet and managed to cut himself. It was such a tiny scratch that I never mentioned it to anyone – didn't want to get into trouble, I guess – but afterwards it left a little scar. If this is Noble Warrior, he'll have white hairs in the shape of a W beneath his chest.'

Blake Wainright opened the stable door. 'Ken, could you do the honours?'

Running a soothing hand down the chestnut stallion's foreleg, the exercise rider crouched down and examined the area carefully. 'No W here.'

When he stood up, he was trembling. 'How could this happen? We were all there, weren't we Mitch? We were all watching.'

Everyone turned to the trainer. Laura opened her mouth to say, 'While we're on the subject of identical twins, this is not Mitch, it's his lookalike brother,' but she was too late. The man posing as Mitch was long gone.

Blake Wainright sank down onto a nearby stool. 'So that's it then. My best horse has been stolen and the trainer I'd counted on to help us win the Derby and save Fleet Farm may be the architect of our ruin.'

Kit ran to his side and put her arms around him. 'Don't despair, Gramps. We can fix this, I'm sure we can.'

He raised eyes in which all hope had been extinguished. '*How*? As you well know, I'm not one to give up without a fight, but our cause seems lost.'

Beside him, Garth Longbrook was a broken man.

'For starters,' Laura said. 'Mitch is *not* involved.' She held up a hand as Ken protested. Quickly, she related what she'd seen through the vent of the Haunted House – Ivan and the man she'd believed to be Mitch embracing like brothers.

'So what you're saying is that the man you saw at the circus wasn't Mitch at all – couldn't have been since he was enjoying a steak dinner with me?' Garth Longbrook asked.

For the first time since they'd met, he was staring at Laura with real respect and interest. 'Your theory is that the person you saw was in fact his identical twin, the no-good brother who is always borrowing money from him? That with Ivan working as the inside man, they hatched a plan to switch the horses and make thousands of dollars in illegal gambling? I suppose it was Ivan who slipped me some kind of poison at the diner yesterday, making it easier for them to get away with it?'

'I expect so,' said Laura, since he seemed to be addressing the question to her. 'If you send a search party, you'll probably find that the real Mitch is locked in a barn or store cupboard at Fleet Farm.'

'I suppose this means that Ivan and Mitch's brother were involved in Red Bishop's accident?' Kit said in disgust. 'They must be sick. Have they no conscience?'

Laura hated to disillusion her friend, but it was the obvious conclusion. She nodded. 'I'm sorry, Kit. Proving it might be difficult though. We still don't know where they got the wildcat potion from.'

Ken started as if he'd been pricked with something sharp. 'What are you talking about? What wildcat potion?'

Throughout the exchange, Tariq had been watching the exercise rider carefully. 'Remember that day when Honey bolted and almost hurtled off a cliff, nearly taking Laura and Kit with her? Well, we found a plastic phial in Honey's bridle that smelled like a lion or a tiger in a zoo. The same smell was on my jacket sleeve the first time I met Noble Warrior. That was why he attacked me. We figure that whoever did those things was also responsible for sending Red Bishop so mad with fear that he threw Kit and—'

'No!' Ken had tears in his eyes. 'I would never in a million years have harmed Bishop. I loved him. But it *is* my fault that Honey bolted with you, Laura.'

Blake jumped to his feet. 'I can't bear it. Not you as well, Ken. You're like a son to me.'

Ryan was aghast. 'How could you, Ken?'

Ken looked at his best friend, shame written all over his face. 'I did it for you, Ryan. I was so angry that Mr Wainright was bringing over a strange boy, some kid who knew nothing about racing, to look after Warrior that I wanted to scare him off. I put a few drops of this stuff called Horse Away on the sleeve of a jacket I planned to give Tariq. I knew Noble Warrior would react badly to it. After all the work you'd put into preparing him for the race, I didn't want someone else stealing your thunder while you were in hospital if Noble Warrior really did win the Derby.

'It didn't work, which says a lot about Tariq's courage and how good he is with horses, so I gave up. I knew it was a bad thing I'd done, because Tariq could easily have been injured and I felt guilty about it. Problem was, I forgot I'd left a phial of the Horse Away in the pocket of my jacket. Roberto called me and asked me to take a look at the fetlock of one of his mares. As I was about to open her stable door, I remembered the phial. I didn't want to upset the mare so I put the little bottle on a ledge near the tack room. When I came back for it, it was gone.'

'Why did that bother you?' asked Laura.

'Because I knew from what had happened with Noble Warrior how dangerous Horse Away could be if it fell into the wrong hands. I'd become convinced that the theft of Goldie was an inside job and that someone at Fleet Farm was on a mission to ruin Mr and Mrs Wainright. When the phial was taken and Honey went berserk, I was sure, especially when the quarry gate was left open and Laura and Kit were almost killed. Someone didn't want Laura asking difficult questions. I suspected Ivan, but I couldn't tell anyone without revealing my own guilty secret so I kept quiet. I've beaten myself up about it at least a thousand times since that day. I'll never forgive myself for being so stupid.'

A tear rolled down his face. 'I'm sorry, Kit and Laura

and Tariq. I can't say that enough. Mr Wainwright, I'm handing in my notice right now.'

'Don't even think of it, Ken,' snapped Blake. 'Where will I find another exercise rider as talented as you are? Yes, you've disgraced yourself and you're very fortunate that these girls didn't end up in A&E, but I've no doubt that you'll learn from this and be a kinder, more generous-spirited person.'

'You'd better be,' Ryan said pointedly, 'or you'll be finding yourself a new best friend. I, for one, am glad that Tariq is here.'

He put a hand on the younger boy's shoulder. 'Anyone who cares enough about Warrior to put his neck on the line the way Tariq did this morning can be my assistant and share my thunder any time.'

'You've told the truth and you're genuinely sorry,' Kit told Ken. 'That's good enough for me.'

'And me,' Laura responded with feeling. 'Just one thing. The wildcat potion – this Horse Away – where did you get it?'

'Ivan brought a big tub of it to the farm just over a year ago,' Ken told her. 'He claimed that a friend of his – some zoo owner in Eastern Europe – was trying to patent it. Said it was real useful when it came to keeping horses away from poisonous weeds or stallions from breaking through fences.'

'Meanwhile, he and Mitch's evil brother really wanted to use it to terrify Red Bishop and stop him from winning the Derby,' Kit said furiously. 'Only their plan backfired when Gramps decided that I should be the one to exercise

Bishop. That's why 'Mitch' got so angry. It wasn't Mitch at all, it was his brother. It suddenly came home to him that if Bishop went crazy, they might have *my* death or broken bones on their conscience as well.'

Her grandfather looked as if he'd had all the shocks he could handle for one day. 'So it's a tale of twins, one fast and one slow, one good and one wicked beyond imagining. How did you guess that Mitch had an identical twin, Laura?'

'It was something Mitch said. He commented that no matter what Noble Warrior did in his life, no matter what he won, he'd never escape the shadow of his twin. Since I'm pretty sure that the last thing on Warrior's mind is his brother, it made me think that he might be talking about himself. It was Mitch who lived in someone's shadow.'

Blake was exhausted. The strain of the past few weeks showed in the sharp-etched lines on his kind face. 'Will we ever see Noble Warrior again, Garth, or do you think they've already spirited him across the Atlantic like the men who stole Goldie?'

A ghost of a grin crossed the security manager's face. He turned to the children. 'If you were me, where would you start looking, Laura Marlin? Any suggestions?'

She smiled back. 'I'd begin with Nathan Perry's farm. I have a feeling that you'll find Noble Warrior standing in Valiant's stall wearing a halter with a broken silver V on it.'

His mouth dropped open. 'How could you possibly know . . . ? Oh never mind. When this is over, I want a few private investigator tips from you. I'm also going to be buying a whole stack of Matt Walker novels.'

He extended his hand first to Laura, then to Tariq. 'I apologise unreservedly for calling you an amateur, Laura. You could run rings around most professionals, including me. And, Tariq, thanks to you and Ryan we might yet be in with a chance to enter a horse in the Derby. Now if you'll excuse me, I have a racehorse to rescue.'

~ 20 ~

'HEY, GUYS, what do you think? Do I pass muster?' asked Kit, emerging from the hotel bathroom. Tariq, sprawled on the bed in a borrowed suit, gave a teasing whistle, but Laura was momentarily speechless. Gone was their farm kid friend with the wild hair, ripped jeans and worn boots. In her place was a dazzling young woman in a figure-hugging white dress patterned with red roses. On her head was a navy blue hat with a wide brim and a matching white and rose scarf twisted around it. She wore white Roman sandals and had painted her toenails crimson.

'You look sensational,' Laura said in awe. 'Like a supermodel.'

150

Kit giggled and hugged her. 'Until tomorrow morning, when I'll put on my cowboy boots and jeans again and be glad to do it. But today is a special occasion. Everyone in Kentucky dresses up. You look very pretty yourself by the way. And Tariq is going to stop traffic in that suit. Now are you ready for Derby Day?'

When they descended to the lobby to meet the Wainrights, Laura saw what Kit meant. It was crammed with racegoers dressed in their finery, some of it elegant, some of it eye-popping and some of it – Tariq pointed out a woman who appeared to have a bowl crammed with tropical fruit on her head – plain bizarre.

There was a carnival atmosphere. A milliner, with a stall displaying pillbox hats and others adorned with feathers or netting, strutted like a peacock as he marketed his wares. There were tables stacked high with Kentucky Derby hats, T-shirts and mugs. Screened by a wall of lilies and roses, diners tucked into white egg omelettes and two Southern favourites – grits, a kind of porridge topped with melted cheese, and biscuits, which to Laura looked exactly like scones. They weren't served with clotted cream and strawberry jam as was customary in St Ives, but with a creamy pork gravy. Laura, who was a vegetarian, found this incomprehensible.

Outside, they joined the long lines of people streaming down the road to the racetrack. 'The traffic's so bad on Derby Day, anyone who can walks,' Christine explained. 'For the police and Churchill Downs officials, it's a huge operation. During Derby week, there are some twelve thousand employees taking care of around a hundred and seventy thousand visitors and the stables are full to bursting. Fourteen hundred horses are kept in the forty-eight barns.'

'Racing people are superstitious, so there's no barn thirteen,' added Kit with a laugh.

As the twin spires came into view, framed against a crisp blue sky, Laura suspected that everyone in their party was all saying the same silent prayer. After everything that has blighted the fortunes of Fleet Farm, please let it be our day today. She knew too that the Wainrights and Kit were still filled with wonder that they were at Churchill Downs at all and in with a chance.

Tariq had already been to the stables with Ryan and Ken that morning and reported that Noble Warrior was in fine fettle and none the worse for wear after his adventure. 'He's all cocky and pleased with himself, as if he's been on a particularly good holiday. You'd never think that he'd been abducted by criminals.'

Tariq and Laura were the heroes of the hour because Tariq had spotted that the horses had been switched, and Laura's hunch had proved correct. When Garth Longbrook and the police had torn through the gates of Nathan Perry's farm the previous day, they'd found Noble Warrior – identified via his microchip by the racing authorities – happily munching hay in Valiant's stall. As Laura had predicted, he'd been wearing Valiant's halter with the broken silver V.

It subsequently turned out that at least two of Nathan's grooms had been in on the fraud and had long criminal records. There was also evidence to suggest that they'd been involved in the plot to harm Red Bishop, which meant that the case against Blake Wainright would be dropped immediately. Much of the money he'd paid out in legal costs would be returned to him. Nathan Perry was said to be mortified and had already called Blake with a stammered but very sincere apology.

Mitch had been discovered locked in the bathroom of his cottage. He'd yelled himself almost hoarse, but as he resided at the far end of the farm, nobody had heard him. Since he was supposed to be in Louisville, no one had thought to look for him either. When he found that his worst fears had been realised and that his own brother had tried to destroy another Derby favourite, he was devastated. He'd wanted to resign on the spot, but Blake had persuaded him to come to Churchill Downs and do his best to get Noble Warrior ready for the race. They'd talk about his future after that.

Laura had called home to tell Calvin Redfern a carefully worded version of the drama before he read it in the newspapers, but there'd been no reply at number 28 Ocean View Terrace. She kept checking her mobile to see if he'd left a message, but there was nothing. She didn't worry. If he was on a job pursuing fishermen with illegal catches, he could be out most of the night.

At the Churchill Downs' turnstiles, they were whisked through, with many of those queuing for tickets recognising the Wainwrights and wishing them luck. The first races were already underway. Some of the most exquisite horses Laura had ever laid eyes upon were being led around the Paddock.

As graceful as panthers and dainty as ballet dancers, they circled before the watching crowd, champing at the chain shanks used by some trainers to keep their horses under control. In Laura's opinion, it was far too harsh a measure for such sensitive beasts. An overhead screen broadcast the current race live.

Some of those watching rushed away to place their bets before the horses were led out onto the track. Laura could not get over the amount of money that seemed to be changing hands at the tote, the racecourse betting facility, where rows of cashiers were ringing up or dishing out cash. While the Wainwrights went to the Jockey Room to talk to the jockey who'd be riding Noble Warrior that afternoon, Kit gave Tariq and Laura a guided tour of the main building.

Each of the six levels was awash with people in glamorous outfits holding glasses of champagne. They moved between the buffet counters, the bar and the betting counters. Floor four was known as Millionaire's Row. On the stairwell outside the palatial rooms was a glass sculpture of Churchill Downs with four hundred glass figurines of jockeys, horses and spectators, perfect in every detail.

As the friends ascended so did the wealth. The people in the Finish Line suites had their own special room with their own personal waiters and they could put up the colourful silks worn by their chosen jockey. The people with the most money occupied the Gold Rooms on Floor Two and Six. Kit told Laura that these men and women would think nothing of putting on a single horse the kind of cash that would buy a house.

'Where does all this money go?' asked Laura. 'Is it kept in some sort of vault?'

'It goes down to the Money Room beneath the grandstand. It's heavily guarded. You'd have more chance of getting into The White House.'

Laura could tell that Tariq, who came from a desperately poor background in Bangladesh, was uncomfortable with such ostentatious displays of extravagance. They were both happier when Kit took them into the media centre, where the racing reporters were pounding away at their keyboards or out on the balcony, watching the horses cross the finish line on the track below.

They were an amiable bunch, passing the time between deadlines with banter and chocolate chip cookies. A couple of them smiled at the children, but most paid no attention to the trio at all. They'd be kicking themselves later in the day when the news broke about the dramatic raid on Nathan Perry's farm and rescue of Noble Warrior and it hit them that they'd unknowingly had under their noses the three key players in the biggest racing scandal of the year.

For now, however, they were oblivious.

As Kit pushed open the balcony doors of the media centre, the roar of the crowd came at them like a wave. The air practically crackled with anticipation. Each race was preceded by a trumpet blast known as the Call to the Post. Pony Boys, who were not boys at all but men and women on trusty steeds, accompanied the racehorses and their jockeys to the starting gates. They were outriders. Their job was to help any rider battling with an excitable mount, or to pick up loose horses after falls.

Tariq leaned over the rails, enraptured, as a line of horses burst from the gates on the far side of the track. On the huge screen behind the finish line, they could see them travelling at electrifying speed round the track. Finally they came into view and a jockey in yellow urged a powerful grey named Wanderlust to victory.

It was while Tariq was hanging over the side, trying to see the winner being presented with the trophy that Laura heard him draw a startled breath.

'What is it?' She knew immediately that something was wrong.

He pointed. 'At the bottom of the grandstand, next to the track rail. See those people dressed in stars and stripes, like an American flag. The woman beside them wearing black, like a widow.'

Laura shielded her eyes from the sun. 'Janet Rain!'

'The monster woman!' cried Kit. 'Where? Oh, I see her. She doesn't look like a kidnapper who enjoys torturing children. She looks like someone who just stepped from the pages of *Vogue*. Are you sure it's the same person?'

Their faces told her everything she needed to know. 'Got it. Well, what do you want to do about it? Confront her? Call the cops?'

In the split second it took for Laura to reply, Janet Rain had gone, melting into the crowd.

Tariq's eyes met Laura's. 'As we came through the turnstiles this morning I thought I saw Ivan on the other side of the glass. I wasn't sure because he looked so different. His long blond hair seemed to have been cut short and dyed black. The sun was shining on the glass, which made it difficult to see, and when we went through he was gone. I didn't want to say anything in case I'd made a mistake.'

Laura turned to Kit. 'When Goldie was stolen, was there anything left behind in the Fleet Farm lorry? Any clue. Maybe something a bit surprising.'

Kit shook her head. 'Nothing. Not a fingerprint, not a trace of DNA. It was as if a ghost had taken him. Oh, wait. After the detectives had gone, Ken found a playing card wedged behind a bench, a Joker, but we figured that it was probably one of Ivan's. You know how he's always doing card tricks.'

Laura went quite still. 'Of course! How obvious. How could I not have figured that out sooner? The Joker might have belonged to Ivan, but if it did it's because he's a member of the Straight A gang. The Joker is their calling card. It's their way of laughing at the police. They leave it when they think they've got away with something.'

She took a deep breath. 'So it was them all along. They've been behind everything. Ivan and Mitch, and the father and son arrested for stealing Goldie in the UK, they're all linked to the Straight A's. And now at least two of the gang are here at the Kentucky Derby'

'I don't understand,' said Kit. 'What does this mean?'

'It means that they're up to something,' replied Laura darkly, 'and whatever it is, it's going to be huge.'

'WE WARNED YOU, *Laura Marlin* . . .'

The words brushed the back of Laura's neck like an ill wind as she stood in a shadowy corridor near the Paddock. She was waiting for Kit who was attempting to wash a coffee stain out of her dress in the bathroom. At the time, Laura was texting her uncle yet again. He wasn't fond of the phone, but he was as reliable as snow in winter when it came to returning messages. The fact that he'd been silent for nearly twenty-four hours was worrying her.

For that reason, her reactions were slower than normal. Before she could blink Janet Rain had a grip on her like an anaconda crushing a mouse. 'You thought you could escape me, Laura Marlin, didn't you? Well, you thought wrong. No one ever escapes Janet Rain. If that imbecile, Ivan, had been quicker off the mark in the Haunted House, he'd have got to you before your boyfriend turned up and you'd have joined the ranks of the disappeared.'

As Janet swooped, her hand moving in to cover Laura's mouth, Laura let out a piercing scream. Janet gave a winded gasp and her grip abruptly loosened.

'Stay away from her, you . . . you black widow spider,' yelled Kit, who had karate-kicked Janet in the solar plexus. 'Security! Somebody please help us! *HELP!* Fire! FIRE!'

In the ensuing chaos, when a fire crew burst from nowhere, accompanied by several burly crowd members, and Kit had to explain about a hundred times that she'd only screamed fire because it was an emergency and not because the grandstand was actually burning to the ground, Janet Rain fled.

The firemen were angry because their time had been wasted. In Laura's opinion, they were mostly annoyed because two shrieking girls had dragged them away from the television screens showing the latest race, but she couldn't exactly say that. And anyway, they weren't the only people in a huff.

The Churchill Downs' officials were in a flat spin because they were worried that a child abductor was on the loose. And the racegoers were furious because a race was delayed without explanation. As if that wasn't bad enough, a couple of pompous cops made fun of Laura when she tried to tell them that a female member of the world's most notorious gang was at the Derby and up to no good.

'Let's put it this way, kid, she's not alone,' one laughed.

'Somehow we've got to keep this from Grandma and Gramps,' Kit whispered to Laura as they tried to slip away from the throng. 'Promise me, you won't say anything. They're so overjoyed to be here, and so looking forward to seeing Noble Warrior run, that I can't bear to upset them. Besides, if Gramps has any more shocks this week, he'll have a heart attack.'

'But Janet Rain needs to be stopped,' Laura told her. 'If you hadn't turned out to be a martial arts expert, who knows what would have happened to me. They're big fans of chloroform, the Straight A's. One sniff of that stuff and you're out stone cold and you don't know a thing until you wake up hours later with a headache.'

'I know, but please wait until after the race,' implored Kit. 'In an hour's time, I'll do whatever you want me to. I'll shout it from the roof of the grandstand. Just promise me you won't do anything till then. What difference is sixty minutes going to make?'

You have no idea how much difference an hour can make with the Straight A's is what Laura wanted to say. But she refused to ruin this long-awaited moment for the Wainrights with her hunches and flights of fancy. She'd been wrong many times before. Why not now?

She gave Kit a big smile as they turned to go. 'I promise.'

'Not so fast,' barked the cop. 'Where are your parents? We need to have a serious talk.'

Kit said politely but firmly: 'We're with my grandparents,

but I really don't think it's a good idea to disturb them right now, Officer.'

He drew himself up to his full height, which wasn't very high. 'And why is that?'

'Because,' Kit told him, 'that's our horse, Noble Warrior, being led into the Paddock as we speak, and my Gramps has waited all year for this special moment. Besides, I may have exaggerated a teeny weeny bit about the emergency. You see, this woman we don't like was being horrible to Laura and it was the only way we could think of to get rid of her.'

The other cop shaded his eyes. 'Noble Warrior? Isn't he the favourite to snatch the Derby from Kindred Spirit?'

Kit beamed with pride. 'That's right. And he will win too.'

The man looked at his partner. 'Is there any law against betting in uniform?'

'If there is, I've forgotten it.'

'Okay, girls, thanks for the tip. Give your Grandma and Gramps our best for the Derby. Oh, and remember, never ever waste police time. While you're making up stories, real criminals could be getting away with murder.'

'Yes, Officer, sorry, Officer,' giggled Kit. She looped her arm through Laura's. 'Let's go and see Noble Warrior run.'

Laura had never felt prouder of anyone in her life than she did watching her best friend lead Noble Warrior around the Paddock, watched by millions around the world. Tariq grinned at her as he passed and her heart contracted. To see him so happy made everything worth it. She'd go through all of it again – well, maybe not the death-defying ride on Honey – just to make him smile.

Noble Warrior looked magnificent. His muscles rippled beneath his fiery coat and, despite his smallness, he carried himself regally and held his head high. To Laura, he seemed more than a match for his main rivals – the strapping bay, Kindred Spirit, and a tall, excitable grey, Speed Merchant.

'The media has those two as his biggest threats,' Blake explained to Laura, 'but there are a couple of outsiders I fear. Avatar and Comic Timing.'

'Don't forget Monsoon,' Ryan put in, enviously watching Tariq parade Noble Warrior around the Paddock. Tariq had fully expected Ryan to do it himself, but Ryan had refused. 'Nobody wants to see someone on crutches hobbling around the Paddock, trying to hang on to a keyed-up stallion. This is Warrior's moment to shine. And yours, for that matter.'

'In other words,' Kit was telling Laura, 'it's an open field. That's what makes the Derby so great, anyone can win.'

Across the Paddock, Garth Longbrook was watching Noble Warrior's every move, flanked by two plainclothes' detectives. Pride had caused him to make many mistakes over the past few months, but he'd been well and truly humbled, and Laura was sure that in the future there'd be no better head of security in any racing stable.

'You were right about what happened on the first night

you arrived,' he'd told her earlier that morning. 'There *was* a second lorry. Ivan and the men from Nathan Perry's farm rehearsed unloading Valiant, switching him over, and then driving away again, all before the CCTV camera clicked to the barn. It took longer than they expected so that's when they made the decision to switch the horses while Warrior was in transit. There was a false compartment, exactly as you'd surmised.'

Kit nudged Laura. 'Don't you just love the racing saddles? They're feather-light, like children's toys. For most races, the declared weight of the jockey – that's his or her weight and the saddle – has to be under a hundred and twenty pounds. If I become a jockey, I'll have to stop eating Anita's waffles.'

A photographer interrupted them. 'Excuse me, ma'am, sir,' he said to Christine and Blake. 'Would you mind if I took a photo of the two of you with your pretty granddaughter? It's for the society page of the local paper.'

Kit rolled her eyes at Laura as they were led away. 'Back in a sec.'

Laura had been standing on her own for less than a minute when her neighbour tapped her on the shoulder. 'Miss, a young man just slipped a note into your pocket.'

The goosebumps stood up on Laura's arms. 'What man?'

But whoever it was had gone. Laura scanned the crowds for Janet or Ivan, but could see neither. Cautiously, she put her hand in her pocket. It wasn't a note but a playing card. A malevolent Joker, grinning fiendishly.

Her blood ran cold. Whatever the Straight A's were

planning was about to happen. With minutes to go until the Kentucky Derby, what else could it be but the race. They must be planning to rig it somehow.

She looked over at Kit and her grandparents, posing and laughing for the photographer, and at Noble Warrior, prancing beside Tariq. She'd promised Kit that she wouldn't spoil this moment for them. She had no intention of going back on her word.

Suddenly Laura felt very alone. If only her uncle was here. He would know what to do. He would take charge. She checked her phone for the hundredth time. No message. Where was he?

And then, like a mirage, she saw him. He was striding through the crowds, instantly recognisable, not because his grey suit was plain in comparison to the resplendent outfits surrounding him, but because he, like Noble Warrior, carried himself in a way that made him stand out from the crowd.

He swept Laura off her feet and swung her round until she was dizzy and laughing. 'Sorry not to call, but I wanted to surprise you,' he said when he set her down. I did talk to Blake yesterday and I gather that you and Tariq have been very busy. In fact, I gather that if it weren't for the two of you, Noble Warrior would not be running in the Kentucky Derby.'

Laura looked sheepish. 'We did do our best to stay out of trouble, it's just that . . .'

He grinned. 'Don't tell me, it's just that mysteries kept needing to be solved.'

'In a way.'

The horses' girths were being tightened and the jockeys – tiny men and women with leathery skin, wearing colourful silk jerseys – were being hoisted into the saddle. They were so strong they looked bionic. The Wainright's jockey, wearing an ultramarine blue and white silk jersey, was hovering nervously beside Noble Warrior.

Calvin Redfern's face was suddenly serious. 'Laura, to be honest, I'm not only here for pleasure. I'm here because the police have had a tip-off that the Straight A's are planning something at the Derby. Our only problem is that we haven't a clue what it is, but we imagine it's something to do with the race itself.'

It was then that Laura a light bulb moment. She had a flashback of Ivan doing his sprint training in the heat of the day.

'It's not the race,' she cried. 'It's all been an elaborate smokescreen. Maybe not the theft of Goldie, but the swapping of Noble Warrior, the hints that somebody somewhere was going to try to fix the race. They were red herrings – distractions.'

'Distractions from what? That's what police intelligence has failed to discover.'

'It's not the horses that they're after,' Laura told him. 'It's the money. You once said to me that the Straight A's don't bother themselves with thousands. They're interested in millions or even billions. I think they're planning to raid the Money Room during the two minutes that the Derby is being run, when everyone's attention – including the guards – is likely to be on the race.'

Her uncle's eyes widened. 'Of course, that's it. How

could we have been so blind? They're after the money. Every cent of it.'

He pulled a radio from his pocket. 'Attention all units. Stand by for orders.'

Laura smothered a grin. Her uncle had been in Kentucky a matter of hours and yet he had already taken command. After the nail-biting tension of the past few days, it was nice to hand the reins of the investigation to someone else.

Kit came rushing up. 'Is everything all right?' she demanded, looking suspiciously at Calvin Redfern.

'It will be now,' Laura assured her. 'Uncle Calvin, this is my friend, Kit. Kit, this is my uncle, Calvin Redfern. Uncle Calvin, please let me come with you.'

He gave her a quick squeeze. 'No, Laura, you've done more than enough and this could get ugly. Go and enjoy the race with your friends. Kit, it's a pleasure to meet you, albeit briefly. The very best of luck to Noble Warrior.'

And with that he was gone.

~ 22 ~

LAURA BLINKED AS a dozen cameras clicked and whirred, and flashbulbs popped once again. 'Over here, please. Big smile, ma'am! Kit, how about a kiss on the nose for Noble Warrior? Oh, that's adorable. Again, if you wouldn't mind?'

If there hadn't been a wall of photographers in front of her, and cameras beaming her image into millions of homes across the globe, Laura would have had to pinch herself. At Sylvan Meadows Children's Home she'd spent hundreds of hours dreaming of a time when she might travel to exotic places and have adventures, but never in her wildest imaginings did she think that on the day she'd

167

helped foil one of the most audacious robberies in racing history, she'd also be in the Winner's Circle with the stallion who'd swept all before him in the Kentucky Derby.

Not that Noble Warrior hadn't given them a heart attack or two. The instant before the starting gate had opened, the jockey in the adjacent stall sneezed. Whether it was because the red stallion momentarily lost concentration or because he got a fright, he broke last. Within seconds, he'd been left behind and a gap had opened up between him and the rest of the field.

'What a disaster,' cried Blake.

'Unbelievable,' Christine said despairingly. 'That's it. The race is over before it's begun.'

'The race isn't over until it's over with Noble Warrior,' Ken comforted her. 'Nothing he hates more than seeing the quarters of the horse in front of him. Nothing he likes more than a challenge. Look closely. You can see him gathering himself. Now watch him go.'

'Ken's right,' Mitch agreed. 'Warrior has the heart of a lion. He's inherited all Goldie's courage and more. He'll never give up.'

Laura strained her eyes. She wanted to see every detail of the horses thundering down the track. They powered towards her, dirt spraying from beneath their mighty hooves, nostrils flaring, veins popping, one with his tongue hanging out of the side of his mouth.

The roar of the crowd was like nothing she'd ever heard. It filled her ears. The air crackled with electricity. Elegant women were jumping up and down in their stilettos. Men in thousand dollar silk suits were screaming their favourites' names like teenagers at a pop concert.

'Come on, Speed Merchant!'

'You can do it, Kindred Spirit!'

'Show them who's boss, Avatar!'

And the Noble Warrior fans:

'Oh no!'

'This is a tragedy.'

'Oh, dear.'

Their partners were berating them: 'Didn't I tell you to put money on Speed Merchant? Didn't I? But you never listen. As if that little red horse is any match for him.'

Speed Merchant and an outsider called Tearaway were dominating the race, burning up the track, when Noble Warrior suddenly seemed to find an extra gear. He closed the gap and began to streak through the field.

'Noble Warrior is making a move,' the commentator yelled excitedly. 'My goodness, they don't call him the Pocket Rocket for nothing. But it may not be enough. Speed Merchant has a commanding lead and now Avatar is on the attack. Kindred Spirit is being pulled up by his jockey. His saddle seems to have slipped. Look at Warrior go, though. He is flying. It's hard to believe a horse so small can take a stride that comes close to matching Man o' War's legendary gallop, but he does.'

'Go Warrior!' screamed Kit.

Laura felt as if her heart might burst out of her chest with excitement. Tariq was jumping up and down as if he was on a trampoline, and Ryan was waving a crutch in the air.

'I don't believe it,' cried the commentator. 'He's ridden

down Speed Merchant and Tearaway, both flagging, and he's going after Avatar. Can he do it? Oh my word, he has, and by a neck. It's Noble Warrior from Avatar and Comic Timing, with Speed Merchant back in fourth place. Ladies and Gentlemen, Noble Warrior, firstborn son of the legendary Gold Rush, wins the Kentucky Derby in heroic style.'

In the grandstand, everyone seemed to be in tears, including Laura. Kit grabbed her and Tariq and the three of them danced around in an ecstatic circle. Christine and Blake were hugging each other. Ken and Ryan were already on their way headed down to the track to wait for Noble Warrior.

Shortly afterwards Laura found herself in the Winner's Circle in front of the world's press and racing audiences from Cornwall to China. Tariq, Ryan, Ken and Laura stood on one side of Noble Warrior, while Kit, her grandparents, Garth Longbrook and the jockey beamed on the other. Mitch had hung back at first, still gutted that his own brother had been involved in a deception that had almost cost them the race, but Christine insisted he join them.

'You're your own person, Mitch,' she told him. 'You are not your brother. It's because of your brilliant training that Warrior was able to win. That's what you need to remember.'

Beside her, the red stallion arched his neck and preened and posed. Draped around his neck was the garland of crimson roses.

Despite the joy of the occasion, Laura had a knot in her stomach. Where was her uncle? Was he safe? She was terrified that he'd be hurt trying to stop the Straight A's. During his years as a detective, he'd had plenty of experience in dealing with the gang, but there was no end to their cunning and in recent months they'd gone to enormous lengths to try to take revenge on him. Each time he – with the help of Laura, Tariq and some unlikely friends – outwitted them, they became angrier and more intent on vengeance.

'That's enough guys,' said the media officer, holding up his hand to the photographers like a traffic policemen. 'The scribes need to hear the story too. We're going to escort the Wainrights up to the media centre.'

He turned to Blake. 'I believe that you have quite a tale to tell, sir. One of stolen stallions and a devilish plot by an identical twin to switch identical twins. As incredible as that is, another story is breaking which might rival it for front page news. Would you believe that while the Derby was being run, a gang of international thieves tried to rob the Money Room. They didn't succeed because the cops had received a tip-off. Several of these gangsters are being led away in handcuffs as we speak. I caught a glimpse as I dashed down here. One looked quite familiar. You didn't have a boy called Ivan working for you, did you?'

As the Wainwrights were led away, Laura turned her phone on. There were two messages. The first was a text from her uncle.

Hey Laura, thanks to you, we caught 'em red-handed. Put it this way, you'll not be hearing from Ms Rain ever again.

*Have some loose ends to tie up, but will see you at Fleet Farm
tonight. Love, Uncle C x*

Her mobile beeped again. This time it was from an
unknown sender.

*Bravo, Laura Marlin! You are a worthy adversary. Until we
meet again . . . Mr A*

It was a glorious afternoon, but Laura suddenly felt chilled
to the bone. The fact that the elusive head of the Straight
A's, leader of one of the world's most notorious criminal
empires, knew her phone number was, frankly, chilling.
'Until we meet again . . . ?' She didn't even want to think
about what that meant.

She glanced around quickly. Somehow she knew
beyond doubt that he was here at the Derby, watching her.
She refused to show she was scared. 'Sooner or later, we'll
catch up with you,' she mouthed silently. 'Sooner or later,
justice will be done.'

'Why are you looking so serious?' demanded Kit,
extricating herself from a crowd of well-wishers and
putting an arm around Laura's shoulders. 'We have so
much to celebrate. As soon as Grandma and Gramps are
done with the media, we're going back to Fleet Farm and
having a dinner party with every treat you can think of.

'Oh, I'm so happy that you stepped into our lives, Laura
Marlin. It's because of you and Tariq that Goldie is safe,
that Warrior had a chance to win the Derby and that Fleet
Farm will now always belong to Grandma and Gramps.

And that's not all. You've also given me back my life. I can ride again. I can dream again. That's wonderful, but it's not the best part. The best part is that I feel as if I've gained a friendship that will last forever. I feel . . . I hope you don't mind me saying this . . . as if I have a sister and brother in you and Tariq.'

'That's cool with me,' Tariq said with a laugh, as he came over to join them. Someone had put one of Warrior's red roses in the buttonhole of his suit. 'I feel the same way about you.'

'And so do I,' Laura agreed heartily. 'Now, you mentioned something about a celebration . . . '

Author's Note

When I was a child in Africa, my father spent several years working for Thomas Beattie, a farmer who was a highly successful racehorse owner. They'd become friends when Dad rode for him as an amateur jockey, and as a consequence of the thrilling stories they told and my daily encounters with the magnificent thoroughbreds that grazed in fields around our house, I became captivated by horse racing.

The highlight of the trip I made to the US to research this book – apart, obviously, from going to the Kentucky Derby – was visiting the Kentucky Horse Park, where I saw the statues of Man o' War and Secretariat, two of the greatest racehorses of all time. I also visited some of the Lexington farms. It was there that I met two stallions worth $80 million and $65 million. They lived in palatial comfort in a sort of house. When we drove up, one was looking out of the window.

For champions like Noble Warrior and Goldie, the life of a racehorse is very good indeed, but they are in a tiny minority. As Laura discovered, racing has a dark side. Horses are not fully grown until they are eight years old, which is why most riding horses do not begin their training until they are three or four. Racehorses, on the other hand, are routinely 'started' at eighteen months and raced at two years old. They are babies being pushed to their physical and mental limits.

Because their bones are not yet fully developed, these young horses frequently pull ligaments, strain tendons or fracture limbs. It's estimated that in North America alone up to eight hundred horses a year die from injuries sustained while racing. Even if they do stay fit, their fate depends on their performances. Those that don't make the grade are seldom lucky enough to go to kind homes, racehorse retirement homes or sanctuaries. The majority are sold to owners who can't handle them, euthanised, sent to slaughterhouses to be turned into pet food, or shipped abroad to countries to be sold as horse meat.

Racing is expensive. One survey of the Australian racing industry showed that fewer than ten per cent of racehorses make a profit for their owners. That means that some unscrupulous owners force their horses to run even when injured, masking the pain with things like cobra venom or cone snail venom. Anyone who read *Kidnap in the Caribbean* will remember the latter as one of the deadliest toxins on earth. Exhausted horses are sometimes forced on by jockeys who can whip them as many as thirty times in a race.

That said, it's important to remember that across the world there are numerous trainers, owners and jockeys who love the horses in their care and do their very best to treat them with respect and compassion. And there's no doubt that the horses who are treated right love to run. Go to YouTube and watch Australian wonder horse, Black Orchid, in action. She lives to race. Or see the movie,

Secretariat. The red stallion loved to run so much that when he finished a race he was often halfway round the track before his jockey could pull him up.

If you enjoy watching horses compete in any sport, whether it be racing, showjumping or eventing, try to do your part to ensure that the horses have the life they deserve. Sponsor charities like World Horse Welfare, or hold cake or car boot sales to help support racehorse retirement homes or sanctuaries. Whether or not they're champions, every horse is precious.

Lauren St John,
London
2012

A LAURA MARLIN MYSTERY
RENDEZVOUS IN RUSSIA

Lauren St John

Illustrated by David Dean

Orion
Children's Books

For my mother, who gave me three of the greatest gifts
you could give any child: a love of reading and travelling,
and a belief in the power of dreams

~ 1 ~

'CUT!' YELLED THE director. 'Cut, cut, cut!'

He was a gaunt man with a receding hairline and small, round glasses that perched high on the bridge of his beaked nose, giving him the air of a worried crow. Leaning into the sea wind, his face turning fire-engine red, he bore down on the hapless dog handler cowering on the edge of the film set. Actors and assorted crew scurried from his path.

'You imbecile! You absolute dunce! Call yourself an animal trainer? You couldn't teach a mouse to eat cheese. You couldn't teach a horse to graze grass. You couldn't teach a bird to fly, or a cheetah to chase antelope, or a fish

183

to swim. What did I tell you yesterday, Otto? For the fiftieth time, I instructed you to find me a dog I would love, a dog with attitude, a dog that will have cinema audiences across the world cheering one moment and reaching for the tissues the next. And what do you do? You produce a greyhound with the attention span of a goldfish. We've also had an obese golden retriever too lazy to do a single trick, yet with all the energy in the world when it came to gobbling three trays of smoked salmon sandwiches from the catering unit. We've had a border collie with rickets, a deranged spaniel and a bull terrier that almost amputated the hand of my supporting actress. If she hadn't been an animal lover, the lawsuit would have bankrupted the studio.'

He shook his fist. 'One more chance, my friend. If the next mutt you bring me isn't capable of winning an Oscar, you're fired.'

A crowd had gathered behind the ropes keeping onlookers from wandering on to the set. The woman beside Laura rolled her eyes. 'Oh dear. If the next scene goes wrong, I'm afraid that Brett will spontaneously combust. I don't suppose you'd consider volunteering your dog for the role? He's an extraordinary looking animal. A bit like a wolf, only kinder. Anyone would fall in love with him.'

Laura glowed with pride. She hugged Skye, her three-legged Siberian husky, and his tail thumped ecstatically. 'You'd be surprised. I think he's the most amazing dog on the planet, but—'

'And so do I,' put in Tariq, her best friend.

'But what?' asked the woman, who was dressed simply in jeans and a pale blue shirt but had the poise and photogenic features of an actress.

'Well, I think Skye is perfect, but not everyone feels the same way,' Laura said. 'Your director sounds very fussy. If he can't cope with a fat retriever, I doubt he'd want a husky with a missing leg.'

The woman laughed. 'Oh, don't pay any attention to Brett. He's all bluster. Beneath it, he's a bit of a geek. And he's super talented – one of the hottest movie-makers in Hollywood. There's a lot of excitement about our film. We've only been shooting for a week and already there's talk of awards.'

'What's the title of your movie?' asked Tariq. He and Laura had been overjoyed to discover, on the first day of the summer holidays, that a film set had mushroomed overnight on the outskirts of St Ives, their seaside home town. As a special treat, they'd begun the morning with breakfast at the Sunny Side Up cafe, but as soon as they'd swallowed the last delicious bite they'd begged permission from Laura's uncle to go out onto the cliffs and watch the filming.

'No running off to Hollywood now,' Calvin Redfern joked as they'd left.

'The title of our film is *The Aristocratic Thief*,' the woman told them. 'It's set in the nineteenth century and is about a wealthy man, renowned and respected in the highest circles in the land, who steals a priceless painting from the Hermitage Museum in St Petersburg, Russia. That's where we're filming next.'

'If it's set in Russia, what are you doing in Cornwall?' Laura wanted to know.

'We're shooting the English bit of the movie. In the story, the child heroine of the film is an orphan who comes from a beautiful seaside town. She has a dog she adores. This pet plays a vital role in the film, which is why it's a disaster that we're having so much difficulty finding the right one.'

She smiled. 'I haven't introduced myself. I'm Kay Allbright.'

Laura shook her hand. 'I'm Laura Marlin and this is my best friend, Tariq, and my husky, Skye. Do you mind me asking if you're an actress?'

'Was. A long time ago. Now I have the job of my dreams. I'm a screenwriter. I get to research and write the film itself. It's challenging and frequently frustrating, but I'm passionate about it.'

Skye stiffened. His blue eyes were locked on the dog handler, who was carrying a yapping Pomeranian onto the set. Laura took a firm grip on his collar. 'Behave yourself, Skye,' she scolded. 'You've already had breakfast.'

Beyond the cameras was an encampment of tents and caravans, plus a catering trailer with a red and white striped awning. The door of the largest caravan opened and out came a girl of about twelve or thirteen with long flaxen hair, wearing a ragged dress of white muslin. Her striking prettiness was marred by a bored scowl. Fortunately for the dog handler, it vanished as soon as she saw the Pomeranian.

'Oh he's so cute!' she cried in an American accent. 'What's his name?'

The man looked relieved. '*Her* name is Britney. She's quite the little actress. Loves attention. I should have used her from the start. You even have the same hair colour.'

'That's Ana María Tyler, who plays the orphan heroine of the story,' Kay whispered to Laura and Tariq. 'She's barely in her teens and she already has five movies under her belt.' She added under her breath: 'And an attitude to match.'

The director strode onto the set. 'Is this the best that you could come up with, Otto – a Pomeranian? Give me strength. How many times do you want me to explain that we need a dog capable of saving a young girl's life, or stopping an arch villain? This one couldn't scare a canary.'

Ana María pouted and clutched Britney to her chest. 'Yes, but she is a dog that audiences will go gooey over and you said that's important too.'

'True,' acknowledged Brett. 'Very true. Okay, we'll give Miss Britney a shot. Let go of her so that Otto can put her on her marker. Crew, take up your stations. Ready, Ana María? Action!'

The cameras rolled. As Laura and Tariq leaned forward eagerly, a low growl rumbled in Skye's throat. Laura soothed him with one hand and took a firmer grip on his collar with the other. He seemed to think that Britney would make a yummy mid-morning snack.

Ana María strolled along the cliff in the sunshine, admiring the view over the shining sea. The Pomeranian was with Otto, out of sight. Ana María bent down to pick wild flowers from the waving grass. One, a poppy, was slightly out of reach. She leaned closer to the edge and stretched for it.

Laura knew she was only acting but it was nerve-wracking to watch.

As Ana María's fingers closed around the poppy, there was a horrible cracking sound. The section of cliff on which she was kneeling suddenly disintegrated, catapulting her, screaming, over the edge.

Laura gave an involuntary shriek.

'Don't worry,' whispered Kay. 'It's all part of the show. She's landed on a specially constructed ledge and is quite safe. There's also a net beneath should anything go wrong.'

'I hope they've secured them well,' Tariq said worriedly. 'If she did fall, she'd almost certainly be killed. If she wasn't crushed on the rocks, she'd be drowned. The currents around here are incredibly strong.'

Laura couldn't repress a shudder. Tariq was speaking from experience. Barely six months earlier, he and Laura had come close to dying at Dead Man's Cove, only a stone's throw from where they were standing. Even now she could feel the power of the sea as it had sucked at her, trying to drag her into its freezing black depths.

Ana María was clinging to the rocky ledge by her fingers. 'Help!' she screamed. 'Help!'

Britney the Pomeranian went tearing across the cliff top, yapping for all she was worth. Her role was to run to Ana María's aid, realise there was a problem, and race away to get help. At least, that was the plan.

Unfortunately, nobody had communicated that to Skye. The husky took one look at Britney bounding like a bunny through the long grass, wrenched out of Laura's grasp and tore after her.

Laura clapped her hands to her mouth in horror. She dared not call him while the cameras were rolling, but how else was she to stop him? Kay and Tariq were also frozen to the spot. All they could do was watch the disaster unfold.

As Britney neared the screaming actress, some sixth sense warned her of approaching danger. She glanced over her shoulder and let out an audible squeak when she saw the husky bearing down on her. Realising that escape was impossible, she chose to leap over the cliff, landing on the ledge that Ana María was holding onto.

'Ouch!' screeched Ana María as Britney's claws dug into her hand. She let go. That shouldn't have mattered because she was standing on a wide wooden platform which had been cleverly painted to blend in with the rocks and was invisible to the cameras. Unfortunately, the jolt to the plank caused the fastenings that secured it to the rock to loosen. It only slipped a couple of millimetres, but it was enough to make Ana María lose her balance and come close to falling. This time, her blood-curdling scream had nothing to do with acting.

'CUT!' yelled the director, but no one appeared to be listening.

'Skye!' yelled Laura. 'Skye!'

She ducked under the ropes and sprinted to the edge of the cliff, followed by Tariq and Kay. Chaos broke out on the set.

'Do something!' Brett Avery shouted at the stunt

coordinator. 'What do you think I pay you for? Go down and get her. Call the coastguard, call the fire brigade, call the Queen if you have to, just get my star back on solid ground.'

Cautiously, he leaned over the cliff. 'Ana María, honey, whatever you do, don't look down.'

Ana María immediately glanced at the sea churning far below and screamed even louder. The Pomeranian whimpered and whined.

The stunt expert was trying to wriggle into a climbing harness while yelling at his assistant to get a rope that the actress could hold on to until he reached her. Ana María's mother, who'd appeared out of nowhere, added to the din by crying hysterically and threatening to sue.

The weight of people gathered on the clifftop caused a further loosening of the unstable edge. Pellets of gravel rained down on Ana María and the Pomeranian. Britney yapped madly. Ana María sobbed and shook.

'What the devil's taking so long?' yelled the director, but the stunt coordinator didn't answer. He was staring at his climbing harness in confusion. 'I don't understand,' he mumbled. 'I don't understand.'

'Something is wrong,' Tariq whispered to Laura as the adults began to argue. 'He looks as if he's lost something.'

Ana María gave a screech that could have shattered a pane of glass. The wind was picking up and threatening to suck her off the cliff.

The stunt assistant came racing up with a spare rope. 'Grab this and hang on tight,' he called down to Ana María. 'Try to stay calm. A lifeboat is on its way and there is a safety net below so you're not in any real danger.'

The words had barely left his mouth when the catastrophe happened. A gust of wind launched Britney into space. Ana María, who was clinging desperately to the rope at the time, was unaware that the Pomeranian had fallen until Britney's furry body flew past her. The little dog hit the water and flailed briefly before disappearing beneath the waves. For an already petrified Ana María, the shock was so great that her legs crumpled beneath her. She swung out over the void, past the safety net.

The stunt coordinator was frantic. 'Hang on tight, Ana María,' he yelled as the actress twirled on the end of the rope, bouncing periodically off the cliff face. 'We're going to pull you up. Whatever you do, don't let go.'

But try as she might, Ana María didn't have the strength to obey. At the first tug of the rope, her hands slipped and she plummeted downwards. She hit the boiling surf and disappeared.

'Now that,' Kay said, 'was not in the script.'

~ 2 ~

ANA MARÍA'S MOTHER, who was Colombian and quite excitable at the best of times, fainted. The director dropped to his knees and appeared to be praying. Otto, the animal handler, was so distressed that he plucked out at least half of his remaining twenty-six strands of hair.

With the humans going into meltdown, it was perhaps not surprising that the husky was the first to recover. Before Laura could take in what was happening, Skye had twisted from her grasp, taken three rapid strides and leapt off the cliff.

'No, Skye!' she shouted, but it was too late. A plume of spray kicked up and then the ocean swallowed him

192

whole, just as it had Ana María and the Pomeranian.

'Skye!' screamed Laura at the same time as dozens of people started yelling for Ana María and one lone voice for Britney. 'Skye! Somebody call the lifeguard. I have to get down there. I have to save him.'

'I think it's a bit late for that, kid,' the production manager, Jeffrey, announced cruelly. 'Your pet will be fish food by the time we've rescued Ana María. I'm sorry, but that's the way it is.'

Tariq was a mild-mannered boy but he gave the man the most murderous glare he could manage. 'Don't pay any attention to him, Laura,' he said. 'Skye is the smartest dog in the world. He wouldn't have jumped if he didn't think he'd make it.'

Kay let out a cry of disbelief. 'Laura, look!'

A hundred metres below them, Skye had surfaced, swimming strongly. He carried a piece of white cloth in his mouth. There was so much foam that it took a few seconds to make out that it was Ana María's dress and that the barely conscious actress was inside it. Fighting the current, he swam to the rocks and hauled her out of the punishing waves. She lay limply on a boulder as if she was dead.

By now, a crowd numbering well over fifty had gathered on the cliff top. They called encouragingly to Skye as he searched for the drowning Pomeranian. A cheer went up when he plucked the tiny dog from the water and placed her on the rock beside Ana María just as a lifeboat came roaring around the corner.

In a matter of moments, a beefy, white-bearded lifeguard

had Ana María on board and was reviving her with warm blankets and hot, sweet tea. The other, younger lifeguard lifted Skye and the shivering Britney into the boat and they too were wrapped in rugs. As the boat sped away, cheers followed it.

When the crowd had dispersed, Brett Avery said in a shaky voice, 'That husky – where did he come from? Who does he belong to? Will somebody find me his owner and bring them to me RIGHT NOW!'

Laura shrank behind Kay. She had visions of Calvin Redfern, her uncle, who had very little money, being sued for all he owned. They'd lose their home at No.28 Sea View Terrace and have to leave St Ives for somewhere cheaper. Social Services would get involved and drag Laura back to the Sylvan Meadows Home for Girls, the desperately dull orphanage where she'd spent the first eleven years of her life.

'The husky belongs to this young lady here,' Kay said with a smile, pushing Laura forward. 'Wasn't he marvellous? You couldn't make it up. It just goes to show that truth is always stranger than fiction.'

Laura stammered, 'I'm s-sorry Skye messed up your scene and caused such havoc. I was holding him, I promise I was, but you see he's incredibly strong and he saw Britney and . . . Mr Avery, my uncle doesn't have much money so we can't pay you. Maybe I could make it up to you by washing dishes in the catering trailer or something?'

'Pay me? *Pay me?* Kid, I'm the one who should be paying you! Have you any idea what a gift you've just given the studio?' He gave an incredulous laugh. 'You have no idea what I'm talking about, do you? Allow me to explain.'

He gestured to a runner. 'Hey, Chad, do me a favour and bring a couple of catering's best smoothies for our friends.'

Minutes later, Laura and Tariq were sitting in chairs that had in their time seated several legends, chatting to their new friends Kay Allbright and Brett Avery, one of Hollywood's most famous directors. They were sipping mango and coconut smoothies and listening with growing astonishment as Brett talked. It turned out that the cameraman had not stopped filming when the director shouted cut, but had recorded the entire drama.

'Do you know what that means?' Brett demanded. 'It's movie gold. Pure movie gold. With some judicious editing we can use the entire sequence in the film almost as if Kay had written it like that in her screenplay.'

Laura was taken aback. 'But what about Ana María? She could have been killed. Surely she wouldn't want that footage being seen by movie audiences?'

Brett Avery laughed. 'On the contrary, she'll love the publicity. Mark my words, she'll get an Oscar for that performance.'

He put a hand on Laura's arm. 'Which is where you come in, my dear. I must have your hero dog for my movie. Obviously, we couldn't use any of these scenes if we had to find a replacement dog. We could get another husky, but it's unlikely we'd find one with three legs. Besides, this particular dog is the exact dog I've been searching for – a dog with attitude, a dog movie audiences will adore. I want to buy him. How much will you take for him?'

'He's not for sale. I wouldn't part with Skye for all the money in the world.'

Brett said smoothly, 'Of course you wouldn't. But you haven't heard my offer yet. I'm prepared to pay you a thousand pounds for him.'

Laura did her best to hide her shock. 'He's not for sale. Not for any price.'

'Ah, a lady who drives a hard bargain. Five thousand. I'll give you five thousand for him.'

Laura thought of her uncle and what a difference such a sum of money would make to him, but Skye was just as important to her. She shook her head.

The smile left the director's face. 'You obviously love your dog and that's great, but maybe you should think what the money might mean to others. You mentioned that your uncle doesn't have much. I'm prepared to pay you ten thousand pounds for your husky. That's my final offer. It might change your uncle's life.'

'Skye means as much to Laura as her uncle does,' Tariq informed him. 'He's family to her. You don't sell family.'

Brett Avery lost his cool. 'Don't be ridiculous. Animals are not as valuable as people. They can be sweet, yes, but there's no comparison—'

'How about a loan?' Kay interrupted hastily. 'Laura, how would you feel if we borrowed Skye for a couple of weeks of filming in Russia? The studio will pay you and your uncle a handsome fee and you'll have your dog back before you know it. And when *The Aristocratic Thief* opens in cinemas later in the year, you'll be able to boast to your friends that your husky is famous.'

Before Laura could answer, the lifeguard's four-wheel drive came bouncing up the slope, and out stepped Ana María, looking pale, fragile and furious. Her golden hair hung in wet rat's tails.

'We tried to persuade her to go to hospital . . .' the lifeguard told Brett Avery, 'but she insisted on talking to you first.'

The director embraced the sodden actress, then pulled her aside and started talking to her urgently in a voice too low to hear. Laura wondered if he was telling her that the cameraman had recorded every detail of her fall and that she'd doubtless win an Academy Award for it, because her countenance suddenly became sunny. At one point, she turned and stared hard at Laura and Tariq.

Laura was so transfixed by the scene that she was almost bowled over by a damp and sandy Skye, who'd bounded out of the lifeguard's vehicle and raced towards her. She squatted down and he put his left paw on her shoulder and licked her face until she was almost as wet as he was.

'You,' she told him, 'are a total hero. You're the best and bravest dog on earth and I wouldn't part with you for all the money in Hollywood.'

'Watch out, Laura,' Tariq warned. 'Here comes Brett Avery again. Bet he tries to talk you around.'

'He can try. He's not going to get anywhere.'

Brett Avery was all smiles. He pushed his glasses up on his nose. 'Sorry about that, kids. Had to check on our star. What a trooper. A bit bruised and suffering from mild hypothermia, but the show must go on and all that.

Needless to say, she's fallen in love with Skye. You'll be pleased to hear that she's in total agreement with you. Won't hear of the dog being taken away from you, even if it's merely on loan.'

Laura was surprised. 'Really? What about the rescue footage? Will you be able to find another three-legged dog?'

Brett Avery ushered them back to the chairs and called for ice creams. 'Sit down, kids, sit down. What were your names again? Laura Marlin and Tariq Ali. Is that right? Fabulous. Kids, you won't believe this, but even in her traumatised state Ana María noticed something that I should have spotted at once – and in fact would have done had it not been for the crisis.'

'What's that?' asked Tariq, declining the ice cream. His early life as a quarry slave in Bangladesh had made him distrustful of the motives of grown-ups.

'I should have noticed that you're great looking kids. You'd be perfect for my movie. You're an eye-catching pair – Laura with her peachy skin and pale blonde hair, and Tariq with his black hair and caramel skin. Knockout. You're born to be actors.

'We'd have to get permission from your guardians, of course, but how would you feel about starring in my movie, along with Skye? We're wrapping up filming here tomorrow, but at the end of the week we're off to St Petersburg, Russia. We'd need you for about ten days of shooting. We'd pay you handsomely, take care of all your expenses, and you'd essentially have a free holiday in one of the most beautiful cities in the world. Best of all, Skye would be with you. How about it?'

During her years at the orphanage, when it seemed that she'd be stuck in a grim, grey town for ever, Laura had longed for a life of excitement and adventure. More than anything, she'd yearned to travel and see exotic places and few countries seemed more exotic or mysterious than Russia. She glanced quickly at Tariq. Though he was trying hard not to show it, his eyes were alight with excitement. Tariq came from a background even tougher than hers and he too dreamed of seeing the world.

She put an arm around Skye. 'I'd have to ask my uncle's permission and Tariq would need to speak to his foster parents, but I think it's something we'd consider, Mr Avery.'

'Brett. Call me Brett.'

As she made her way back to Sea View Terrace with Skye, Laura was walking on air. For as long as she could remember, she'd dreamed of becoming a detective when she grew up. Unlike many of the girls she knew, she'd never had any desire to become a famous actress. Now the opportunity had unexpectedly landed in her lap. Acting would not have been her first choice of career but, Laura mused as she strolled home, it was always good to have options.

'*EXTRAS?* BRETT AVERY didn't say anything about us being extras. He told us he was going to make us stars.'

Calvin Redfern smothered a laugh. He filled one mug with hot chocolate and another with black coffee and carried them over to the kitchen table, side-stepping Lottie, his wolfhound, who was basking in the warmth of the Aga. 'Welcome to Hollywood, Laura. Mr Avery tried to tell me the same thing, but I'm afraid I'm rather more cynical. When I pressed him for a job description, he said that while Skye would definitely have a starring role in the movie, you and Tariq would be what he called "background artistes".'

'What does that mean?'

'You'll be crowd scene extras who show up in the credits described as "Girl in Red Hat" or "Boy Pushing Cart." When the film comes out at the cinema, if you blink you'll miss yourselves.'

'Oh,' said Laura, feeling deflated. She'd been looking forward to the expressions on her classmates' faces when she and Tariq returned from the summer holidays as famous film stars. 'Didn't you hear about it?' she'd planned to say airily. 'We were discovered after my husky saved Ana María Tyler's life. The director said we were naturals.'

'Don't look so glum,' said her uncle. 'Since when have you cared about fame and fortune? As far as I know, all you've ever dreamed of is becoming a detective like Matt Walker in those books you love so much. Don't tell me that's changed after one small brush with stardom?'

Laura gave a sheepish smile. As everyone who knew her knew, she was obsessed with both fictional investigators like Detective Inspector Walker, and real detectives like her uncle. He'd been Scotland's top detective for five years running before he'd lost his wife while leading the hunt for the Straight As, one of the world's most notorious gangs. Devastated and blaming himself, he'd quit his job and fled to Cornwall. Now he worked as an undercover investigator for the Fisheries Inspectorate.

'Of course I'm not going to give up on my dream. It's just that acting did sound fun, that's all, and it would have been cool to see our names up in lights. Plus Tariq was practically turning cartwheels he was so excited about seeing Russia. Now I suppose you're not going to let us go.'

'On the contrary, I'd love you to go.'

Laura gave a squeal of delight. 'You're kidding?'

Calvin Redfern cut two slices of their housekeeper Rowenna's legendary apple pie, doused them in custard, and pushed a bowl over to Laura. 'No, I'm not. To tell you the truth, I have some news myself. I've been trying to pluck up the courage to break it to you.'

'What news?' The last six months had been the best of Laura's life. Living in glorious St Ives with the uncle she'd come to adore and her beloved husky was nothing short of magical. Meeting Tariq had been the icing on the cake. A little part of Laura was always slightly fearful that some twist of fate would return her to the Sylvan Meadows Home for Girls.

'Don't worry. It's not bad news, just bad timing. You may have heard that Britain's Deputy Prime Minister, Edward Lucas, is going on a rare state visit to Russia in the next couple of weeks. He'll be in Moscow, not St Petersburg, which is where you'll be filming if you do decide you're willing to be an extra. The two cities are a considerable distance apart, so it's unlikely that you'll even be aware he's in the country. That's probably not a bad thing. There's always tons of security surrounding these events.'

'I don't understand. What does Ed Lucas' visit have to do with you?'

Her uncle swallowed a mouthful of pie. 'As you know, I had a lot of experience working with criminal gangs like the Straight As when I was in the police force.'

Laura said nothing. Just the name of the gang was enough to make the hair stand up on the back of her neck. The Straight As were criminal masterminds with their fingers in hundreds of evil pies. Depending on your point of view, they were the best of the best or the worst of the worst. From bank robberies and horse race fixing to slave labour and black market dealing in endangered species, they were involved in all of it. On three occasions, she and Tariq had made the mistake of crossing them. Each time they'd almost paid with their lives.

'Go on.'

'A month ago, I was contacted by MI5. They've had reliable intelligence that the Russian mafia is planning an assassination attempt on Ed Lucas during his visit. For diplomatic reasons it's essential that the trip goes ahead so the Foreign Office has asked me, as an expert on criminal networks, to work with them to keep him safe.'

'How are you planning to track the potential assassin down?' Laura said excitedly, momentarily forgetting the Straight As. She loved intrigue. 'Do you have to go to Moscow?'

'No, I don't. But the powers that be do want me to base myself in London while Ed Lucas is in Russia so that I can head up the British side of the security operation. I did my best to refuse the assignment on the grounds that I've left that life behind, but they've gone to great lengths and offered me quite a bit of money in order to persuade me to agree.

'I'm sorry, Laura. I've been dreading telling you that I'd be away for several weeks in the middle of your school holidays. I know you think I'm a workaholic.'

'Yes, you are,' Laura scolded.

He smiled wryly. 'But don't you see that if you and Tariq are interested in working on the film, it could be the perfect solution for everyone? I've checked out the film studio, Tiger Pictures, and they have a good reputation in the business. They had some financial trouble but they're fine now. Brett Avery is a temperamental character, but he's generally well-liked and respected. He has also given me his word that Kay Allbright, your screenwriting friend, would be personally responsible for your welfare. We had a long conversation this morning and she seems a lovely person. Perhaps most importantly, you'd have Skye with you. And as Ana María Tyler discovered, there could be no better bodyguard.'

Beneath the kitchen table, the husky's tail thumped a happy rhythm. Laura rubbed his ears. Tariq's foster dad, a vet, had examined him thoroughly after his hundred and twenty-seven metre leap. Incredibly, he was no worse for wear. His heroics had made him the talk of the town, and the local paper had sent a photographer round to snap his picture.

'So there's only one question remaining,' Calvin Redfern was saying.

'Which is?'

'Would you like to go to Russia or not? Do you want to spend ten days working as a background artiste in one of the world's most fascinating cities – all expenses paid and with Skye and Tariq at your side – or would you prefer to spend your whole summer on the beach in beautiful St Ives?'

Laura glanced at the rain pouring down outside the window. If sunshine could be guaranteed, there'd be no contest. She'd choose to laze away the holidays on Porthmeor Beach. Annoyingly, it had been the wettest June since records began and now July was looking equally dismal.

On the other hand, St Petersburg, a city that conjured images of great monuments, magical nights at the ballet and long visits to the Hermitage Museum, a treasure house of art, sounded impossibly glamorous. So did working on a film set, even if she and Tariq did occupy the decidedly unglamorous roles of 'Girl in Red Hat' and 'Boy Pushing Cart.'

She smiled. 'I'd love to go to St Petersburg, but only if Tariq can come too.'

Her uncle poured more custard on her pie. 'Oh, I don't think you need have any worries on that score. Tariq's foster parents are both busy people and they think this would be a wonderful opportunity for him to see St Petersburg for free and have an unforgettable experience. Besides, they know the two of you are inseparable.'

There was a moment of silence as each contemplated that the reason Rob and Rena were so relaxed about Tariq's adventures with Laura was that they were blissfully unaware they'd frequently included encounters with kidnappers, bank robbers, volcanoes, sharks and other lethal things. For reasons of national security, those had been kept secret.

'So that's settled,' Laura said. For reasons unknown, butterflies started flapping around her stomach. She'd been uneasy since she'd left the film set the previous day, but she couldn't figure out why.

Her uncle carried the plates and mugs to the sink and began to wash up. 'Yes, that's settled, but on one condition.'

'I thought there might be a catch.'

'No catch but I want you to promise me you'll stay out of trouble. All foreign countries have the potential to be dangerous, but Russia is more deadly than most.'

Laura hopped up and pretended a sudden interest in drying dishes. How could she give him her word when trouble had a habit of seeking her out? Her day on the film set was a perfect example. One minute she was happily watching a young actress pick wild flowers, the next her husky was embroiled in a life and death drama.

'Laura?'

Her dimples deepened. 'Oh Uncle Calvin, there's not going to be any trouble. We'll be on a Hollywood film set, being taken care of twenty-four/seven. And as you said, Skye is the best bodyguard in the business.'

He laughed as he handed her a plate, his powerful forearms soapy with suds. 'I'm sure you're right. At least promise me that you'll make a holiday of it and enjoy yourself and not go looking for mysteries where there are none.'

Laura relaxed. Now that she could do. 'I promise.'

~ 4 ~

'**WILL IT BE SNOWING**, or should I take shorts?' asked Laura, gazing helplessly into her wardrobe. 'What about jeans? Will I need two pairs or three? And how on earth am I going to fit Skye's food dish and doggie treats into my suitcase? I've barely started packing and already it weighs a ton.'

Tariq was stretched out on her duvet, using the husky's furry hindquarters as a pillow. He glanced up from the pages of his Russian guidebook.

'According to this, St Petersburg is the world's northernmost city and we're going to be there during the famous White Nights. Apparently it's light almost

207

twenty-four hours a day and the sun barely dips below the horizon. How cool is that? Some people don't bother going to bed at all. They stroll along the Neva River or hang out in cafes or at the Hermitage, which is one of the largest art museums in the world. It has over three million works of art.'

'Sounds great, but now I'm even more confused. Are they called the White Nights because they're freezing, or is it like summer all evening long? Or something in between?'

'The guidebook says the temperature could be anywhere from thirteen degrees to twenty-three. I've taken every bit of clothing I own, which isn't very much, and you should do the same. I don't think it'll be hot enough for shorts and you probably won't need treats. They do have dogs in Russia, you know. There are bound to be pet shops selling food.'

'Yes, but these are his favourites and— '

The doorbell drowned the rest of the sentence. Lottie's booming bark echoed up the stairs.

Skye bounded off the bed and out of the room. Tariq sat up. 'Are you expecting someone?'

Laura shut the suitcase. 'Not as far as I know. My uncle would have mentioned it before he left for work this morning. Maybe it's the postman.'

She hurried down, followed by Tariq. Skye and Lottie were growling and snuffling at the front door. Laura peered through the spyhole. A bouquet of flowers blocked the way, obscuring the person holding them.

Laura backed away from the door. The last time someone

had come to number 28 with a delivery, it was a ruse by the Straight A gang to kidnap her. It was not an experience she was anxious to repeat.

'What is it?' Tariq peered through the spyhole as the doorbell rang again and Lottie let off another volley of deafening barks. 'That's weird.'

'What's weird?'

'It's the stunt coordinator from the film set. What do you suppose he wants?'

'I don't know, but whatever it is it must be urgent.'

Laura unlocked the door and opened it with a smile. The man was already halfway down the steps. When she called out to him he turned with a strange reluctance, almost as if he'd changed his mind and would have preferred there to be no one home.

'Excuse me! Sorry it took me so long to answer the door. Can I help you?'

'I, um, these are for you, Miss Marlin.' He thrust the flowers at her. 'To say thanks. I don't know if you remember me from the set. I'm Andre March, the stunt coordinator.'

Laura was astonished. She stared up at him through a fragrant thicket of poppies, roses and cornflowers. 'It's very kind of you, but I can't think of anything I've done to deserve them.'

He looked from her to Tariq, who stood protectively at the top of the steps gripping Skye's collar. 'It's not so much what you've done, it's what your husky did. He saved Ana María's life. If it hadn't been for him, I'd never have worked again in this industry. My life would have been ruined. As it is, I'm quitting. Brett Avery hasn't fired me, but it's been made clear to me that I should go.'

Laura's heart went out to him. 'I'm so sorry. I feel responsible. You see, Skye, my husky, he sort of caused the accident by chasing the Pomeranian. He thought she was a toy. It's my fault. I should have been holding him tighter.'

A storm was closing in and a sharp, cool breeze preceded it, yet beads of sweat had broken out on Andre's forehead. He wiped them away with the sleeve of his shirt. Glancing with agitation at Laura's neighbour, Mrs Crabtree, who'd chosen that exact moment to dash into her garden and rescue her laundry from the line, he said in a low voice: 'Is it possible to go inside so we can talk more privately?'

It was on the tip of Laura's tongue to refuse. Stranger danger and all that. But then he added: 'Your friend and dogs are welcome to hear what I have to say. I mean you no harm. I only want to return the favour you have done me.'

'Gorgeous flowers, Laura!' cried Mrs Crabtree, Laura's neighbour, who was dressed entirely in purple. 'Are those from the film studio? Don't tell me you're getting the star treatment already? Does that extend to "background artistes"? In my day, there was no such thing. People who appeared in crowd scenes were known as extras and appeared in the credits with titles like "Girl Sweeping Street" or "Limping Pickpocket". They didn't get flowers and free holidays to St Petersburg. But perhaps that's your reward for Skye's heroics. That Ana María what-you-may-call-it could have plunged to her death . . .'

Pellets of rain splattered down on Laura's arm.

'Excuse us, Mrs Crabtree,' she said, virtually shoving Andre up the steps. 'We have an urgent appointment with the film's stunt coordinator.'

'Stunts? I do hope you're insured . . .'

Mercifully, the rain came slanting in, forcing Mrs Crabtree to pick up her washing and flee. Laura and Andre bolted inside, followed by Tariq and Skye. Lottie growled and barked until Laura quieted her. Ordinarily she would never have dreamt of inviting a near stranger into the house without her uncle present, but she had plenty of protection, plus her neighbour as a witness.

'Can I offer you a drink? We have tea or coffee or juice. I think it's mango.'

Andre shook his head vigorously and held his position near the door. 'I can't stay. I wanted only . . .' He stopped. 'This is a mistake. I should go.'

'It's okay,' Tariq reassured him. 'The dogs won't bite and nor will we.'

'Are you sure I can't get you a glass of water?' asked Laura. 'You don't look well at all. Do you have a migraine or something? Please don't worry about returning any favours. I'm glad that Skye saved the day, but he acted on instinct. It had nothing to do with me.'

'Maybe, but he's your dog. I owe you both. The only thing is . . .' His sleeve flew up and mopped more beads of sweat. 'Well, I'm not sure you'll thank me for it. You'll think I'm mad, just like the rest of the crew.'

Laura exchanged glances with Tariq. She regretted allowing Andre to enter the house. He was acting so oddly that she couldn't blame his colleagues for believing he was slightly deranged. 'Of course we won't think you're mad,' she lied. 'What did you want to tell us?'

'Go on,' Tariq encouraged.

Andre took a deep breath. 'Do you know that there are films which are said to be cursed?'

'I've never heard of a movie being cursed, but I've just done a school project on Egyptology and that involved a curse,' said Tariq. 'When the archaeologist, Howard Carter, opened Tutankhamun's tomb in 1923, loads of spooky things happened. Almost everyone who was at the opening of the tomb later fell victim to accidents, unexplained illnesses and even deaths.'

Andre was impressed. 'I actually worked on a documentary about Tutankhamun so I'm familiar with the stories about an ancient curse sent to destroy anyone who disturbed the boy king's tomb. Our research proved that almost all of them were conspiracy theories. I mean, Carter himself died of old age. The only really creepy story is the one about Lord Carnarvon, the man who financed the dig. He was bitten by a mosquito during the opening of the tomb. The bite became infected and he fell seriously ill. At the exact moment that he passed away in Egypt, his dog in England gave a series of blood-curdling howls and dropped down dead.'

Skye, who'd been regarding Andre with his vivid blue eyes, cocked his head and whined, sending a shiver up Laura's spine. The stunt manager nearly jumped out of his skin.

'Yes, but what does that have to do with your film?'

demanded Laura, determined to keep the conversation in touch with reality. 'Are you saying that *The Aristocratic Thief* is cursed?'

'Not the film, the set. For years, I've heard stories about film sets that seem to attract one disaster after another. Most relate to horror films like *The Crow*. Not being a fan of them myself, I've always taken these tales with a pinch of salt. Some are more believable than others, but I've always believed that even those that are proven to be genuine are linked only by coincidence.

'When the film *The Crow* was being made, there were lots of bizarre happenings, including a fire and an electrocution and Brandon Lee, the son of martial arts legend Bruce Lee, was tragically killed by a gun that was supposed to be loaded only with blank cartridges.

'When the James Bond movie, *Quantum of Solace*, was being filmed, Daniel Craig, who plays Bond, cut his face and needed eight stitches. A week later he sliced off the top of his finger doing a stunt. There was also a fire on the set and two stuntmen were hurt in separate car accidents. One mysteriously drove an Aston Martin sports car into Lake Garda in Italy.'

Sensing Laura's impatience, he said quickly: 'I am getting to the point. You may have noticed that when Ana María was in trouble on the cliff yesterday, I seemed confused. Normally, I can assure you I am the opposite. My job depends on my staying calm in a crisis. Every day I supervise stuntmen and actors as they set themselves on fire, endure car crashes and throw themselves off cliffs.'

Tariq was puzzled. 'But none of those things are real, are they? They're all staged for effect.'

'Yes, they are. But many stunts can be life-threatening if they're not done correctly.'

'What went wrong yesterday?' asked Laura.

A small smile lightened the gloom on Andre's face. 'You mean, apart from your husky deciding that Britney would make a delicious snack?'

'Yes, apart from that.'

'Three things – all potentially lethal.' He counted them off on his fingers. 'One, the ropes on my harness were cut.'

The blood quickened in Laura's veins. Finally, they were getting somewhere. 'Deliberately? I mean, they weren't worn out or anything?'

He gave her a cutting look, as if to say, Give me credit. I'm a professional.

'They had been sliced with a knife *on purpose*. You don't get much more deliberate than that. Two, when I abseiled down the cliff later that day to try to work out why the stunt had been such a disaster, I found that the ledge Ana María was standing on – a ledge I'd built myself – had been unscrewed in two places. That meant it was unable to support her weight. Three, the centre of the safety net had been carefully frayed with a razor. Even if she'd landed in it, she'd have fallen straight through.'

Tariq was aghast. 'Someone was trying to kill her?'

'If those were the only things that had gone wrong since we started filming, I'd have jumped to the same conclusion. But they're not. There have been so many strange incidents that I hardly know where to start. On the night before we left Los Angeles, five of our crew members came down with food-poisoning so severe we had to leave them behind.

'And it didn't end there; on our first evening in St Ives, our cinematographer tripped over a chair that had been overturned in a dark passage and broke both his wrists. Then yesterday an unidentified car travelling at high speed veered in front of our equipment truck, causing it to overturn. Incredibly, the truck driver suffered only minor injuries. However, thousands of pounds worth of equipment was destroyed.'

'Do you have any idea who or what is behind this?' Laura asked. 'You talk about the set being cursed. Do you think it's haunted?'

He gave a hollow laugh. 'Miss Marlin, I do not believe in ghosts, evil spirits or anything else supernatural or fantastical. I *do* believe that someone – a human being – wants the film stopped, and will go to any lengths to make that happen.'

'But who would take such desperate measures?' asked Tariq.

'And why?' added Laura.

'I don't know and I don't plan to hang around and find out.' Andre glanced anxiously at his watch. 'I'm leaving on the 2.33 p.m. train to Newquay. I can't miss it. The sooner I'm back in LA, the better I'll like it. But I couldn't go without warning you. You and your husky must quit the film at once. If you go to Russia,

I believe that something terrible will happen.'

Laura almost laughed. 'We can't. We've signed a contract.'

'And the film company have given us our plane tickets and booked our hotel rooms,' added Tariq. 'There's a car taking us to the airport tomorrow. It's all arranged.'

'Then unarrange it. Your lives may depend on it. You're only extras. It's not as if you'll be missed.'

'Gee, thanks,' Laura said drily, 'but aren't you forgetting something?'

She put a hand on Skye's head. He was watching their faces as if he understood every word. 'We might not be missed, but Skye will. Brett Avery has paid a fortune in visa fees and transport arrangements for him. I doubt if one penny of it is refundable. Even if we wanted to get out of the contract, which we don't, he'd probably sue my uncle. There's no way I'm going to let that happen just because of a few weird incidents that may not even be connected.'

'Nor me,' Tariq said firmly.

Laura smiled. 'Thanks for coming here today, Andre. We'll go to St Petersburg, but don't worry, we'll be careful. What's that saying? "Forewarned is forearmed". We'll watch our backs.'

Andre's mouth set in an angry line. 'Well, so be it. Let no one accuse me of not doing my duty. I'll go with a clear conscience, but I believe you're making a serious mistake. There are many ways you could get out of your contract. You could feign illness or even wrap your husky's paw in a bandage and claim it's broken. If you do nothing and something bad happens, you only have yourselves to blame.'

He pulled open the front door with an expression that was close to dread. 'Good luck, Miss Marlin. You'll need it.'

~ 5 ~

LAURA PRESSED HER nose to window of the British Airways jet and gazed out at the Russian landscape rising to meet them. It was flat, parched and dotted with factories. A bronze lake sparkled in the distance. As the plane touched down on the runway, spiky fir trees, like upended brooms, sped by.

'Do you think we've done the right thing – ignoring Andre's warning and coming here?' Tariq asked as they waited for their luggage. Their passports had been stamped by an unsmiling official with stars on the epaulettes of his white uniform.

'Firstly, we didn't exactly have a choice,' Laura said. 'We

had signed a contract and the tickets were bought and everything was arranged. Secondly, we have a mystery to solve. It'll give us something to do during the long hours when we're not needed for filming. Sounds as if there'll be quite a few of those.'

'I thought your uncle told you to stay out of trouble.'

'He did, but he also instructed us – several times – to look after each other and keep each other safe. If I didn't at least do a little bit of investigating to make absolutely sure that somebody isn't about to drop a brick on your head or poison Skye, I'd be breaking my promise to him.'

'What's all this talk about poisoning and dropping bricks?' demanded Kay, coming over to them with a trolley. 'You've been reading too many detective novels. I visited St Petersburg when I was researching *The Aristocratic Thief* and found it one of the most civilised cities on earth and among the most beautiful. Quite glorious. Wait until you see it.'

For most of the long drive from the airport, Laura thought that both Kay and the author of the guidebook needed glasses if they considered the place attractive. Initially, everything seemed a universal grey. Soulless concrete buildings crowded wide motorways, over which flyovers looped like fighting snakes. A giant statue of Vladimir Lenin, the communist revolutionary who rose to become ruler of the Soviet Union in the 1920s, towered over the traffic. A thick coating of brown dust made the cars and buildings look duller still.

Laura cuddled Skye, who'd jumped into the back seat between her and Tariq after they'd collected him from the cargo division and bared his teeth when the film company driver, a surly Russian who spoke little English, objected.

Laura had apologised but refused to move her husky, explaining that he needed to be close to her after the long, scary flight. 'He's very gentle really. It's just that he's been travelling for about twenty-four hours and he's out of sorts.'

Kay supported her by telling the driver that Skye was no ordinary husky. 'Back in England, he saved a young girl's life. What's more, he is about to become as famous as Lassie. Have you heard of Lassie? No? Look, if it makes you feel better, he can sit on my coat, but we are absolutely not leaving the airport without him. He's one of us and he's going to ride with us.'

As the driver started the engine with a snarl that rivalled Skye's, Laura warmed to Kay even more. There was something so straightforward, decent and warm about the screenwriter that it was impossible not to like her.

It wasn't until they swept through the city gates that a sense of wonder came over Laura. It was as if they'd stepped through a magic curtain into another world. Within moments they were cruising along tree-lined boulevards overlooked on all sides by magnificent architecture. It was as if the best buildings and monuments from Paris, Rome, Prague, London and other great cities had been scooped up by the founder of the city, Tsar Peter the Great, and deposited in St Petersburg.

The colours changed too. A mansion of dusky pink, edged with cream, flanked a pale green restaurant. In among the statues, there were museums, homes and shops painted rusty red or baby blue or mustard yellow. As they drove into the city centre, further delights awaited them. Horse-drawn carriages clip-clopped past canals alive with riverboats, swans and wild ducks. It was nearly 7 p.m. and yet the sun was still shining and the sky an electric blue.

'Would you believe that the city's name has been changed three times?' said Kay. 'In 1914 it was renamed Petrograd, then a decade later it was altered to Leningrad. It wasn't until the 1990s that it was called St Petersburg again. Personally, that's my favourite.'

The drive took nearly an hour and Laura was glad to reach the Pushka Inn, which would be their home for the next ten days. She was even happier when she saw the room she'd be sharing with Kay and Skye. A chandelier twinkled on the ceiling, and red velvet drapes framed the French doors. She chose the bed by the window, which was so soft it almost swallowed her when she sat on it. The bathroom was pink and white and had a Jacuzzi-style tub.

Best of all was the balcony, which overhung a canal. Skye rushed out and growled hungrily at a swan gliding by.

'I'll feed you in a minute and take you for a nice walk,' Laura told him, 'but only if you promise to stay away from all small creatures. And large ones. They have bears in Russia. I don't want you being eaten.'

Tariq, who was in an adjoining single room on his own, came out to join her. 'My bed is so big I'm worried I might get lost in it. Would it be all right if I borrowed Skye for the night?'

'Sure. As long as you understand that it's like sleeping with a furry hot water bottle. Given half a chance, he'll try to share your pillow.'

'Isn't this wonderful?' cried Kay, stepping out into the sunshine. 'We're on the roof of the world. That's where St Petersburg is on the map, you know, level with Helsinki in Finland. We're so close to the Arctic, we could almost reach out and touch it.'

She hooked her arm through Laura's. 'Come along, roomie. Let's feed your beautiful wolf and then I'll treat you and Tariq to dinner.'

It was after ten when Laura finally brushed her teeth and put on her pyjamas. She was physically weary but somehow wide awake, which might have had something to do with the hot chocolate she'd had with her meal. It was so thick she'd had to eat it with a spoon. On the basis of that alone, Laura had already decided that, next to St Ives, St Petersburg was her favourite place in the world.

'It's awesome,' she'd told her uncle when he'd called as they were walking back to the hotel. 'The hotel is beautiful and the food is delicious. I thought we'd be eating boiled cabbage and potato soup every night, but we had beetroot soup. Borscht, it's called. You eat it with sour cream and black rye bread. It sounds revolting, but it's totally divine. Then we had apple pie and this hot chocolate to die for.'

He laughed. 'I'm happy to hear it. St Petersburg has

always been high on my list of cities to visit. Well, spare a thought for your poor uncle. I'm staying in a London hotel that has all the charm of a maximum security prison and working round the clock to organise the security for Ed Lucas' visit. It's a nightmare. *He's* a nightmare. You'd think he actually wanted to be assassinated. He's behaving as if he's going on holiday. Wants to visit this museum and that gallery, and eat at such and such a restaurant. He leaves for Moscow early tomorrow morning and the arrangements are not even fifty per cent completed.'

'He sounds like a pain in the neck. But if anyone can protect him, it's you.'

'I hope you're right. Sleep well, Laura, and say hi to Skye and Tariq. I miss you all.'

'We miss you too, Uncle Calvin. I wish you could be with us.'

'So do I, Laura. So do I.'

Laura rinsed the toothpaste out of her mouth and studied herself in the bathroom mirror. Her uncle often remarked that with her cap of short blonde hair and serious grey eyes, she was the image of her mother, his sister, who'd died when Laura was born. Of her father, reputed to be an American sailor, there'd never been any sign. For years Laura had dreamed that he'd materialise one day at the Sylvan Meadows Home for Girls and take her away to a loving family home. Now she was glad he hadn't. Calvin Redfern was the best dad any mystery-mad girl who had ambitions of becoming a detective could ever have hoped for.

For that reason, she felt guilty that she'd said nothing to

him about Andre's visit, let alone his warning. She'd justified this omission by telling herself that her uncle had other, more important, things on his mind. But the real reason she hadn't mentioned it was that she was scared he might ban her and Tariq from getting on the plane to Russia.

There was a rap on the bathroom door. 'Are you okay in there, Laura, or have you disappeared down the plughole?'

Laura emerged with a grin. 'Sorry, Kay. The bathroom is the place where I do my best thinking.'

'In that case, *I'll* be using the bathroom first in future. Then you'll be able to do your thinking at your own leisure.'

Laura laughed and hopped into the wonderfully soft bed. Skye was in the room next door with Tariq. It felt strange to be thinking of sleep when the sun was still beaming outside. She picked up the guidebook and began to read about the famous St Petersburg White Nights. She must have dozed off almost immediately, because she was awoken a few minutes later by Kay's voice.

'Did you put this here, Laura, or do you think it's a peculiar local custom to welcome guests with a card?'

Laura's eyes snapped open. Kay was sitting on the edge of her bed, holding a playing card. It wasn't just any playing card. It was a meticulously painted Joker wearing a malevolent grin.

Her blood ran cold. 'Where did you find it?'

'Here – tucked between the pillow and the duvet. Why? What on earth's wrong? You look quite ill.'

Before going out to the restaurant, Laura had left her pyjamas lying on Kay's bed. Anyone entering the room – a spying member of the housekeeping staff, for instance –

would have automatically assumed that she'd be the one sleeping on that side of the room, not Kay. Laura's face felt as frozen as a death mask, but she forced a smile. 'I think the long day has caught up with me. I'm shattered. Uh, would you mind if I looked at the card?'

Kay yawned. 'Be my guest, but it's lights-out time in about thirty seconds. If I stay up any longer, I'll turn into a pumpkin.'

Laura took the card from her, feeling a shiver go through her at the mere touch of it. It was like holding a small slice of evil. Kay couldn't know – and Laura was not about to enlighten her – that the Joker was the calling card of the Straight As. Nor could she know that the gang had sworn vengeance against Laura, Tariq and Calvin Redfern for their role in the capture of various high-ranking members.

Throughout these arrests, the mastermind behind the Straight As, a mysterious figure known only as Mr A, had remained elusive. For those seeking justice, it didn't help that no law enforcement officer anywhere in the world had any idea what he looked like. Even his own gang members claimed never to have seen him. He controlled every division of the Straight As from afar, via the Internet and coded messages – a spider at the centre of a sinister web.

Rather chillingly, Mr A did, it seemed, recognise Laura. He'd even texted her in June after she'd helped foil a bank robbery in Kentucky. It was those words that returned to haunt Laura now.

Bravo Laura Marlin! You are a worthy adversary. Until we meet again . . . Mr A

'Night night,' Kay said sleepily, switching off the light. 'Sweet dreams.'

But dreams of any kind were impossible for Laura. She lay stiff and cold in the darkness, wishing Skye was with her and not sleeping beside Tariq in the next room.

The card was a message meant for her, of that she did not have a sliver of doubt. The Straight As knew she was in Russia. They were waiting for her.

~ 6 ~

'**WE SHOULD NEVER** have come,' Laura told Tariq over breakfast when Kay left the table to visit the buffet counter. 'We should have taken Andre's advice and made up some excuse about Skye being ill or injured. There are thousands of Siberian huskies in Russia. One of them must have a missing front leg.'

She paused as the waitress arrived with two plates piled high with golden crêpes. Tariq's smile could have lit up the room. He immediately spooned honey and sour cream over his portion. Laura regretted ordering hers. She felt ill with tiredness and worry.

'We could have made up a story to get out of our

227

contract,' conceded Tariq, 'but it would have been dishonest. Besides, we were excited about coming. You said it would be an adventure.'

'That was before I knew that the Straight As were lying in wait for us. Now I want to catch the next flight home.'

Tariq's fork paused on the way to his mouth. 'Laura Marlin, I can't believe you just said that. Is that what Matt Walker would do in this situation – run away?'

Laura studied a speck on the tablecloth. 'It wouldn't be running away, it would be . . . sensible.'

Tariq put a palm on her forehead. 'Your skin feels hot. I think you might be coming down with something. Either that, or a Russian alien has abducted my best friend.'

Laura pushed his hand away. 'Tariq, be serious. Think about what the Straight A gang have put us through. Because of them, we've been kidnapped twice, nearly drowned and almost been fried to a crisp by a volcano.'

He picked up his knife and fork and started work on the crêpes again. 'Yes, and we've survived all those things because of you. You're an amazing detective – at least as good as Matt Walker. Okay, let's say the card was a message for you. Calvin Redfern says that the Straight As leave the Joker as a kind of joke. It's their way of telling the police or anyone else trying to catch them that they've got a big job planned and they're confident they're going to get away with it.'

'And your point is?' Laura dipped a square of crêpe into the bowls of honey and sour cream and cautiously put it in her mouth. The combined flavours were unexpectedly wonderful.

'What would Matt Walker do in this situation?'

Laura ate a few more bites of crêpe as she considered. Her detective hero often took jobs that would allow him to keep an eye on a suspect until they made a move. Then he'd pounce. 'I guess he'd do what we're doing. He'd get a job that would allow him to blend in with the crowd and observe without being observed. He'd work undercover as a film extra, say.'

'Background artiste,' put in Tariq.

'Sorry, I keep forgetting. Yes, he'd work as a background artiste. And while he was doing that he'd also look into the string of accidents on set and find out whether or not there was anyone or anything behind them. I suppose the good thing about us having obscure parts in the movie is that we'll have plenty of time to slip off and explore St Petersburg and try to find out what the Straight As are up to. Unfortunately, the Joker card means that the Straight As are already watching us. That takes away any element of surprise. Unless . . .'

'Unless we pretend you never received it?'

'Exactly. If we act all happy and excited and continue as if absolutely nothing has happened, chances are they might let down their guard. In the past, they've only ever tried to harm us when we've got close to one of their operations. We could pretend that we're so caught up in the Hollywood dream and the wonders of St Petersburg that we no longer have any interest in solving mysteries.'

Tariq said teasingly, 'Does that mean that you're not going to be getting on the next plane back to England after all?'

'What – me? Of course not. Well, okay, it did cross my mind briefly, but then I remembered that Matt Walker has never walked away from anything in his life. Nor has my uncle. But, Tariq, we do need to be careful. If we see anything suspicious, we are absolutely not going to get involved. We are going to call Uncle Calvin immediately so he can alert the authorities.'

He saluted. 'Aye, aye, captain.'

'What are the two of you grinning about?' asked Kay, sitting down with a tray loaded with healthy options like plain yoghurt, fruit and muesli. 'You have a mischievous air about you. What are you planning?'

Laura gave her an angelic smile. 'Mischievous, us? Never. We're just preparing for our new roles. We might only be background artistes but we're going to be the best background artistes we can possibly be.'

To Laura, there was something surreal about emerging from the hotel to find that the ordinary street of the previous evening had been transformed into a historical scene by the film crew. There were stagecoaches and men striding about in smart waistcoats and breeches. A woman in a long red gown and fancy hat was talking on her mobile phone while drinking a coffee outside the catering trailer.

Nearby, an actor in a top hat played computer games on his iPad.

'To me, one of the peculiar delights of working on a period drama like *The Aristocratic Thief* is scenes like this,' said Kay. 'I find it funny when actors in nineteenth-century costumes do twenty-first century things like sit around eating hamburgers and drinking Coke, or playing *Angry Birds* on their mobiles.'

'What are you filming today?' asked Tariq.

'It's the scene where Oscar de Havier, the aristocratic thief of the story, meets the orphan girl, Violet, and her three-legged husky, Flash. As you already know, the girl is being played by Ana María and Flash will be played by Skye. In the scene, Violet almost goes under the wheels of Oscar's carriage. A confrontation ensues.'

She lowered her voice. 'That's William Raven, the actor who's been cast as Oscar de Havier – a controversial choice.'

Laura followed her gaze. A silver-haired man in a long black coat and boots polished to a high shine was talking to the director. Brett Avery had a notebook in his hand and was scribbling frantically. In theory, it was Brett who was the boss, not the other way round, but the actor's height and his handsome, arrogant face gave him a presence that made Brett's wiry frame seem shrunken and rather nerdy.

The director looked up and spotted them. Or rather, he spotted the husky. 'Kids! Kids! Bring Skye over here.'

'Any actor featuring in the next scene would usually be in hair and make-up by now, but Skye is gorgeous enough as he is,' Kay said with a laugh. 'Go and meet William Raven. I'd be interested to hear what you think.'

Not a lot, was Laura's opinion as they approached. The man's chilly gaze crawled over her and Tariq with the probing intensity of a prison searchlight.

'This is the dog I was telling you about,' Brett Avery was saying with boyish enthusiasm. 'And these are the lovely kids who own him. Fine young actors. Kids, meet the star of our film, William Raven – a future Hollywood legend if I have anything to do with it.'

Since he'd never seen them act, Laura suspected the director was exaggerating their importance to disguise the fact that he had obviously forgotten their names.

Brett patted Skye rather gingerly on the head. 'What do you think, William? He's quite a find, even if I say so myself. Audiences will be coming in droves to see him. Saved Ana María's life, you know. Jumped off a cliff and dragged her from the boiling sea. Extraordinary thing.'

The actor gave a practiced smile. 'So I heard. I hadn't realised he was disabled.'

Laura's temper flared. 'He's not disabled,' she snapped, 'and so what if he was. A car hit him when he was a puppy and they couldn't save his leg, but he's fifty times fitter, stronger and faster than most dogs with four legs, and a lot more useful than any human being I've ever come across – famous or not.'

Brett Avery became quite agitated. 'Of course he is, of course he is. Isn't that what I was saying? Umm, I hadn't realised how late it was. Would you excuse us, William?

I'm sure Laura didn't mean any offence. Apologies, sorry, umm, see you shortly.'

He steered the children away, gripping Laura's shoulder until she winced in protest. As soon as they were out of sight of the actor, he stopped and glared at them. Shoving his milk-bottle glasses up over the beak of his nose, he looked more like a cross crow than ever.

'You're new on the set, so I'm going to let you off with a warning. If you dare to speak to my star actor that way ever again, I'll have you escorted off the set by security and put on the first plane back to England. Do I make myself clear?'

'But he insulted Skye,' Laura said indignantly. 'I didn't offend him. He offended us.'

'I don't care if he says that your Great-Aunt Bertha resembles a whale. You grin and bear it. William Raven pays our salaries. At least, his movie producer brother does. Mr Raven is a man of – how shall I put it? – great sensitivity. As it is I'm going to have to do some fast-talking to prevent you being fired. If you upset him again and he walks out, the movie is finished and one hundred and fifty-six actors, extras and crew are out of work. Do I make myself understood?'

'Yes,' they mumbled in unison.

'Sorry,' added Laura.

'All right, let's put it behind us. If Mr Raven says jump, the only question you should be asking is: "How high?"' He checked his watch. 'Take Skye to Otto, the animal trainer, as quickly as you can. He's needed in the next scene.'

'What about us?' asked Tariq. 'Are we needed?'

'Most definitely not. You're lucky I haven't thrown you off my set. Stay away from my crew and my actors and don't speak unless you're spoken to.'

~ 7 ~

'YOU WERE BARELY out of my sight for five minutes – how on earth did you manage to upset the great William Raven?'

Laura's heart sank. The last thing she wanted to do was fall out with Kay, their only friend in Russia. She was about to launch into a stumbling apology when the scriptwriter poked her in the ribs and giggled.

'Don't fret. I don't blame you in the least. What a nerve the man has. Skye is worth a hundred of him. Anyway, I'm glad someone finally stood up to him. Ever since filming began, he's been treating everyone, including Brett, as if they were the hired help. Look at the way he's being helped into the carriage for the next scene. Anyone would think

235

he was a real aristocrat, not an actor merely playing one.'

Putting her arms around their shoulders, she led them over to a silver equipment case, where they could perch and watch the production team set up a street market scene. The carriage was parked some distance away. Tariq, who adored horses, was transfixed by the magnificent black pair being hitched to it. It was a warm blue day and their necks were already streaked with sweat. A worried groom wiped them down and combed their manes.

Across the street, Skye was sitting obediently beside Otto, the animal handler. For Laura, it was an odd feeling watching someone else handle Skye, but it helped knowing that Otto genuinely loved animals. The husky seemed quite content. From time to time, he glanced at Laura, but for the most part he, like Tariq, was riveted by the frenetic activity on the street.

As they waited, Chad MacFarlane, a teenager from California, grudgingly delivered a cold drink to William Raven. Chad had the head-turning good looks of a high school football star or a boy band member, but his whole demeanour seemed to say that he considered his job as a runner – a film set dogsbody – beneath him. Laura got the feeling that he was only doing it in the hope of being snapped up by a talent scout and turned into a superstar. According to Kay, his coffee was undrinkable and his sandwich-making skills non-existent.

William Raven settled back in his carriage seat and put on the hat and cape that transformed him into the aristocrat, Oscar de Havier.

Laura said casually, 'Kay, you told us earlier that

Mr Raven was a controversial choice for the role. Why is that?'

Kay glanced over her shoulder. 'If I tell you, it's confidential and can go no further than the three of us. Deal?'

'Deal.'

'You have our word,' Tariq assured her.

'It all started six weeks ago, the day before we were due to fly to the UK to begin filming. The movie was cast, the crew was hired, and we were packed and ready to go. Next morning we arrived at the film studio to find several staff members in tears. Tiger Pictures had gone bust, seemingly over night. As if that wasn't bad enough, our lead actor, a huge Hollywood star – I could tell you his name but I'd have to kill you afterwards – had pulled out with no explanation.

'We were all devastated, particularly Brett and I. We'd spent about five years fighting to get the movie to happen. The *Hollywood Reporter* ran a story on our woes. Within days, something miraculous happened. We were approached by a new production company. Not only were they prepared to finance the film, they were prepared to release the money overnight. To begin with, we kept looking for a catch, but there was none. Mick Edwards, the new producer, had only one condition.'

'He wanted you to cast a family member or friend as the star of the film,' Tariq guessed.

'Smart boy. That's exactly right. William Raven is a fine actor, so it wasn't his talent we doubted, but for marketing reasons we'd rather have had an established Hollywood star. We also knew that the reason Mr Raven hasn't become a household name is that audiences tend to react badly to him. They find him cold.'

Laura watched the actor climbing into the carriage in preparation for the next scene. He was too far away for her to see his expression, but she could still recall how her skin had crawled under his piercing stare. 'Yes, I can imagine.'

'Unfortunately, we didn't have a choice. We were basically ordered to hire him. At the time he was working as a conjurer and that didn't exactly fill us with confidence, but we were between a rock and a hard place. Either Brett and I walked away from everything we'd spent five long years working towards or we agreed to have William be our star. For better or worse, we said yes.'

'Which has it been so far?' asked Tariq. 'Better or worse?'

'To be truthful, apart from being a bit of a prima donna, William has been great. He's the least of our worries. There've been a string of other incidents that have caused us much more of a headache. Nothing you need to concern yourself with. They're trifling things really. Oh, look, they're about to start shooting.'

Before Laura could press her on the headache-causing incidents, which she guessed were the ones that had so unnerved Andre March, someone yelled 'Action!' The cameras rolled.

Ana María, dressed once more as the orphan Violet, led Skye along a pavement packed with raggedy market traders. There were stalls laden with fruit and vegetables, and others selling cheese, sausages, oil lamps, and reams of colourful cloth. A boy with a grubby face begged for bread.

Along the cobbled street came the shining carriage, pulled by the proud black horses. Their necks arched and their manes flew as they trotted past the market stalls, urged on by the driver's swinging whip. Oscar de Havier was visible only as a shadow in the rear of the carriage.

As the carriage rattled up the street, a man carrying a load of chickens swung his crate and knocked Ana María into the path of the horses.

That part was scripted. Unfortunately the crate door flew open and one of the chickens flapped out. It tore squawking into the street. The horses shied violently, unseating the driver, who crashed to the ground. William Raven's terrified face appeared briefly at the window before the carriage careered away down the street, dragged by the out-of-control horses.

Everyone started shrieking and panicking at once.

Kay sprang off the equipment case. 'Oh my goodness. This can't be happening. Laura, quick! Run and grab Skye before he adds to the chaos by chasing the chicken.'

'Do something, Otto,' screamed Brett Avery. 'Stop the horses! Save William! If the carriage reaches the main road, they'll all be killed.'

Unfortunately, Otto was a beachball of a man who became short of breath if he saw someone running on the television. He was not physically equipped to be a hero. All he did was bleat despairingly and clutch at his few remaining tufts of hair. Further along the road, a couple of brawny crew members tried to grab the reins as the horses galloped by. The beasts swerved, causing the carriage to rock wildly.

Their groom pursued them, but he was a tall, ungainly man, not built for running, and the horses effortlessly outdistanced him.

William's desperate cries grew fainter. 'Somebody save me! HE-ELP!'

'I'll do it,' Tariq said suddenly.

Before Kay could stop him, he was sprinting across the production unit car park, dodging trucks and hurdling fat coils of black cable. He was taking a shortcut in a bid to reach the horses before they got to the main road.

With the exception of Kay and Laura, nobody noticed him. Most people were too busy watching the carriage being dragged full-pelt toward certain disaster.

Brett Avery was apoplectic. 'Do something, you idiots!' he yelled at no one in particular. 'Oh, I'm ruined. Totally ruined.'

Laura held tightly to Skye's collar and squinted into the sunlight, her heart in her mouth. It didn't seem possible that Tariq could reach the crazed horses before the traffic engulfed them. Even if he did, she dreaded to think what would happen to him. The few people brave enough to attempt to halt the horses had either been tossed aside or trampled. One had a bad cut on his leg and the other looked as if he'd been attacked by wild boars. The coach driver was unconscious.

Kay was beside herself. 'What does Tariq think he's doing? If he winds up in the emergency room, it'll be my responsibility.'

Overhearing her, one of the cameramen swung his lens in the direction of the running figure. The red recording light glowed. 'Now that's impressive. I don't think I've ever seen a kid run so fast. He's like an Olympic sprinter. I wouldn't worry about his health though. He has no chance of cutting off the horses. By the time he's crossed the bridge, they'll be . . . I don't believe it. I don't believe the evidence of my own eyes.'

Neither did Laura. Realising that he had no chance of cutting off the runaways if he used the canal bridge fifty metres away, Tariq had leapt off the riverbank onto a moving barge. Ignoring the outraged shouts of the tour guide, who was in the midst of explaining the wonders of St Petersburg to twenty-eight Japanese tourists, he ran the length of the vessel and jumped onto a moored speedboat.

From there, he sprang onto a rowing boat. It was bucking on the waves generated by the barge and Tariq almost went headfirst into the water, but managed to save himself by grabbing an iron rung in the canal wall. By the time he'd hauled himself onto the bank, word had spread across the film set. The cameras were rolling and everyone was transfixed.

'He's going to get hisself killed, no question about it,' said a woman dressed as a market trader.

Tariq stood directly in the path of the horses, close to the thundering traffic. Kay had her hands over her eyes and was peering through her fingers. 'Please tell me he's not going to offer himself up as a sort of human shield. He'll be crushed to death.'

'You don't know Tariq,' Laura said loyally. 'He has a gift

with horses – with all animals. They won't hurt him. They can't.'

Kay gripped her hand. 'Let's hope you're right.'

A hush had fallen over the film set. All eyes were on the Bengali boy as the horses bore down on him.

There was a heart-stopping moment when the angle of the carriage and horses momentarily obscured him and Laura thought he'd been trampled underfoot. Then something incredible happened. The carriage slowed and came to an abrupt, jerky halt. When the horses came into view once more, they were being led by Tariq. A hand waved weakly from the carriage window.

William Raven had survived his ordeal.

A cheer went up. Dozens of people rushed forward to offer their sympathies to the actor and praise Tariq, but a shout from the director stopped them in their tracks.

'If you value your jobs, you will stay where you are until the carriage is safely back on the set, the horses are secured and William is on solid ground. If you surround the carriage, you could start another stampede.'

Laura was dying to rush to Tariq's side, but she didn't dare. As he neared, she could see his lips moving as he talked to the animals, soothing them, telling them they were safe. It was only when he reached the set and was able to hand the horses over to Otto and the groom that Laura saw how pale and shaky he was.

She threw her arms around him and gave him a bear hug. 'I'm so proud of you. You're amazing – a total hero.'

'Yes, you are,' agreed Kay. 'If it weren't for you . . . If the horses had reached the main road . . . If—'

Tariq flushed. He hated being made a fuss of. 'It was nothing. Anyone would have done the same.'

'Yes, but you were the only one who did.'

William Raven offered Tariq his hand. 'Thank you, young man. You averted a catastrophe. At the very least you saved me an extended stay in hospital.'

He seemed sincere in his gratitude, but his eyes were icier than ever. Laura wondered how many people would lose their jobs over the incident before the day's end.

Tariq looked uncomfortable, but he shook the actor's hand. 'No problem, Mr Raven. I'm glad I could help.'

Brett Avery came rushing up. 'Help? You didn't just help, you saved the man's life. That's twice in one week that you and Laura Marlin here – or should I say her husky – have inadvertently plucked one of my stars from the jaws of death. I do hope it's nothing more than coincidence that whenever you show up on my set, drama ensues!'

He chuckled. 'Only joking. Seriously, I'm in your debt. The cameraman kept filming throughout so we now have even more Oscar-worthy footage. Don't you agree, William? We owe these kids.'

The actor's white teeth flashed again. 'We do indeed owe them – and I always repay my debts.'

As the men walked away, Laura thought how odd it was that words that were supposedly meant kindly managed to sound so ominous.

IN AN IDEAL WORLD, Laura would have begun her investigation into this latest accident immediately, but she didn't get a chance. Brett Avery used a megaphone to announce that shooting would be suspended for the rest of the day while the set was made safe and measures were taken to ensure that no similar disaster could happen ever again.

'That's the official reason,' remarked Kay. 'The real reason we have the rest of the day off is that William Raven doesn't want to be around when Brett carries out his orders to fire Otto, the animal handler, or the extra who let the chicken escape, or the groom who didn't catch the horses, or . . . you get my drift.'

Laura was horrified. 'But surely Brett isn't going to listen to him and sack all of those people?'

'Of course he isn't. Brett can be a bit hot-headed, but underneath it all he's actually very kind. However, he will have to shuffle the culprits into different positions in order for our star to feel that his wishes are being taken seriously. My only worry is that if we have many more of these . . . incidents, there'll be nobody left in the crew.'

'What incidents?' Laura asked innocently.

Kay could no longer hide her concern. 'All film sets have their share of drama – you know, fires, injuries, rows – but we've had more than our fair share. Coincidence, I'm sure, but for the sake of crew morale we could really do with a few days where everything goes smoothly.'

'Is that what you believe – that it's nothing more than coincidence?' asked Tariq.

She stared at him in surprise. 'What else could it be? I mean, who could have predicted that the chicken would hop out of the crate at that exact moment and scare the horses? It's bad luck – that's all. Now, since you have the afternoon off, how about I arrange a visit for you to the Hermitage Museum?'

'Bad luck? Coincidence? Personally, I don't believe in either of those things, and neither does Matt Walker,' said Laura as they crossed the canal and walked the short distance to the Hermitage.

She lowered her voice so that she couldn't be overheard by Vladimir, their Russian guide, or the motley bunch of film set folk he was escorting to the museum. 'These "incidents", as Kay calls them, could only be caused by someone with detailed knowledge of each day's schedule for filming. How else could they plan each "accident"? We need to find out who that person is, and if there's more than one of them, before someone else gets seriously hurt or worse.'

'What if we can't?'

'We will,' Laura said, with such determination that even Tariq, who thought of his best friend as the kindest person he knew, felt a chill go down his spine.

At that moment they rounded the corner and saw the Hermitage, one of the greatest, and largest, museums on earth and all other thoughts were forgotten. What made it particularly thrilling was that a marching band in bearskin hats was high-stepping across Palace Square, overlooked by an angel on a skyscraping pillar. Laura and Tariq stood beneath her and gazed at the green, gold and white museum.

'Follow me, follow me,' cried Vladimir, a jolly man with an unruly black moustache. Using a combination of charm and brute force, he cleared a path through the tourists cramming the entrance to the museum. A grinning guard waved them through the barriers.

Vladimir puffed up the Jordan staircase, a dazzling stairway of granite, marble and gold. 'Of all the magnificent attractions in St Petersburg, the State Hermitage Museum is among our proudest creations. It was founded in 1764 by Catherine the Great and has been open to the public since 1852. There are over three million works of art in the collection . . .'

'Three million?' exclaimed Laura. 'We could be here for days.'

Vladimir's moustache twitched. 'Only a fraction of which you will see today . . .'

Laura loved art and had been looking forward to seeing the Hermitage as much as Tariq had, but nothing could have prepared her for its epic scale or for its treasures. Vladimir's monologue had them gasping and laughing as he guided them expertly through the four historic buildings that made up the part of the museum open to the public.

Each was more magnificent than the last, although Laura's favourite was the Winter Palace, once the state residence of Russian emperors. She also loved a Van Gogh painting that seemed to move as if a great storm was brewing in it. Tariq was fascinated by the Egyptology section, which had hieroglyphics, mummies and a statue of Pharaoh Amenemhat III, who'd lived 2100 years BC.

They saw frescoes by students of Raphael, and the carriage used for the coronation of Catherine the Great. Tariq, a gifted tapestry artist, was captivated by the religious tapestries, while Laura loved the boldly coloured paintings of Matisse, Gauguin and Kandinsky. Another highlight was Michelangelo's statue of a crouching boy. It was so real that Laura almost expected the boy to stand up and walk away.

By five o'clock they'd been walking for three hours. Laura

could have wept with relief when Vladimir suggested a stop for a hot chocolate and a pastry. Her new boots had given her a blister.

At that time of day, the coffee shop was quiet and they found a table easily. After Vladimir excused himself to talk to a friend, Tariq helped Colin, a skinny extra with a sweet, sleepy face, to drag more chairs across. The group sat together in a slightly awkward circle, lit by an overhead skylight.

Laura stole a glance at the other occupants of the cafe. Ever since Kay had found the playing card, she'd been keeping an eye out for anyone who might be a spy for the Straight As. So far, she'd seen nothing unusual, but it was important to be vigilant.

Her thoughts turned to the issue at hand. Who or what was terrorising the film crew? She was trying to decide how best to bring up the subject of the runaway carriage when Peggy, a curly-headed fifty-three-year-old from Norfolk, did it for her.

'You're the hero of the day, Tariq. What's *your* opinion? Should the police be called in, or is it the Ghostbusters that we need?'

'Excuse me?' stalled Tariq, startled to find himself the centre of attention.

'What I was wondering,' Peggy said loudly, 'is, do you think that criminals are behind this latest "accident" on the film set, or is something supernatural at work?'

She stabbed her pastry with a fork. 'You and Laura have no idea what I'm talking about, do you? Allow me to update you. What happened this morning, with the horses going berserk and nearly dragging William to his death, is the fourth or fifth catastrophe we've seen since filming began. We've had people poisoned, a couple of broken wrists and lost half of our equipment in a crash. And if it wasn't for your husky, Laura, lovely little Ana María might have drowned in Cornwall.'

'People are calling it a *cursed* set,' said Colin in a hushed tone.

Sebastian Wright, a young British actor tipped to be a future star, was amused. He leaned back in his chair and put his hands behind his head. 'You can't seriously believe in all that superstitious hokum?'

Chad MacFarlane looked up from his slice of pizza. 'What are you saying – that you don't believe in curses?'

'I'd sooner believe in Father Christmas and the Tooth Fairy. No, my friend, I deal only in fact. There are two options here. Either some fruit-loop is on a mission to destroy our film, and what possible reason would anyone have for doing that? Or it's down to sheer incompetence on the part of the production team.'

'Maybe they're jokers by nature as well as by name,' said Bob Regis, a retired insurance salesman from Hull. He'd explained to Laura that his wife disliked travel. Working as a 'background artiste' had been his passport to seeing the world.

'Take what happened this morning,' continued Sebastian, paying no attention to him. 'Somebody didn't secure the chickens' crate properly. If I was directing this film, I'd have used a whip to give the horses a proper fright and then we would have been rid of that fool William Raven for good.'

There was a shocked silence.

'That's a terrible thing to say,' Peggy managed at last. 'William can be a bit full of himself, it's true, but surely you're not suggesting you'd like him dead?'

'Oh, come on Peggy, don't be naïve. Everyone on the set wants something bad to happen to the man. I'm the only one honest enough to admit it. He's insufferable.'

Chad said eagerly, 'If something were to happen to old Raven, would Tiger Pictures bring back Jon Ellis-Harding?' Laura and Tariq had discovered that he was the Hollywood star who'd been replaced in the lead role after the film studio went broke.

'That old has-been,' snorted Sebastian. 'We'd have more luck casting Skye in the role. The dog's a better actor.'

'You remind me of someone, Chad,' said Bob Regis. 'It's been plaguing me since we met. Are you by any chance related to Hugo Porter, who starred in that film about the lighthouse keeper?'

Incensed by Sebastian's comments, Chad ignored him. 'How can you say that? Jon Ellis-Harding is one of the greatest actors who ever lived. He's a thousand times better than you are.'

Bob Regis stood up. 'I think I've heard quite enough. If anyone needs me, I'll be in the gift shop.' Laura smiled at him and Tariq shifted his chair, but the others didn't acknowledge his departure.

Laura watched the young men squaring off as if at any moment they might challenge one another to a duel. In a way, it was hardly surprising. They were opposites. Sebastian was a Cambridge graduate from a wealthy family and a rising star, frequently featured on the covers of magazines. In *The Aristocratic Thief*, he'd been cast as an ambitious young artist who is persuaded to use his talents to fake a masterpiece.

Chad, on the other hand, was a runner, one of the lowliest positions on set. Laura had heard several people making fun of him. 'Not the brightest light in the harbour,' one had said.

To judge by appearances, Chad was the one more likely to succeed as a film star. He had dreamy blue eyes, perfectly behaved blond hair, golden skin and the body of an Olympic swimmer. Sebastian, on the other hand, was small and had pale slim limbs, devoid of muscle. His face was dominated by long-lashed, basset-hound eyes.

Yet Kay had explained to Laura and Tariq that they were mistaken if they thought that any talent scout worth his salt would choose Chad over Sebastian. The former, she said, looked like ten thousand other wholesome, all-American boys.

'Walk down Sunset Boulevard in Los Angeles and you'll see so many perfect people you'll be convinced they're making them in a factory.'

To be a great actor, she told them, you had to be different. The camera adored Sebastian. On the street he might pass unnoticed, but on film he was a chameleon – as capable of being soulful and romantic as he was of playing a darkly magnetic villain.

'The furthest Chad is ever likely to go in acting is if someone casts him in a cereal commercial, whereas for Sebastian the sky is the limit.'

Sebastian, who was well aware of that, was busy rubbing salt into Chad's wounds. 'At least I'm being paid to actually act in films. I'm not spending my days making rubbish coffee and cleaning up horse poop.'

Chad's fists bunched at his sides. He pushed his chair back, his handsome face twisting in anger. 'You—'

'Have we had a lovely, relaxing break?' asked Vladimir, striding across the cafe towards them, a broad smile on his face. 'Have our feet recovered? Have we enjoyed the pastries? Very fine, are they not? Good. Then you are ready for a special treat. I am taking you to see what is arguably the most special painting in the Hermitage. For centuries it was feared lost. When it was found, the whole art world wept with happiness. It is a masterpiece, its worth beyond price. Mere money cannot convey how precious it is, how unique, how profound, how mysterious . . .'

'For goodness sake, man, get to the point,' said Peggy. 'Are you going to show us this painting or not?'

Vladimir looked indignant. 'Or course I am, Madam. But we are talking about art, not groceries. At all times there must be respect. Now, please, come this way.'

~ 9 ~

AFTER VLADIMIR'S BIG build up, Laura's initial response to the painting was one of disappointment. Indeed she was more impressed by the salon in which it was housed, the Leonardo da Vinci Room.

The quality of the light in the gallery and the size of the windows was the first thing that struck her. From the moment she passed through the tortoiseshell veneer and gilded brass-decorated doors, the airiness of the space set it apart from every other section of the Hermitage. Every detail seemed enhanced, as if through a special filter. The lapis-lazuli insets in the marble fireplace were the exquisite blue of Porthminster Beach on a clear day. The ceiling paintings seethed with life.

By contrast, the masterpiece in question, Leonardo da Vinci's 'Madonna and Child with Flowers', famously known as the 'Benois Madonna', was almost dull. Laura stood on tiptoe to try to glimpse it through a gap in the procession of visitors and couldn't understand what the fuss was about.

It was of much more interest to her that the painting was situated right beside a window with no security bars on it – a partially ajar window overlooking the Neva River. She supposed that the picture was alarmed and that there were guards patrolling the halls who would spring into action if anyone tried to snatch it, but it seemed quite vulnerable. However, Vladimir assured her that the Hermitage was impregnable.

'Through the centuries, there has only once been thieves here and they were insiders, working for the museum. They stole some bits and pieces – some ceramics and little statues and such like – over many months. Believe me when I tell you that their punishment has served as a deterrent to others.'

Stifling a yawn, Laura bent down to loosen her bootlaces. She was debating whether to limp across to the 'Madonna Litta' when an elderly man caught her attention. He was sitting on a bench clutching the wooden handle of a mop. Laura had the impression that, without it, he'd collapse at the waist. His head wobbled constantly like one of those nodding dogs in car windows. His face was as wizened as a peanut but he grinned aimlessly and toothlessly at everyone who passed. He seemed far too ancient to be employed as a cleaner, and yet by all appearances that was what he was.

'That's Igor,' said Vladimir, coming over to check on her. 'He is senile and rarely speaks, but he once scribbled his name on some paper. Because he is so decrepit, the museum staff found it quite amusing that his name means Warrior. They can be a bit like naughty children sometimes. They make up stories about Igor's past, each more funny and fantastical than the last.'

'He doesn't have a family?'

'Not that we know of. He appeared about a year ago – a starving street person. He was always sweeping and trying to clean windows in a desperate attempt to make a few roubles. The police kept chasing him off, but winter came and the director of the Hermitage felt sorry for him. He gave Igor small jobs cleaning some basement rooms. To everyone's surprise, Igor turned out to be quite competent and reliable. Eventually, he was given responsibility for washing or polishing the floors throughout the museum.'

He lifted a hand to Igor, 'Good day, my friend,' he said in Russian.

Igor beamed and bobbed his head enthusiastically.

To Laura, Vladimir murmured, 'He is fixated with this room. Museum staff often find him sitting here with tears in his eyes. They believe that the paintings of the Madonna and Child – there are two, as you can see, the 'Benois Madonna' and the 'Madonna Litta' – perhaps remind him of the family he has lost.'

'He's lost his family?' As an orphan, Laura felt great compassion for anyone who was alone in the world.

'We might never know. He can't exactly tell us. He arrived on the wind and he may leave the same way.'

Vladimir gestured towards the 'Benois Madonna'. 'Now, I see you were not very taken with our special painting. Might I have the privilege of explaining to you why it is one of the greatest works of art the world has ever known? It is thought it was the very first painting Leonardo completed on his own in 1478. It was believed to be lost for centuries before it was exhibited in Russia in 1909 by the architect Leon Benois, causing a sensation. Even now mystery surrounds it – no one knows for sure whether it is definitely the work of Leonardo, or if it's even finished.'

As he steered her towards the painting, Laura glanced back at Igor. A family with a boisterous toddler passed him, gabbling loudly. The child was wailing for sweets. In a desperate bid to snatch them from his mother's bag, he tripped over Igor's mop.

The old man's hand shot out so fast that Laura registered it only as a blur. He grabbed the toddler's arm and stopped him from falling flat on his face. The child's mouth opened in a shocked O. His mum and dad were noisily discussing a painting and didn't notice until their son, back on his feet and frightened, let out a piercing screech. Embarrassed, they scooped him up and left the room in a hurry.

Igor heaved himself to his feet. Listlessly, he headed for the door with his mop. No one but Laura noticed him go. All of a sudden the meaning of his name – Warrior – didn't seem quite so funny. Whatever the story of his past, she had a feeling that the museum staff hadn't come close to guessing it.

'You may think you've seen all the treasures the Hermitage could offer, but I have one more surprise for you,' said Vladimir.

Peggy groaned. 'Oh no you don't. I'm bowing out. I've loved every minute but my feet feel as if they've been through a mincing machine.'

'I'm with you on that,' agreed Bob. 'Amazing experience, but another surprise would put me in A&E.'

Vladimir was dismayed. 'But you don't even know what I am going to show you. This will be the icing on the cake of your year. It will be a once in a lifetime experience – a story to tell your grandchildren. It will—'

'Sorry old chap,' interrupted Sebastian. 'It's been a blast, but it's time for some dinner and a stiff vodka. I'll bid you das-vee-DAN-ee-yah. Isn't that the Russian word for goodbye?' He looked pointedly at Chad. 'Besides, I have lines to learn.'

The American boy scowled. 'Thanks, Vlad, but some of us have real work to do.'

Vladimir seemed so crushed that Laura didn't have the heart to tell him that she, too, was desperate to get back to the hotel and attend to her blisters.

'Tariq and I would love to see your surprise, whatever it is,' she told him.

Tariq gave the best smile he could manage. He'd landed awkwardly while leaping from the moving barge that morning and after four hours of walking his knee was killing him. 'Definitely. Sounds great.'

'Young, enquiring minds,' Vladimir said triumphantly to the departing group. 'What could be better? This is the most satisfying part of my job.'

Peggy waved him away with a weary hand and in another minute they were alone.

Vladimir beamed. 'I am so delighted you decided to stay. I promise you won't be disappointed. Follow me.'

Laura and Tariq might have had enquiring young minds, but after the rigours of the day their bodies felt at least a decade older. Clutching each other for support, they limped after their inexhaustible guide. Mercifully, a lift hidden behind a velvet curtain whisked them down to the basement, saving them a trek down the stairs.

The basement had nothing of the grandeur of the museum upstairs. It was shabby and poorly ventilated, with wooden floors that could have done with a polish. At one point a reinforced steel door swung open to reveal a storeroom stacked from floor to ceiling with rolls of canvas and statues swathed in linen sheets.

A hunched man with wild grey hair glanced up to see them staring and slammed the door in their faces.

'It is nothing personal,' Vladimir told them. 'There are riches in that room that could rival the Bank of England. It's his responsibility to keep them safe.'

They came to a locked door. Their guide suddenly became deadly serious. 'Can you keep a secret?'

Laura almost laughed – it was a bit cloak and dagger. 'Of course we can. Why, what are you going to show us – another lost masterpiece?'

Tariq grinned. 'Maybe it's the old headquarters of the KGB spy network.'

Vladimir threw up his hands in disgust. He stalked away down the corridor. 'Nothing. I will show you nothing. Come, let's go. Even though you are only children, I thought you were different. I trusted you. I—'

They limped after him.

'Vladimir, we're sorry,' said Laura. 'Please forgive us. We're tired. That's what we do when we're tired – make jokes.'

'I apologise too,' added Tariq. 'Whatever it is you'd like to show us, we're really interested. Don't worry. We're good at keeping secrets.'

Vladimir took quite a lot of persuading, but eventually he relented. 'Okay, I show you, but be aware that nothing you see here can be revealed outside of this room. If your friends from the film set had come along, they too would have been privy to it. Since they are not . . .' He shrugged. 'How do you say it in English? They are outside the circle of trust. Understand?'

They nodded eagerly.

Vladimir typed a code into a wall panel. The door opened, releasing a pungent odour of oil paints, canvas and turpentine. It was a smell that Laura associated with the artists' studios of St Ives and she felt a wave of homesickness.

The room was a cluttered sea of half-finished canvases,

oozing tubes of paint and used brushes. In the midst of them, a young man with masses of curly black hair was bent over a canvas. He was painting the mane of a chestnut horse with a brush as fine as a cat's whisker.

When he saw Laura and Tariq, he spat a volley of Russian at Vladimir. Reassured by the response, he resumed his task and paid them no further attention.

The guide led them to a canvas draped with a white sheet. When he lifted it, Tariq gasped. 'The 'Benois Madonna'! But we've just seen it upstairs. How did it get here so quickly? Is it a copy?'

Vladimir laughed. 'It is a fake, yes, but you've only guessed that because it is not ten minutes since you saw the original. This painting would fool many of the world's greatest art experts. The artist, Ricardo, who like Leonardo da Vinci is an Italian, is a genius.'

He held up a hand. 'Don't get me wrong. Ricardo is not in the business of faking great paintings in order to deceive or to put money into the hands of thieves. He uses his gift only for good – to restore damaged masterpieces or provide near-perfect copies of the works of the masters as a record in case they are ever ruined by fire or accident or age.'

Tariq leaned closer to the painting. 'It looks a perfect match. It even seems old and a bit faded, like the one upstairs.'

'That is part of Ricardo's brilliance. He uses techniques so sophisticated that they have fooled numerous experts in carbon dating. That's the process used to calculate the age of a painting. We are fortunate that he has chosen to work *with* the Hermitage and not against us.'

Laura studied the picture. Straining to catch a glimpse of it between the jostling tourists earlier, its beauty had been lost on her. It was only now that she saw that Leonardo's (or in this case Ricardo's) use of line and light in depicting the Virgin Mary cradling her child gave the painting an ethereal quality that was almost spiritual. It had an atmosphere. She felt as if she were looking through the window of history at a real life scene.

'This is fascinating, but is there a particular reason why you've brought us here?'

'Because, Laura, this painting is the subject of the movie you are working on. Don't you remember how in the story a priceless picture is stolen by a gentleman thief? For obvious reasons, the Hermitage would not give the film company permission to shoot the stealing of Leonardo's actual painting. Instead the museum recommended that Brett Avery commission Ricardo to make an exact replica. He is expensive, but as you can see he is worth every rouble he has been paid. The director is delighted with the result. I think that is why he has given me permission to show a small number of people the finished picture.'

Tariq was amazed. 'To me, the paintings look identical. How do you tell them apart?'

Vladimir laughed. 'It is impossible to tell with the naked eye. That is how talented Ricardo is. His attention to detail is second to none. Come, watch him paint this horse's mane. He gives it the quality of silk.'

Laura stayed looking at the 'Benois Madonna'. Acccording to the guide not everyone was convinced that it was the work of Leonardo. Some experts believed that, even if it was, it appeared to be unfinished. To her, that only added to its mystique. It also had a sumptuously creamy texture that begged to be stroked.

Impulsively, she touched it.

It was wet. Jerking back, she shoved her guilty fingers into the pocket of her jeans. There was a tiny smear on a flower in the painting. It was so miniscule that it was doubtful anyone would detect it, but to Laura, now feeling sick to her stomach, it was glaringly obvious. Ricardo would surely spot it and tell Vladimir, who'd report her to Brett Avery. Laura would be in disgrace. She'd be fired and put on the next plane back to London.

'Everything all right?' Vladimir asked.

'Fantastic!' squeaked Laura. 'I'm having a wonderful time.'

Tariq's eyes met hers. Something told her he'd seen what had happened.

'Thank you for a great afternoon, Vladimir, but we should probably go,' he said. 'We have a long day of filming tomorrow. The sooner we get back to our hotel, the better.'

'The sooner the better,' Laura agreed weakly.

~ 10 ~

'"**HURRY UP AND WAIT**", that's what we call it in the trade,' said Kay, smothering a yawn. 'You spend hours and hours doing nothing, bored out of your mind, and then all of a sudden it's as if someone has lit a fire under the director's chair. There's frenzied activity and occasional hysteria, followed by an intensive burst of filming sometimes lasting only seconds. Then you're back to waiting around again.'

The screenwriter was sitting cross-legged in an ancient leather armchair in the draughty storeroom which, for the duration of the shoot, would be doubling as a space for the actors and senior crew to hang out in between takes. It was known as the Green Room. Laura and Tariq were sharing a sofa with no springs, using Skye as a backrest. Piled on a crate in front of them were numerous coffee mugs, water bottles and paper plates strewn with crumbs.

'I can't understand why most actors aren't the size of houses,' Laura said. 'If I had to do this for a living, all I'd do is lie about eating and reading.'

'Because, darling, most of them are on the latest fad diet,' said the costume designer, overhearing her as he sashayed past to the coffee machine. 'If they're not fasting – i.e. starving themselves – they're drinking grapefruit and celery smoothies three times a day, or popping Amazonian jungle pills chased down with miso soup. Trust me when I tell you that you're better off eating cake. Anyway, you'll be pleased to know that I'm here with a message. You and Tariq are required in make-up. Your scene starts shortly.'

'Hurrah,' said Laura, getting up with rather more enthusiasm than she felt. Ever since the disaster with the painting, she'd been convinced that the long arm of the law was going to descend on her at any moment and that she'd be dragged away and either locked up by the authorities or bellowed at by Brett Avery. It was hard to decide which was worse.

Tariq had been no help. For some reason he found the whole thing hilarious.

'I'm not laughing about the fact that you left a fingerprint on a Leonardo da Vinci masterpiece,' he'd protested as she pretended to punch him. 'I'm laughing because your expression after you touched it was priceless. You looked like a kid caught with their hand in the cookie jar.'

'It's the painting that's priceless, not my face, and I'll probably be forced to pay for it,' Laura said in annoyance. 'I don't see what's funny about that.'

'I'm sorry. But firstly, it's not priceless. It's only a copy. Secondly, the smudge is so small you'd need a magnifying glass to find it. Nobody is going to make you pay for anything. They'll never know, for starters. Even if Ricardo were to notice that a flower petal is slightly uneven, he's unlikely to connect it to you. Given the state of his studio, he'll probably think a rat walked across it or something.'

Laura knew that he was right but her conscience gnawed away at her. They were on their way to the wardrobe department with Skye when she suddenly stopped. 'Tariq, I think I should tell Brett Avery what happened and face the music.'

'Laura,' Tariq said gently, 'if you'd done something to the real Leonardo painting or even damaged the fake one in any noticeable way, I'd be the first person to tell you to confess to Ricardo or the museum authorities. But you haven't. I understand that you're upset about it and I feel bad for you, but what you did was an accident. Tell Brett if you really want to, but it's almost guaranteed that the whole thing will blow up out of all proportion. Without even looking at it, Brett will decide that you've ruined his specially commissioned painting and cost him thousands of dollars and he'll go off like a nuclear blast. Our lives won't be worth living.'

The make-up artist poked her head out of her caravan and waved to them. 'Hey guys, I'm ready for you.'

'Thanks, Gloria,' Laura called. 'We'll be right there.'

She started to move, but Tariq held her back. 'Laura, why don't we keep quiet about the painting for a day or two and see what happens? If Ricardo finds the mark and everyone gets angry, I'll say that it was my fault too and we can face the fallout together. If nobody ever says a thing, then it'll be our secret. When we go to see the film at the cinema, we can have a laugh about how you contributed to a Leonardo masterpiece, even if it's only a copy of one.'

Laura felt a weight lift off her shoulders. What Tariq said made sense. There was no point in provoking Brett unnecessarily. It was not good that she'd left her fingerprint on a petal, but it paled beside the more serious issues the director had to worry about, such as the stars of his film falling off cliffs and nearly being dragged to their deaths by runaway horses.

'You're right,' she said. 'Let's do as you say, except for one thing. If Ricardo does notice the damaged petal and it turns out that it's a massive disaster, you are not taking any share of the blame. It's my fault and mine alone. If there's a price to be paid, I'll have to find a way of paying it."

After the drama of the past few days, it was not only Laura and Tariq who appreciated an afternoon without incident. They learned that filming could be fun as well as frustrating and, on occasion, dull.

That afternoon two crowd scenes were being filmed. In the first one, Laura played the daughter of rich parents and had to walk between them in a dress that made her resemble a Christmas tree fairy. She and Tariq, who was dressed as a choirboy, teased each other about who looked more ridiculous.

Still, when the cameras rolled it all felt terribly exciting, especially since they were filming in and around the Church of Our Saviour on Spilled Blood. The cathedral owed its name to one of the bloodiest moments in the city's history: Emperor Alexander II was assassinated on the site after revolutionaries threw a bomb at his carriage.

Despite its violent history, there was a fairytale aspect to the church's gold and candy-striped domes and exquisite mosaics. The extras – Laura refused to call herself a background artiste – spent most of the time milling around in the sunshine. From time to time, the director yelled and everyone jumped to attention while the cameras rolled. Laura felt quite important and actorly as she trotted between her make-believe parents, one of whom was retired insurance salesman, Bob Regis.

'Enjoying yourself?' he asked her, and she suddenly realised that she was.

'I am. How about you? Are you having a good time?'

'Oh, I'm in my element. I'm rarely happier than when I'm in a foreign country making films. I know I'm only a lowly background artiste, but some days I feel as if I'm a proper actor. Tomorrow I actually will be. I have my first ever speaking part. Three quite dramatic lines. I've been practicing them in the mirror.'

Chad went by with a tray loaded with coffees and sandwiches. His handsome face was sullen.

'That's it!' cried Bob. 'I've got it, boy. It's in the eyes. You look uncannily like—'

'Bobby Regis! It *is* you, isn't it?' A woman in a yellow hoop dress was rushing in their direction, trying not to trip over her petticoat. 'It's Evie Shore. Don't you remember? We did that Romanian vampire movie together.'

Laura left them to their reunion and went to find Tariq. He was having his hair waxed for the next scene. When he glanced up and saw her, he grinned sheepishly, knowing she'd tease him later.

Both he and Laura had been repeatedly told that, while hundreds of hours of film were shot, only a couple were used. There was a strong likelihood that their fleeting appearances would end up on the cutting room floor.

'Who cares. We're here, aren't we?' Laura said to Tariq. 'We're in St Petersburg and we're experiencing another culture and seeing great art and creating memories. That's all that matters.'

Her friend agreed. He was overjoyed to be with Laura and in exotic St Petersburg, but he'd not lost his suspicion of the entertainment business.

'It is all that matters. Who cares if no one ever sees us on the big screen. Fame is overrated anyway. All it means is that people take photographs of you in your swimming costume when you're looking really fat and put them on the front covers of magazines. I think I'd rather be poor and obscure.'

By the day's end, they were so tired they were ready to drop. The second crowd scene, in which they played grubby urchins piling fruit onto a market stall, had gone on for ever. Skye had also been kept busy. His stomach was rumbling.

As they walked through the lobby of their hotel with Kay, Laura's phone rang.

'Hi, Uncle Calvin,' she said, handing Skye's lead to Tariq. 'How's it going in London?'

'It's given me a new appreciation of St Ives. Everyone is so grumpy here and they all behave as if life is a competition or a race. They sprint up and down the escalators on the Underground, throwing back lattes and gobbling breakfast, lunch and dinner on the run. I admit that I'm a workaholic, but these people make me look positively laid-back. How's it going in sunny St Petersburg?'

'Oh, you know, it's non-stop glamour,' Laura joked. 'We're getting the red carpet treatment all the way. Limousines, banquets, five-star catering . . .'

Her uncle laughed. 'Yes, I can imagine. Well, as long as they're treating you well and you're having fun.'

'We're having lots of fun. Yesterday, we spent the whole afternoon in the Hermitage.' She didn't add that the reason they'd been given time off to visit the museum was that William Raven had almost been killed in an on-set accident. There was no point in worrying him unnecessarily.

There was an audible groan on the other end of the line. 'Don't talk to me about the Hermitage. I've spent the last forty-eight hours trying to reschedule Ed Lucas' state visit to Moscow after he decided that he wanted to do a side trip to St Petersburg to see some art. Our security team in Russia has been having a nightmare trying to keep him safe over there. Anyone would think that he actively wanted to get into trouble.'

Laura's opinion of the Deputy Prime Minister took a further dip. He seemed a thoroughly obstinate, egotistical and inconsiderate man. With people like him running the United Kingdom, it was hardly surprising that the newspapers were always complaining about the country being in a mess.

Even so, it intrigued her that any politician would so blatantly flirt with disaster. 'The film set is only a block or two from the Hermitage,' she said. 'Maybe we'll get to see him.'

'I'm relieved to say you won't,' was her uncle's frank response. 'We've arranged for him to have a closed visit. I can't tell you when it is for security reasons, but I can tell you that it won't be on the same day as the film company do their shoot there. I made sure of that. The only public appearance Mr Lucas is likely to make will be at the ballet tomorrow night. That, too, is top secret. Not a word about any of this to anyone.'

'Of course not,' said Laura, crossing her fingers behind

her back. She and Tariq told each other everything and Mr Lucas' St Petersburg trip would be no exception. 'But I do think it's a shame that the Deputy Prime Minister is going to be in St Petersburg and I'm not going to see him. I'm quite curious.'

'Laura, trust me when I tell you that it's a good thing you're not going to get to see him. Keep it that way. We've had so many nightmares arranging his visit that we've codenamed it Operation Misadventure.'

Tariq caught her eye and rubbed his stomach. Kay was talking to a colleague on the other side of the lobby. Laura grinned. 'I have to go, Uncle Calvin. This acting business is hard work and we're starving.'

As she clicked off her phone, Kay came over. 'Ready for dinner, superstars? I know I am. Let's go out and celebrate a day where absolutely nothing went wrong. In fact, everything went right. Smooth as silk. And to top it all, I have some thrilling news. Just remember, you heard it here first.'

'What is it?' asked Tariq, trying to hang on to Skye who'd spotted a waiter with a tray of food.

Kay lowered her voice, 'You may have read in the papers that the Deputy Prime Minister of Britain has been on a state visit to Moscow while we've been in St Petersburg.'

'I did hear something about that,' Laura said vaguely.

'Well, it now turns out that he's going to be coming to St Petersburg! Apparently he's always had ambitions to see the Hermitage.'

Laura resisted the urge to say that she already knew that and had heard it from a member of the inner circle of his security team, the man responsible for plotting every last detail of Ed Lucas' Russian tour.

Except, it turned out, for one unscheduled stop.

'Edward Lucas has another ambition too,' Kay reported triumphantly as they headed across to the lift. 'Brett Avery has just received a personal phone call from him. Your Deputy PM wants to visit the set of *The Aristocratic Thief* tomorrow. Isn't that fabulous? We couldn't hope to buy that kind of publicity. More amazingly still, he's agreed to host the reception we're giving at the Hermitage the night after tomorrow.'

Laura took the opportunity to press the lift button so that her face didn't give away her shock. 'How cool. I hope I get to see him.'

She felt guilty even as the words left her mouth, because it was obvious that this latest detour would be yet another headache for Calvin Redfern. She planned to text her uncle with the information as soon as she returned to the room. Clearly, he hadn't been informed about it or he'd have mentioned it on the phone.

It was only as the lift doors closed and the party was whisked upwards that it occurred to Laura that the malicious prankster who'd been causing mayhem on the film set had yet to be caught. If it was attention that he or she was seeking, there could be no better time to stage an attack than during a visit from one of the world's most high profile politicians.

And what about the Straight As? She hadn't forgotten the Joker in her hotel room. They were a gang who liked to broadcast their misdeeds from the rooftops. It would be typical of them if they chose the visit of a British statesman to a film set in Russia to do something audacious.

There was also the mafia to consider or perhaps a lone assassin . . .

But no, her imagination was running away with her again. Operation Misadventure was only a codename, not a prediction.

AT BREAKFAST LAURA managed to spill half a cup of coffee down the front of her jumper and had to run upstairs to change while Kay, Tariq and Skye waited for her in the lobby. It took her three outfit trials to decide that her pink checked shirt was the only other thing suitable for meeting a visiting head of state. She was rushing to rejoin her friends when her eye was caught by something on the housekeeping trolley parked in the corridor. In among the miniature bars of soap and bottles of shampoo was a deck of cards. The empty box that had contained them lay beside it.

Laura stopped dead. The door beside the trolley was

open and a vacuum cleaner was being tugged around the corner of an unmade bed. As if in a dream, Laura picked up the cards. She'd have known the design on them anywhere. The Straight As had left her a Joker with that same intricate blue and red pattern on the back in at least three other locations over the past few months. Each time it had been a warning from the gang and each time it had spelled disaster.

Further along the corridor a door opened and an empty breakfast tray was shoved out. The door slammed shut. Laura fanned through the deck of cards. She was half afraid that all fifty-two of them would be Jokers, but it was a perfectly ordinary mixed pack. If housekeeping were doling them out, it must have been pure coincidence that Kay received the Joker.

The vacuum cleaner was switched off. Before she could move, the maid appeared in the doorway. Her smile changed to a frown when she saw Laura with the cards. Laura put them down quickly.

'I'm sorry. I was just looking. I . . . I don't suppose you happen to know where these cards came from?'

The maid shook her head. 'No English.'

Laura tapped the cards. 'Do you have any more of these?'

'Ah, you take. Yes, yes, you take.'

'No . . . umm, where does the hotel buy them? If I wanted more, where could I get them?' To prompt her, Laura picked up the empty box and pointed to a label saying Made in China.

The maid smiled with relief. She flung open a side compartment in the trolley and gestured inside. Stacked neatly were at least forty identical boxes of cards.

As soon as she stepped into the lobby, Laura was pounced on by Tariq. Kay was near the reception desk talking animatedly on her mobile.

'Where on earth have you been? Kay thought she'd have to send out a search party. She's on the phone to Otto, who is beside himself because Skye is needed in about five minutes.'

'Sorry, I had to investigate something. You know how I was fretting that the Joker card Kay found in our room was a warning to me and that the Straight As were planning some awful crime? Well, we don't have to worry about them any longer. They're not following us in St Petersburg. I was mistaken.'

'How do you know?'

Laura was briefly explaining her rather humiliating discovery that the cards, far from being unique, were actually made in China and widely available, when Kay came running up.

'Good grief, Laura, what were you doing up there – consulting a fashion designer? Otto is having a nervous breakdown. The Deputy Prime Minister is due on set at any moment. I thought you were keen to try to see him.'

'I am. Sorry I took so long upstairs. I couldn't decide what to wear.' She tried not to think about the text she'd received from her uncle that morning about the politician's visit.

L – unlikely that you and Mr Misadventure will cross paths (he prefers big stars) but if it happens stay well away. Fanatics

target people like him all the time and I don't want you and T
anywhere near if something goes wrong. CRxx

'Great,' said Kay. 'Does that mean we're finally ready?'
Laura glanced at Tariq. 'We're ready.'

The film unit had relocated to Palace Square beside the
Hermitage, where anticipation levels had reached fever
pitch. Gone was the relaxed, lackadaisical vibe that had
punctuated the short bursts of filming the previous day.
There were no actors lolling half asleep on sofas, or extras
playing video games and drinking cappuccinos while in
period costume. Instead they rushed about in a state of
high anxiety on a set so scrubbed and organised it was
almost unrecognisable. Russian policemen in bear fur
hats patrolled the fringes.

Everyone not essential to that morning's filming had
been banished for the duration of Ed Lucas' visit. Laura
and Tariq had been told in no uncertain terms that they
were to help Otto with Skye and the horses and leave as
soon as they were done.

'You can forget meeting Edward Lucas,' Jeffrey, the
production manager, said snootily. 'Only Brett Avery and
the stars will be getting to do that. Not the likes of you.'

The door of the trailer behind them opened. Sebastian
exited with feline grace. He was dressed to kill in a dark
blue suit and waistcoat with fancy embroidery around the

edges. Scowling at the production manager's receding back, he said, 'Why does everyone fawn all over William as if he's a superstar, that's what I'd like to know. I'll admit that he's a good actor, but everyone treats him as if he's the greatest talent since Brando. How he got this job I'll never understand. Previously, he was a washed up magician. Scratch the surface and you'll probably find there's nepotism involved.'

'What's nepotism?' asked Tariq. 'Sounds like a disease.'

'It sort of is. Essentially, it's when a relative or a family friend or connection gets you a job you would never have got otherwise and probably don't deserve.'

'You don't think he deserves his role?' pressed Laura.

'No comment. But if I were him, I'd be checking that the gun being used in the next scene is loaded with blanks, not real bullets. In a short space of time, he's managed to make a record number of enemies.'

Chad came striding up in a T-shirt and ripped jeans. 'You're wanted in make-up,' he told Sebastian. 'Hope they have enough of it.'

'Jealousy will get you nowhere. As I've just been telling Tariq and Laura here, connections are what count in this business.'

'Yeah, well, I wouldn't know anything about that,' growled Chad. 'Not having a rich daddy to buy me into films.'

Sebastian's laughter floated back to them as he walked away. He turned to say teasingly, 'Even if you did, MacFarlane, your daddy couldn't afford the price he'd have to pay. Looks aren't everything, you know. By the way, what are you wearing? Are you aware that we have a British head of state coming to see us?'

Chad waited until Sebastian had moved away before muttering, 'One of these days, someone is going to lose patience with that guy and he'll get what's coming to him.'

He spotted Bob Regis emerging from the wardrobe department trailer in a frock coat, breeches and boots. 'Hey Bob, I have a spare coffee and croissant on my tray. Interested?'

'Sebastian criticises William Raven for being full of himself and making enemies, but he's not doing too badly himself,' remarked Tariq as he and Laura walked over to the temporary stables.

'No, he's not,' agreed Laura. 'It's a good thing that the Straight As haven't followed us to Russia. We have enough on our plate trying to figure out who among the actors and crew might actually be a threat and who is simply full of hot air. Let's hope we do it before it's too late.'

~ 12 ~

AT 10.45 A.M. THERE was still no sign of the Deputy Prime Minister and his entourage. Brett Avery, who had delayed shooting a chase scene for nearly two hours in order to have something 'cool' to show his special guest, was ready to burst a blood vessel.

'Can't we call his people?' suggested Kay.

'His people? Are you mad? I wouldn't know where to begin to find them. You don't *call* Ed Lucas. He calls you. No, we have no choice but to start filming now, while the light is perfect, and hope that he comes before we get the last take in the bag. Actors and crew to their stations, please.'

Laura and Tariq crouched unnoticed in a space between two trailers. In the fuss over the missing Deputy PM they'd been forgotten.

Bob Regis passed them on the way to his mark. He caught sight of them and reacted with comical astonishment, doing a double take and putting his finger to his lips. 'Naughty, naughty,' he scolded, bending to their level. 'But don't worry, I shan't tell a shoal. Soul, I mean. I won't tell a shoal. I mean, soul. Oh, whatever.'

He straightened up and marched away like a soldier on parade.

Tariq watched him go. 'Is he all right? He seems drunk.'

'Mmm, I thought so too, but he can't be because I saw Chad taking him a coffee only about an hour ago and he seemed fine then. Anyway, he doesn't seem the type. He was really looking forward to saying his three lines in the next scene. Maybe he's just fooling around.'

'Action!' yelled the director.

Laura forgot about Bob and stood on tiptoes to watch the scene, not wanting to miss a thing. This was Skye's big moment and she was both excited and nervous. It was the part in the story where Violet the orphan realises that Oscar de Havier has stolen a priceless painting. Unable to follow him on foot, she gives chase on a sledge with wheels pulled by her husky. Since a gun would be used in the scene, Otto had devoted time the previous afternoon to getting Skye accustomed to loud bangs.

The cameras rolled and William Raven – or at least his character, Oscar – came running out of the Hermitage, black coat flapping. He fled across Palace Square in the direction of the river. Sebastian emerged next and ran after him. Moments later Ana María, playing the orphan Violet, raced out of the museum and whistled. Skye, who had been waiting for her in a side alley, bounded forward. Violet jumped on the back of the sledge and shook the reins.

'Go, Flash!' she cried. 'Everything depends on you now. Run for your life, boy, run!'

For Laura, it was hard to watch Skye respond to the commands of another girl, but another part of her was thrilled that her husky's cleverness would be captured on film for the world to see. She and Tariq knew how beautiful and brave he was, but it was nice to know that other people would experience it.

With the crew engrossed in the action, the children crept closer in order to get a better view. Only Tariq noticed that a short, pudgy man immediately moved into the space they'd vacated between the trailers.

Oscar de Havier had commandeered a horse and was shooting over his shoulder. In the pursuing sledge, Violet ducked. As the shots continued to ring out, she pulled up her husky, Flash, not wanting to risk his life. They'd caught up to Sebastian, who used the opportunity to jump aboard and use the sledge as a shield.

Bob Regis had explained to Laura that that was his signal to step forward and shout, 'After 'im, Miss! Don't let 'im get away with it. I reckon your dog can take care of himself.'

He got as far as saying, 'After 'im, Mish! Don't let . . .' and then a shot rang out. His body gave an unnatural jerk and he pitched forward and lay still. A trickle of blood ran from his temple and smeared the cobbles.

The film set curse had struck again.

For a couple of seconds, nobody moved. Half the company assumed that the shooting of Bob was in the script. The others were too stunned to move.

The silence was pierced by Ana María's screams. Otto, the animal handler, rushed to grab Skye.

Ana María's mother burst through the ranks of camera crew and lighting operators and flung her arms around her daughter, crying hysterically. Anyone would have thought that it was Ana María who'd been shot, not Bob. Between sobs, she shook a fist at William Raven. The actor had climbed down from his horse and was staring at the gun in his hand as if he had no idea how it had got there.

'You nasty man,' she cried. 'You're mean and nasty to everyone and now finally you kill someone. You go to jail where you belong.'

William Raven was grey with shock. He lowered the revolver to the ground and put both hands in the air as if he were already under arrest. 'It wasn't me. I mean, it was, but it wasn't, I can promise you that. Who loaded the gun?'

'I did,' said the stunt coordinator who'd been brought in to replace Andre March. He looked as shaken as Andre had when he came to see Laura in St Ives. 'But it's been under lock and key the whole time and I double-checked that the bullets were blank before I handed it to Mr Raven. Either he switched them or someone else did.'

'Don't be a fool,' the actor snapped furiously. 'Are you suggesting that I deliberately tried to murder the man? What possible reason would I have for doing that?'

Sebastian looked at him with dislike. 'You might have been aiming for someone different. Me, for example.'

Brett Avery recovered his powers of speech. 'Sebastian, get over yourself. Your ego is getting out of control. Has anyone checked whether poor Regis is really dead?'

The production manager crouched down and felt Bob's pulse. 'If he was any deader, he'd be extinct.'

'Well, that's compassionate, Jeffrey,' said Kay. 'What's wrong with you all? Right, I'm calling the police.'

Laura whispered something to Tariq, who nodded and took out his phone. She stepped forward. 'Before you do that, I suggest you take a closer look at Bob.'

'Will somebody get those children out of here,' ranted the director. 'Good grief. As if we don't have enough to deal with.'

Kay moved to stop the security guard who swooped to grab Laura and Tariq. 'Brett, need I remind you that these kids have already helped save the lives of William and Ana María?'

'That's true,' said William.

'Yes, they did,' agreed Ana María, tugging away from her mother's strong grasp. 'What is it, Laura?'

'It's Bob Regis. He's not dead, he's dead drunk.'

'Please tell me you're joking,' said the director.

Everyone started talking at once.

'Don't be ridiculous,' snapped Jeffrey. 'I checked him. He's as dead as last year's Christmas turkey.'

As if on cue, Bob groaned and writhed. The film set medic, who'd been in the production trailer tending to a background artiste who'd collapsed after mistakenly eating a peanut, belatedly rushed to his side.

'I don't believe it,' said William Raven. 'Here I was thinking that the curse of *The Aristocratic Thief* had struck again, only this time I'd be jailed for murder, as Ana María's mother so helpfully suggested. And all the while we're dealing with an extra who can't hold his drink.'

'I guess that this will be the final straw,' said Chad. 'One too many accidents. I suppose the film will be cancelled now. Closed down.'

'What do you think, Brett?' asked Kay. 'Are we going to admit that our film is cursed and give up and go home with our tail between our legs?'

'I can't answer that until I've spoken to the production company, but I don't think they're going to want to hear that something else has gone wrong. At best, I'll be fired. At worst, they'll cancel the movie.'

Tariq handed his phone to Laura. She read the information on the screen – an old newspaper article – and nodded. It was what she'd expected to see.

'Don't you understand, that's exactly what he wants you to do,' she said to Brett and Kay. 'If you quit the film, he wins.'

The screenwriter stared at her. 'What are you talking about? *Who* are you talking about?'

285

Laura handed her the phone. 'Chad MacFarlane. He's the one who spiked poor Bob's coffee with some drug or other. He's the one who's caused every other so-called accident that's happened on your film set.'

'Liar!' yelled Chad. 'She's lying. She and her friend and their stupid husky, don't you see, they've been ruining everything.'

Kay's faced changed as she read what was written on the screen. She passed the phone to Brett.

'Is this article accurate, Chad?' the director demanded. 'The one in the *Hollywood Chronicle*? Are you the nephew of Jon-Ellis Harding?' Harding was the film legend who'd been booked to play Oscar de Havier before the studio went bust. 'Is that what this is all about – revenge?'

Chad's golden face contorted with rage. 'I don't know what you're talking about. You should be looking at *him*.'

He jabbed a finger in Sebastian's direction. 'He's the one who's always saying that he wishes that William was dead. The coffee I gave to Bob was one I'd made for William that he decided he didn't want. I'd left it on the tray outside Sebastian's trailer while I was fetching the croissants. Maybe Sebastian put something in the coffee in order to set William up to fall off his horse or have an accident with the gun, or something.'

William was startled. 'Is that true, Sebastian?'

'No, of course not! He's obviously out of his mind.'

'So it's not true that you're always wishing I was dead.'

'No! Well, maybe a little bit. Look, I can explain. Chad's jealous, that's all. He's riddled with envy. He wants to be me, walk in my shoes, wear my clothes.'

'Who would want to be in your shoes, you jumped up little nobody?' thundered William. 'Now I wish I had shot you after all.'

'Like you can talk. If it wasn't for your producer friends—'

'Shut up, Sebastian,' Brett Avery said quietly. 'You're really starting to get on my nerves. Chad, have you done what Laura's accusing you of? Did you do it out of revenge or jealousy?'

'You can't be jealous of someone who's stolen your life. You can only pity them and be angry at them.'

Kay went over to him. 'Chad, did your uncle ever promise you a role in *The Aristocratic Thief*?

If she'd punched him in the stomach, she could not have produced more of an effect. He slid to the ground and hugged his knees, rocking slightly. The wail of approaching sirens almost drowned out his next words and Laura and Tariq had to strain to hear him.

'My uncle promised me Sebastian's role. It was going to be my big break. But that wasn't why I did the things I did. I know what you're thinking but I did them because I love my uncle like a father. When the production company went bust and he was told he was no longer wanted for the film, it destroyed him.'

'But we had no choice,' protested Kay. 'Brett and I wanted him for the role. That's why we cast him in the first place. But our new backers were determined that we should have William Raven. I hate to be the one to break this to you, but we're glad they did. William has been fantastic.'

A tear rolled down Chad's cheek. 'But don't you

understand? You've as good as killed my uncle. It's true that he's a legend, but he's getting old now and lots of people think the way Sebastian does, that he's washed up. When he was cast in the role of Oscar de Havier, it gave him a reason to get up in the morning. He put tons of work into researching the role. Then it was snatched away from him with no explanation.'

'Did you not hear what Kay said?' Brett demanded. 'It wasn't our fault. We did try to explain that to him. We also gave him financial compensation – a lot of it.'

Chad ignored him. 'From that day, he changed. He became sadder and sadder. Finally, he ended up in hospital. They couldn't find anything wrong with him. The doctor suggested to me that he might be dying of a broken heart. So I decided I'd get a job on the film, any job, and get it shut down. Stop it happening.'

There was a long silence, broken by the director. 'Chad, I feel sorry for you and I especially feel sorry for your uncle, but your actions could have killed William and Ana María, did put a man in hospital in Cornwall and forced us to leave those crew members with food-poisoning behind in LA, costing them work. You also destroyed thousands of dollars worth of equipment. I'll plead for leniency but I fear a judge might decide it'll take a jail sentence to persuade you to reflect on your actions.'

He nodded to the Russian policemen who had been called by the security guards. As they closed in, Chad kicked and yelled and threatened vengeance. He was borne away at the same time as Bob Regis was carried to a waiting ambulance on a stretcher.

Brett smiled wearily. 'Well, I don't know about anyone else, but I feel as if I've just gone ten rounds with a black belt karate champion. How many of you think that we should admit defeat and quit?'

Nobody stirred.

'How many of you think that we should pick ourselves off the mat, dust ourselves down and make the best movie we can possibly make? Can I have a show of hands?'

A forest of hands went up.

He smiled for the first time that day. 'I guess that's decided then. William and Sebastian, I'm going to have to insist that the two of you shake hands and get over this pettiness.'

The older actor and the young peacock shook hands rather sheepishly. A cheer went up. Brett whooped. 'Well done, boys. Now let's make an Oscar-winning film, people.'

'Aren't you forgetting something, Brett?' asked William.

'Yes, aren't you forgetting something?' demanded Kay.

'Eh? What's that? Oh. *Ohhh.*' The director had the grace to look shamefaced. 'Laura and Tariq, I'm so sorry. If it weren't for you, we'd never have discovered that Chad was the culprit. He'd have continued to terrorise us until he really did bring about disaster and that would have been the end of the film.'

Laura smiled. 'No problem.'

'Glad we could help,' mumbled Tariq.

'I'm curious to know how you worked it out?' asked Kay. 'What made you think it was him?'

'Something Sebastian said about nepotism.'

'Nepo what?' demanded the production manager.

'It's when a family member helps a relative or friend get a job they don't deserve,' explained Tariq.

'It reminded me of the plot of one of my Matt Walker novels,' Laura went on. 'It made me suspect that there might be a reason why Chad was so sensitive to Sebastian's teasing. When Bob collapsed, I was sure. He was getting too close to the truth. He was convinced that Chad was related to a well-known Hollywood actor.'

'No wonder Chad got so uptight when I said his uncle was an old has-been,' remarked Sebastian. 'Which he is. Hardly surprising that he has a fruit-loop for a nephew.'

Brett Avery turned on him. 'Sebastian, if you say one more word that isn't scripted between now and the end of filming, I'll fire you on the spot. Do I make myself clear?'

There was a loud cheer from the rest of the cast and crew.

Sebastian subsided like a pricked balloon. 'Am I allowed—'

'No, you're not. You're not allowed anything. Now get out of my sight.' Brett clutched his head. 'What a morning. The only small mercy is that the Deputy Prime Minister didn't show up.'

The short, pudgy stranger who'd been standing quietly between the trailers stepped forward. 'Oh, but I did. I'm pleased to say that I witnessed the whole drama. Most amusing it was, too. Better than any live theatre I ever paid to see. Bravo.'

~ 13 ~

THE DIRECTOR PRESSED his glasses firmly to the bridge of his nose, as if their positioning had somehow caused him to overlook their famous visitor. He gulped audibly. 'Sir – I mean, Prime Minister . . .'

Kay poked him in the ribs and said under her breath, 'Deputy.'

'*Deputy* Prime Minister. I'm Brett Avery, the director. I don't know what to say. Please accept my humblest apologies. My incompetent security staff did not alert me to your presence, otherwise I would of course . . .'

The politician bowed his head. 'Of course. Please, say no more about it. I especially requested that my tour attract a minimum of fuss. Allow me to introduce myself formally. I'm Ed Lucas.'

William Raven and Ana María Tyler, accompanied by the girl's suddenly cheerful mother and a chastened Sebastian, came forward in a line, displaying a dazzling array of white teeth.

'But how nice to meet you,' gushed Ana María's mother. Her daughter's sulky face momentarily brightened. Sebastian shook hands eagerly, but with the director's words still ringing in his ears he dared not open his mouth.

That left William. 'An honour,' he said in a deep, sonorous tone, as if he was delivering a line out of Shakespeare.

'The pleasure is all mine,' murmured Edward Lucas. As the men shook hands, Laura was surprised to see a look pass between them. From where she stood it was impossible to tell if it was hostile or admiring, but she was certain they'd met before. They knew each other.

Brett Avery lifted his hands in a helpless gesture. 'I'm afraid, Mr Lucas, that you've not seen us at our best. It's been a morning of mishaps.'

The visitor raised an eyebrow. 'Mishaps? I was under the impression that *you* were under the impression that one of your actors had been shot dead. Is that an everyday occurrence?'

'Definitely not, sir, Deputy Prime Minister. It was simply a miscommunication. The production manager wrongly reported that our finest background artiste was deceased when in fact he was perfectly well. That's what led to the confusion.'

'From what I could see, the actor in question was

unconscious and bleeding. Dead drunk. Wasn't that how the young lady over there put it?'

His gaze alighted on Laura, Tariq and Skye, who were in the process of being shooed off the set by the production manager, Jeffrey. Laura was looking over her shoulder at the time, marvelling that such a nondescript little man could rise to a position of such power. When her eyes met Ed Lucas', a strange electrical sensation crawled slowly over her. It was like standing in a magnetic field.

'Laura did use the phrase "dead drunk", but it was inaccurate because Bob Regis hadn't been drinking,' spluttered the director. He was squirming like a schoolboy caught cheating in an exam. 'I don't run that sort of show. The unfortunate man had his coffee spiked.'

But the Deputy PM had lost interest. 'Thank you, Mr Avery, I'll take your word for it. Would you be kind enough to introduce me to the youngsters who discovered that you had a saboteur in your midst?'

'But they're only . . .'

'Yes?'

The director had been about to say that Tariq and Laura were only extras, but thought better of it. 'I'd be delighted to,' he said hastily. 'They're proving to be invaluable members of the cast.'

Jeffrey hid a scowl as he was forced to relinquish Laura and Tariq, whom he'd disliked on sight for no other reason than that he hated all children. To him, every last one of them was a brat, including and especially that precocious monster, Ana María Tyler, who treated him as if he was her own personal skivvy. However, this pair ran a close second. They'd made him look like a fool over the whole Chad business.

'You can leave your hound with me,' he muttered to Laura. 'I'll take it to Otto. I'm sure the Deputy PM doesn't want it slobbering all over him.'

He snatched at the lead and Skye rounded on him, letting out a ferocious snarl.

'I don't think he likes the idea of being dragged away by a stranger,' Laura said coolly. 'Do you?'

There was an explosive laugh. She and Tariq turned to find the Deputy Prime Minister standing less than a metre away from them. He had somehow crossed the set with wizard speed. Brett Avery was hurrying to catch up with him, his expression panicked.

The first thing Laura noted was that Ed Lucas was not a whole lot taller than Tariq, and the second was that the energy that radiated from him increased the closer one got to him.

Jeffrey was reduced to a quivering jelly, especially after the Deputy PM introduced himself as an animal lover first and a politician second. 'I was only . . . I was just . . . I wanted . . .'

'I know,' Ed Lucas said kindly. 'It's much appreciated.'

Then he turned his back and focused on Tariq and Laura. 'As you've probably gathered, I'm the Deputy PM of your country. When I was your age, I found the world of politics intensely boring and I have to say that nothing's changed. I wouldn't blame you in the least if you'd never heard of me before today. You can call me Ed. And you are?'

'Uh, I'm Laura Marlin and this, umm, this is Tariq Ali,'

stammered Laura, conscious that the entire cast and crew were staring at them in astonishment.

The Deputy Prime Minister had the serene smile of a man accustomed to having the world dance to his tune. It was at odds with his watchful brown eyes, which unnerved Laura by looking through her rather than at her, like one of those airport X-ray machines.

'Delighted to make your acquaintance, Tariq. A real pleasure, Laura Marlin. A most unusual surname you have. It might interest you to hear that I have some experience fishing for marlin, and if there's one thing I've learned it's that they're surprisingly elusive.'

His gaze fell on Skye. 'And who have we here?'

Laura tightened her grip on the husky's collar. 'This is my Siberian husky, Skye, but I'm afraid he doesn't like strangers, even if they are animal lovers and in charge of the British Government.'

'He makes up for it in other ways,' Brett Avery said enthusiastically, trying to make amends for earlier blunders. 'The husky, that is. I didn't mean you, sir. You should have seen what he did in St Ives . . .'

He stopped. Ed Lucas had extended a hand towards Skye. With a whine that ended on a sigh, the husky lowered his head. It was hard to say which was more astounding – that the Deputy PM had managed to touch Skye without being snarled at or even bitten or that the husky seemed to be enjoying it. Laura had never seen her dog act so weirdly. It was as if he had been hypnotised.

'Beautiful animal,' said Ed Lucas. 'Radiates intelligence. How did he lose his leg?'

Half of Laura was flattered by his interest in Skye; the other half wished that she'd listened to her uncle's advice and stayed as far from the man as possible. She made a point of not looking at him. She didn't want him hypnotising her.

'There was an accident. He was hit by a car when he was a puppy.'

A smile tweaked Ed Lucas' pale lips. 'Accidents do have a habit of happening, Laura Marlin, especially if you are of a heroic disposition and put yourself in harm's way.'

'If you have a person with a grudge in your midst, they seem to happen anyway,' joked Brett Avery. 'On this set, at least. Although hopefully with Chad's arrest, that's a thing of the past. Now, sir, you might be interested in talking to William Raven, our star, about—'

'I can't think of anything I'd enjoy more, Mr Avery, but if you'll forgive me I do have one more question I'd like to ask of Laura Marlin.'

The director flushed with annoyance. 'Sure, sure. Go ahead.'

'Thank you. Laura, you mentioned that the plot of a Matt Walker detective novel helped you realise that Chad was behind the disasters on the film set. Is this something that interests you, solving mysteries?'

Laura felt like an insect being examined under a microscope. It no longer surprised her that Ed Lucas was the second most powerful man in Britain. He radiated charisma and some quality that made her want to start babbling as if she'd been given a truth serum. It was on the tip of her tongue to tell him that her uncle had once been

Scotland's best and bravest investigator, but she suspected that Ed Lucas would not be pleased to discover that a lowly extra was linked to the intelligence team protecting him.

She covered her hesitation with a smile. 'I like reading mystery novels. My hero is Matt Walker. He's only a character in a book, but to me he's the perfect twenty-first century detective. He's good at dealing with the sort of international criminals and gangs that do evil things in the modern world.'

'Fascinating. Fascinating,' murmured Ed Lucas. 'Yes, I enjoy reading Matt Walker novels myself. They're far-fetched but quite diverting.'

He looked at Tariq. 'And in this world of modern criminals, who do you think will win, Mr Ali?'

'Excuse me?'

'Who will come out on top? The good guys or the bad guys?'

Tariq brushed his black hair from his eyes. 'Whoever's smartest.'

Ed Lucas laughed. 'Clever answer.'

'In the movies, the good guys always win,' interrupted Brett Avery, keen to bring the discussion to a close. 'Everyone loves a hero.'

Laura felt Ed Lucas' strange electricity transfer to the director. 'Yes, everyone loves a hero, don't they?' he said in his soft, firm voice. 'What a shame it is that real life can't be more like the cinema. On the other hand, the conflicting sides of human nature – light versus dark – are what keep things interesting.'

Seizing his chance, Brett Avery said, 'Definitely. That's

certainly true of the cinema. Now, sir, if you'd like to come this way . . .'

Ed Lucas checked his watch. 'Do you know, I appear to have run out of time. Please accept my sincere apologies, Mr Avery. They have me on this ridiculous schedule, you know. It's a curse of high office. However, as we discussed on the phone I would be delighted to host the reception in honour of your film at the Hermitage tomorrow night – provided, of course, that you allow me to watch you shoot a scene or two later. I will also tell my personal assistant to organise personal invitations for Laura and Tariq. So inspiring to talk to such . . . motivated young people.'

He lifted a hand. Bodyguards in dark glasses materialised from the shadows. Laura blinked. The Deputy PM was gone.

~ 14 ~

'WHAT DO YOU THINK?' said Laura, doing a twirl. Ordinarily, she loathed dresses and wore nothing besides jeans, boots, sweatshirts and a jacket with a fake fur collar, but it was fun playing dress-up in the clothes that had been loaned to them by the wardrobe department. In her case, that meant a nineteenth-century cherry-red silk bodice and skirt, under which she'd hidden her lace-up boots. The wax she'd applied to her short, pale blonde hair gave her a slightly gothic look.

'You look like a film star,' said Tariq, who was wearing a white silk shirt with a wide blue collar beneath a black suit. 'Actually no, you look more like a musician. There's a folk singer called Laura Marling. You look a bit like her.'

Laura laughed. 'No, I don't. I look a bit ridiculous. But it's sweet of you to say so. You look quite good yourself. A bit like a rock singer from some eighties band but, you know, it sort of suits you.'

'Gee, thanks.'

'You're both ravishing,' said Kay, emerging from the bathroom in a black cocktail dress that was most definitely not old-fashioned. 'Right, are you ready to go?'

Laura shrugged into a black coat, also on loan from the wardrobe department. She kissed Skye goodbye and he lay on her bed with his nose resting on one paw, looking forlorn. 'We'll be back soon, I promise. No parties.'

Before she left the room, she put her phone in the bedside drawer. That way, if her uncle made a last-minute call to ban her from going, she could honestly say that she hadn't received his message.

The previous evening, she'd had a slightly fraught conversation with him about Ed Lucas' visit to the film set. It began when he called to say that one of the Deputy PM's bodyguards had reported that his boss had had a long conversation with a couple of extras.

'He was sure that one was you. Of course, I sent him away with a flea in his ear. I told him that it was obvious he'd confused you with someone else.'

'It's true.'

'It's true that he confused you with someone else?'

'No, it's true that Ed . . . I mean, Mr Misadventure, spoke to me.'

'You're joking?'

300

'I'm sorry,' Laura said defensively, 'but what was I supposed to do? He made a beeline for me and Tariq and started asking questions about Skye's missing leg and Matt Walker.'

'*Matt Walker*? Why on earth would he ask you about a fictional detective?'

'It's a long story.'

There was a deep sigh. 'Try me.'

'It was because one of the extras was shot.'

'With a gun? In real life?'

'Yes, with a gun in real life, but don't worry, he didn't die. The problem was that everyone thought he was dead and that William Raven had murdered him by mistake while trying to shoot Sebastian. To be honest, it would have been less surprising if Sebastian had killed William.'

'I'm starting to feel unwell. Are you telling me that live ammunition was being used on the set while one of our most prominent politicians was visiting?'

'No, he wasn't there yet. At least, we thought he wasn't. It turned out later that he was there all along, only in secret. But don't panic – Bob, the dead extra, was only drunk. Or drugged. We don't know which.'

A growling noise came down the phone. 'I might commit murder myself. On Brett Avery. He gave me his word that you'd be safe in St Petersburg. "I'll wrap them up in cotton wool" is what he told me.'

Laura tried not to laugh. 'Believe it or not, we've been very well looked after. It wasn't Brett's fault that Chad – he's this runner who had a grudge – turned psychotic. But we weren't in any danger. He only hurt people who'd stolen his uncle's job. Except for Bob, of course, who hadn't done anything.'

'Don't tell me any more. I think I might have a nervous breakdown. Can we return to the original question? How did you end up in conversation with Mr Misadventure?'

'It was me who guessed that Chad was behind all of the supposed accidents, so after he'd been taken away by the police and Bob had gone off in an ambulance, Mr Misadventure asked me if I liked solving mysteries. That's when I said that I liked Matt Walker novels.'

'That's it?'

'Yes, that's it. He did ask Tariq a bit of an odd question. He wanted to know who Tariq thought would come out on top, the good guys or the bad guys. He's quite weird, isn't he? It's hard to imagine how someone like him got to be so important. Maybe it's because he's good at charming people and because he's electrical.'

'Electrical?'

'You must have noticed. There's this strange energy that comes off him. It's not what you'd expect in such a small, dumpy man. It's as if a lightning bolt has somehow ended up in the most unlikely body in the world.'

Calvin Redfern laughed. 'I know what you mean. Oh well, I suppose you satisfied your curiosity and no harm was done. I must say, I can't wait until this assignment is over and Mr Misadventure is back on British soil. Can't wait till you're home safely either. What are you up to tomorrow?'

'We're doing some more filming with Skye in the morning, but then we've been told we have to nap all afternoon so we're not too tired for the reception at the Hermitage in the evening.'

'The one that Ed – our friend – is hosting? No way. I'm not allowing it. Laura, I've told you that it's too risky. As long as he's in Russia, there's a chance that an assassin could strike.'

'Oh please let us go, Uncle Calvin, it's going to be the highlight of our trip. All the stars will be there and we'll be perfectly safe. Kay says there will be lots of interesting people and great food. And afterwards we've been asked to help with the filming in the museum. Please don't stop us from going. I'll be heartbroken.'

Another deep sigh came down the line. 'It's really that important to you?'

'Yes, it is. Anyway, Kay will be there to look after us. She won't let us out of her sight.'

'This Chad character – he's been arrested?'

'Yes, he's under lock and key.'

'All right, you can go. Only Laura . . .'

'Yes?'

'Be careful. Try to remember that you're not in St Ives any more. St Petersburg is a much darker place.'

The lift doors pinged open. Laura followed Kay and Tariq into its fluorescent depths. She thought of Ed Lucas' watchful brown eyes; the way he'd hypnotised Skye and looked through her as he interrogated her. She had the idea that he only asked questions to which he already knew the answers.

'Everything all right, Laura?' asked Kay. 'You seem deep in thought.'

'Everything's fine. I was thinking about tonight. I've a feeling it's going to be unforgettable.'

As they walked through reception, the concierge ran after Kay. 'I thought you had already gone out, Madame. You have just missed a phone call. There is a man who is desperate to get hold of you. He said it's a matter of life and death.'

'Thank you,' said Kay. 'I know who it is and I'll call him later.'

'But . . .'

'It's fine. Really. I'll call him later.'

As they exited through the revolving doors, she said with an eye roll, 'There's this Russian oligarch – an oil trillionaire, in case you didn't know – who thinks he can buy his son a starry career in Hollywood. He's nearly driven me mad over the last few days, calling to see if we can write this boy into the script. I absolutely refuse to allow him to spoil my evening.'

They strolled along the canal, past the pastel painted buildings and cafes offering crêpes. Riverboats packed with jubilant tourists chugged by. The film set had been removed from Palace Square, but the trailers used by William Raven and Ana María Tyler were parked in a side alley, along with the film unit truck containing cameras and lighting equipment.

As they passed it two guards in bear hats moved to let in

a limousine. The electronic gates sighed closed behind it. Four figures climbed out – two bodyguards and the man and woman they shielded.

'The governor of St Petersburg and his wife,' whispered Kay.

As the party moved away into the shadows, Laura saw a gun outlined against the hip of one of the bodyguards. It was a warm evening but she shivered. All along, she'd viewed her uncle's concerns about the possible dangers of Russia as being exaggerated. From what she'd seen since arriving, St Petersburg was a friendly, rather gentile city. Now she realised that was an illusion. It was a beautiful city, but one with a dark heart.

Crossing the shaded courtyard that led to the entrance of the Hermitage, she felt a sudden urge to hear Calvin Redfern's voice. She wanted to reassure him that she was with Kay and Tariq and that he didn't need to worry.

She caught her friend's arm. 'Tariq, I've left my phone at the hotel. Is there any chance I could borrow yours to give my uncle a quick ring?'

The reception guests were filing into the museum in all their finery and both Kay and Tariq stared at her in surprise.

'What, now?' Kay asked. 'Is it something urgent?'

'Sure,' said Tariq, pulling his mobile from his pocket.

Laura was embarrassed. 'I'm sorry. I should have done it earlier. I only wanted to tell him Tariq and I are fine and that I don't want him fretting.'

'You are blocking the way. Are you going in or not?' demanded a man with a stomach so vast it could have seated a party of six. His tuxedo squeaked at the seams.

'I spoke to him first thing this morning,' Kay told her. 'I assured him that this evening would be a lovely treat for you and Tariq. I also told him that he was fussing unnecessarily and in the end he agreed. By the time I put down the phone, he was laughing.'

'You are moving, yes?' boomed the large Russian.

Laura handed the phone back to Tariq and moved forward in the queue. 'You're right. There's not much point in calling now, anyway. London is three hours behind and I don't have any news. I'll text him when we get back to the room and tell him all about the night we got to hang out with the stars.'

15

THE RECEPTION WAS held in the Winter Palace, in a salon illuminated by a chandelier so sparkling it could have been made entirely of diamonds. On one side of the room was a large glass cabinet housing a solid gold pheasant. It surveyed the crowd regally, one claw raised. A single gold feather could have bought and furnished Calvin Redfern's entire house.

On the other side of the room was a small stage, at the top of which was a black screen flanked by two giant vases of flowers and two armed guards. A microphone was being set up by a poker-faced technician.

The room was already packed when they arrived.

Women draped in jewellery so heavy that Laura feared for the health of their necks paraded by on the arms of men who resembled penguins in their tuxedos. Glasses tinkled. A smiling waiter presented Laura and Tariq with a lychee cocktail.

It was 7 p.m. but beyond the velvet drapes that hugged the windows, the summer sun still lit the surface of the Neva River. Laura and Tariq, who'd gone without lunch on the promise of fabulous hors d'oeuvres, stopped every passing waiter and piled their plates high with mini pizzas and quiches and California sushi rolls. There were even tiny ice cream cones for dessert. At one point, a silver bucket heaped with black caviar was offered to them, but they drew the line at that. It smelled foul.

As they ate, they leaned against the windowsill and watched the room. With the exception of Ana María, they were the youngest people there. Much to the disgust of Jeffrey, who had not been invited, they were the only extras.

'It's like seeing an ant colony at work,' commented Tariq. 'Everyone is on a mission to achieve something, but they're all pretending that they're only here to have a good time. Meanwhile, they're desperately trying to network with someone richer or more connected than they are.'

'I'm not sure they're like ants,' said Laura, as she watched William Raven, Sebastian and Ana María's mother move through Russian high society, dispensing charm as if it were chocolate. 'Ants are quite friendly. Sharks would be more accurate.'

As she spoke, there was a commotion. Igor, the ancient cleaner, was trying to enter with his mop. The muscle-bound doormen who, Laura suspected, were either part of Ed Lucas' security detail or Russian ex-Special Forces soldiers, barred his way. When he tried to push past, his grey head nodding, their attempts to dispatch him became firmer. They laughed as he tottered away.

'Do you think we should check if he's all right?' Laura asked Tariq.

'Who's that?' demanded Kay, arriving with two glasses of sparkling elderflower.

'Igor,' Tariq explained. 'He's the old cleaner the museum staff have nicknamed "the Warrior". He's quite decrepit. The security guys were being mean to him.'

'I'll be the worrier if you disappear,' was Kay's retort. 'Laura, your handsome but very stern uncle gave me strict instructions to watch you both like a hawk tonight. I don't know what he thinks is going to happen – the museum is closed to the public and there are more guards than statues in the Hermitage. Nonetheless, you're going to stay right here by my side. Besides, the big event is about to start. You'll be sorry if you miss it.'

The Deputy Prime Minister had been scheduled to make a special presentation at 7.30 p.m., but by 8.05 p.m. he hadn't shown up. Brett Avery, who'd been granted permission for only two hours of shooting at the museum that evening, was becoming more agitated by the moment. Every time he paced past them, a vein popped in his neck.

'Ed Lucas may be a big deal in political circles, but frankly I think he's rather rude,' said Kay. 'I don't care if he's the—'

'Shh!' An elegant woman in a pale turquoise ball gown

glared at her. The chatter in the room cut off so abruptly it was as if a mute button had been pushed. There was a grating noise and an ancient mosaic of a monk detached from the wall and swung open. Through the secret portal stepped the evening's star guest. Cheers and applause greeted his arrival.

Ed Lucas looked slightly more impressive in a black tuxedo and crisp white shirt than he had on the film set in a grey suit. Yet his presence transformed the energy of the room. Everyone snapped to attention. Men looked alive and keen to impress. Women twinkled like candles.

His fluid walk carried him so quickly towards the microphone that, from a distance, he appeared to levitate. He trotted up the steps onto the stage, followed by Ricardo, the artist. They made an incongruous pair – Ricardo with his swarthy skin and wild mop of black curly hair, and Ed Lucas, pale and uninteresting. Yet even when they were joined by the smartly groomed governor of St Petersburg, it was to the Deputy PM that every eye gravitated.

'His eminence, the governor of St Petersburg, ladies and gentleman, boys and girls, let me start by apologising for my late arrival. I hope you will forgive me when you learn that it was because I was overseeing the packaging of some special gifts, which you will receive on your way out. I don't wish to spoil the surprise, but every one of them contains a jewel-encrusted Fabergé egg . . .'

There was a gasp from the crowd.

He grinned. 'Not a real one, I hasten to add . . .'

Lots of laughter.

'I'm honoured to be your host on this wonderful

evening where the great and good have gathered together to celebrate the making of *The Aristocratic Thief*. I don't know about you, ladies and gentlemen, but I love that title. For those of you not familiar with the story, it's about an art heist – a theft. A rich and powerful man steals a painting from one of the greatest treasure houses on earth – the Hermitage. He almost gets away with it, but an orphan girl ruins his plans.'

He shook a finger at the audience in mock warning. 'In case any of the aristocrats here this evening have any ideas of doing something similar, let me assure you that the museum director has tripled the usual security. You'll be dealing with people a lot larger and a whole lot more scary than an orphan girl.'

More laughter.

'Without further ado, I have the privilege of asking William Raven up to the stage to unveil the painting that will be "stolen" from the Hermitage in the film. It is a copy of a Leonardo da Vinci masterpiece, the so-called "Benois Madonna". Ricardo, the artist who took on this project, is a genius himself. I would defy any of you to tell the real painting from the fake, but if you think you can, do let me know.'

William Raven joined him on the stage. Laura watched closely to see if any look passed between the men, as it had done on the film set, but their smiles and handshakes seemed purely professional.

The guards moved the screen that hid the back of the stage. Behind it, propped on easels, were two paintings draped in black cloth.

Ed Lucas beamed up at the actor, who was at least twice his size. 'Would you do the honours, William?'

But as William stepped forward, there was an almighty crash. The waiter carrying the silver bucket of caviar had tripped, sending slimy pellets of fish eggs cascading all over the dresses of the governor's wife, her glamorous daughters and a Russian oil billionaire. The screams that followed were so piercing that Laura was amazed there was a glass left intact.

There were several minutes of bedlam while the mess was sorted out and the angry billionaire and crying women were escorted from the room by the governor and various officials. Laura felt sorriest for the waiter, who would doubtless be fired.

'May I humbly apologise and ask the forgiveness of anyone affected by this unfortunate incident,' said Ed Lucas when the room was finally silent. 'I have promised the governor that I will buy his wife and daughters brand new dresses from a designer of their choice. Of course, it's a promise I may live to regret . . .'

There was relieved laughter.

Once again, Laura marvelled at how effortlessly he won people over with his charm and generosity. She could feel herself warming to him. After all, he had admired Skye.

'Seriously,' he went on, 'it would be my pleasure to make amends. Now if there are no more buckets of caviar to spill, shall we return to the evening's main attraction? William, kindly unveil the paintings.'

The actor swept the cloth from each picture, as if he were a matador twirling his cape. The audience cheered.

'Extraordinary,' marvelled the Deputy Prime Minister, peering closely at the paintings. 'In my opinion, we have two masterpieces here, not just one. But don't take my word for it. If you would be kind enough to form an orderly queue, I'd like to invite you to inspect them at close range. Ricardo will be here to answer any questions. Before I go, I would also like to advise all would-be thieves that the museum knows which painting is the original!'

As he and William left the stage to thunderous applause, they were engulfed by a circle of celebrities.

'Care to see the paintings up close?' Kay asked Laura and Tariq. 'Or are you content with the private view you had on your tour with Vladimir? Of course, you didn't have a chance to compare them. Brett and I were invited to see them side-by-side the day after the copy was completed. To me, they looked identical.'

On the one hand, Laura was curious to see whether her fingerprint was still on the painting, or if it had been noticed and corrected by Ricardo. On the other hand, she still felt guilty about what had happened and was nervous even now of her crime being discovered.

'Once was enough,' she said with feeling.

Tariq caught her eye and smothered a laugh. 'Yes, I feel the same. Besides, we should probably go and find Jeffrey and find out if he has any jobs for us. I'm really looking forward to seeing how you film the theft of the painting.'

Kay smiled. 'So am I, but I can't help feeling that I might be arrested at any moment. I know we've had permission and that the painting we're using is a fake, but it still feels wrong to be filming an art heist at a museum in broad daylight. But I'm being silly. It'll be fun. Tomorrow's shoot will be even more exciting. The submarine we've hired for the getaway scene has arrived and is ready and waiting for us on the river outside. Can't wait to see it.'

'A submarine,' cried Tariq. 'How cool.'

'Kay, honey, there you are,' said Brett Avery, rushing up to them in a state of high agitation. 'I need your help. Ana María's mother is having a fit about her daughter's costume. Says it isn't flattering enough. Would you mind coming to talk to her before I strangle her with my bare hands?'

16

'**DO YOU THINK** anyone will believe us at school when we tell them what life is really like on a film set?' asked Tariq as he and Laura followed the director and screenwriter into the Leonardo da Vinci Room on the first floor.

'No,' said Laura, 'I don't. Even if they did, we should probably avoid the truth in case they have to spend the rest of the term in counselling. We could pretend we're writing a story for a celebrity magazine and give them a rose-coloured version of events. We could say that William Raven is sweet and humble, and that Sebastian is not in the least conceited, and that Ana María's mother never behaves like a crazy stage parent.'

Tariq laughed. 'She's all right, Mrs Tyler. Any parent would go a bit crazy if they saw their daughter fall off a cliff or appear to be involved in a shooting.'

'That's true,' admitted Laura. 'It's just that—'

'Are you two working tonight or would you prefer to stand around idly chatting?' demanded the production manager. 'Because if it's the latter, I can have you escorted back to the hotel.'

'Would you leave these poor kids alone, Jeffrey?' scolded Kay. 'In between saving the lives of our stars, they do deserve to enjoy themselves occasionally. Are you forgetting that they're here at the invitation of the Deputy Prime Minister of Britain? Speaking of which, would you mind fetching Ed Lucas a chair? He's going to sit beside Brett and watch us film the heist scene.'

At the mention of Ed Lucas' name, the hairs on Laura's arms stood up. She didn't like the idea of another encounter with him, but at the same time she didn't want to miss the shooting of the film's most exciting sequence. She couldn't understand why a man of his position was bothering with something so frivolous. It was only a movie. Surely he had more important concerns. World peace, for example.

Then again, even politicians had to have the occasional break. According to Kay, government ministers rarely cared about, or put money, into the arts and it was a coup to find one who did. Still, it annoyed Laura that the Deputy PM had caused so many problems for her uncle during his time in Russia.

She needn't have worried about meeting Ed Lucas again. He entered the room in a bubble that included the film publicist, one of his bodyguards and sundry hangers-on and was escorted to the chair beside Brett Avery. Laura and Tariq were banished to the far corner of the gallery by Jeffrey, who seized them the moment Kay's back was turned and told them that, in his opinion, children on set should be 'unseen and unheard.'

'I'm not sure you mean what you think you mean,' Laura told him. 'Your grammar is a bit twisted.' But he just glowered at her and repeated his threat about dragginging them back to the hotel if they didn't do as they were told.

They were reprieved when there was a sudden buzz on the set and the production manager had to rush away to deal with a crisis involving a missing camera battery.

Screened from the room by a row of tall equipment cases, Laura and Tariq coiled cables as Jeffrey had instructed and peered through the gaps between the boxes as the crew lit the scene. Ricardo's fake painting had replaced Leonardo's original in the spot beside the window. Most other paintings in the room had been replaced by copies or less valuable pictures in case they were damaged during filming.

Old Igor came nodding and creaking into the gallery with his mop.

'Excuse me,' called Laura. 'I saw what happened downstairs. I mean, with the doormen being horrid to you. Are you okay? Would you like to sit with us and watch the filming?'

His head snapped round like a startled turtle and something unreadable flashed through his eyes. He was mumbling something incoherent when Jeffrey bore down on him.

'No, no, NO! Igor, please, we are about to shoot a scene. You have to leave immediately. When it is over, we would be grateful for your services, but not now.'

As the door shut behind Igor, Brett yelled the now familiar word: 'Action!'

Laura and Tariq had moved the equipment cases slightly so they could see better, but their view of the scene was still slightly blocked by cameras, crew and Brett Avery and Ed Lucas. Laura hoped the Deputy Prime Minister didn't melt in his jacket. The studio lights were so intense that the room was like an oven. It was after 9.30 p.m. but the sun still shone outside.

William Raven, dressed once more as the aristocrat, Oscar de Havier, strolled into the gallery and pretended to be admiring different pictures. When he reached the 'Benois Madonna', he paused to study it. A couple with an unruly child passed him. The boy, aged seven or eight, kept complaining that he was bored. He reminded Laura of the boisterous toddler who'd tripped over Igor's mop, except that he was older.

This boy, spiky-haired and spoilt, upset the gallery guard by touching a statue clearly marked 'DO NOT TOUCH!' Oscar de Havier, still standing near the window, scowled his disapproval. It had little effect on the boy. He continued to whine and fuss. When his mother snapped at him, he reacted by prodding a nearby oil painting, setting off the gallery alarm.

The noise was ear-splitting and brought guards running from all over the gallery. They were on the verge of arresting the boy's parents when the aristocrat intervened. It was not their fault, he explained to the guards. They'd done their level best to keep their boy under control, but he'd been determined to cause trouble. Fortunately, no real harm had been done. However, it might be a good idea for them to leave the gallery before they found themselves trying to come up with the money to repair a Rembrandt or a Da Vinci.

The embarrassed parents were escorted out of the room by the guards. Every other visitor had either fled in panic, or been frightened out of the room by the aggressive guards. The alarm was turned off while the crisis was sorted out.

Eventually, Oscar was left alone in the room. A sly smile came over his face. He opened the window and waved a white handkerchief out of it. A masked figure wearing black came abseiling down from the roof of the Hermitage and landed on the ledge outside. A poster roll was strapped to his back.

Oscar took it from him and removed what was supposed to be the Leonardo copy. Kay had explained to Laura and Tariq that it was actually a blank piece of canvas. They would edit in an image of the copy at a later stage. Oscar had to slice the 'original' from the frame and replace it with the fake. He'd been given a spare frame for this purpose. He then rolled up the 'real' painting and handed it to the masked man on the window ledge. Snatching it, his accomplice dropped out of sight.

As Oscar wrenched shut the window, the door of the gallery burst open. A guard ran in.

'What's going on? I heard a noise.'

'Of course you heard a noise,' the aristocrat replied smoothly. 'The alarm went off. It nearly shredded my eardrums. A brat of a boy took it into his head to poke the Rubens over there.'

'I don't mean the alarm. It was a suspicious sound. A scraping sound, as if a window was being opened.'

'That's because it was. By the time every man and his dog had been in to attend to that horrible boy, it was so stuffy in here I started to feel a bit dizzy. I'm afraid I opened the window to gasp for air. Apologies if it's not allowed.'

'It isn't usually, but since it was you, Mr Havier, there is no problem. Forgive me if I was a bit abrupt. Our nerves are all on edge tonight. We pride ourselves on our ability to keep these treasures safe.'

'Don't mention it, my dear man. I quite understand. Now if you'd excuse me, I must be on my way. Goodnight.'

As he swept from the room, he gave a villainous smile.

'Cut!' cried Brett Avery. He jumped out of his seat. 'Great work, William! What a performance.'

'I agree,' said Ed Lucas, marching forward, hand outstretched. 'I don't know about anyone else, but you had me convinced that you could be a master thief.'

'Thank you, Mr Lucas. That's quite a compliment coming from you.'

'I never thought I would hear myself say this, but that was the perfect take,' interrupted Brett Avery. 'We'll do one more, just to be sure, but I'm delighted with how that went.'

He pushed his glasses up the bridge of his nose. 'Mr Lucas, sir, I owe you a debt of gratitude. Your presence inspired our actors to raise their game. They performed out of their skins.'

'The pleasure is all mine, Mr Avery. I shall remember this night for the rest of my life.'

Laura and Tariq, who'd emerged from behind the equipment cases and were diligently tidying cables so that they could listen without appearing to listen, were taken aback when the Deputy PM approached them.

'What did you think of the scene?' he asked jovially. 'Did you enjoy it? Was it clever enough for you? Or would you or Matt Walker have figured out the plot and put a stop to it?'

He winked. 'Personally, I think you might.'

17

'**WHAT WAS THAT** all about?' said Tariq as he and Laura walked into the basement room which was a combined hair and make-up studio and storage facility for all cast and crew. 'Why ask a question and then walk away without waiting to hear the answer?'

Laura helped herself to a chocolate biscuit from a plate near the coffee urn.

'Because he enjoys toying with people. It's not personal. According to Matt Walker, that's what politicians do. They're sort of like cats. Occasionally, they'll be nice to other cats, usually because they want something or because the other cat has sharper claws, but most of the time they prefer to play cruel games with creatures much smaller or weaker than they are. It amuses them.'

'What's this about cats and mice?' asked Kay. 'I hope there are no rats in the museum, nibbling at priceless works of art. That would be a catastrophe.'

She picked up a biscuit. 'Did you enjoy the shoot? In my opinion, the second take was better than the first, but Brett disagrees. Ideally, we'd have liked longer to work on the scene, but the museum want us out of here as soon as we're done with the shoot on the main staircase – that's the one where Violet pursues Oscar. Brett is filming it now and I have to join him. You're welcome to come and watch, but it's one of those hurry up and wait scenes. We'll shoot for twenty seconds, then spend twenty minutes setting up again.'

Laura, who had already concluded that the life of an extra was not for her, was unable to conceal her lack of enthusiasm.

Kay smiled. 'I understand completely. Filming days can be long and, for the most part, quite tedious. Don't worry, it'll all be over soon. If you're tired or cold, why not stay here and have a hot chocolate. You'll be quite safe. If the make-up artists don't scare off any would-be assassins . . .'

'We heard that!' called Gloria, a towering blonde woman in red stilettoes.

'See what I mean? If Gloria doesn't frighten any bad people away, the guard will. He's here to keep an eye on the "Benois Madonna" until it's returned to the Leonardo Room shortly.'

It was only then that Laura noticed that beyond the area where the make-up artists and stylists were working, a lone guard watched over the painting. The picture was covered once more with the black cloth.

'Before I go, I have something interesting to tell you,' Kay was saying. 'When Ed Lucas visited the museum earlier today, he noticed that Igor's toes were sticking out of his shoes. He sent one of his lackeys to buy the old boy a pair of top-of-the-range trainers – only black. Presented to the cleaner when we finished shooting after everyone but me had left the Leonardo Room.'

'That's very kind of Ed Lucas,' said Tariq. 'You wouldn't think that a man with that much power would even notice a cleaner.'

'That's what I thought, but Brett told me that he was orphaned when he was a baby and that he apparently comes from very humble beginnings. It's good to know he hasn't forgotten them. Igor was almost beside himself with happiness. He put the shoes on immediately. When I left the gallery, he was cleaning the floor around Ricardo's painting and beaming from ear to ear.'

'Where's Ed Lucas now?' asked Laura.

'Already tucked up in his hotel bed, I expect. He said he was worn out and ready for a long holiday somewhere sunny.'

The new runner – Chad's replacement – came rushing in. 'Kay, Brett needs help with a script change. He says it's urgent.'

Kay picked up her bag. 'Heaven help me. See you shortly, kids.'

'Actually, I think I will come with you, if that's okay,' said Tariq. 'I'm curious to see how they do the scene. Do you mind, Laura?'

Laura took a sip of hot chocolate. 'Not if you don't mind if I stay here and chill. I can talk to Gloria if I'm lonely. Have fun. See you in a bit. Oh, Tariq, can you leave me your phone so I can text my uncle?'

Left to her own devices, Laura ate another biscuit and texted Calvin Redfern to say that the evening had gone off without a hitch and they'd had a great time. *Looking forward to bed tho!* she added. She had just pressed send when the phone started buzzing. It was a call from an unknown number. She didn't answer. If it were Tariq's foster parents, their names would have shown up. It was more likely to be a marketing person in the UK trying to sell double-glazing and if she picked it up Tariq would incur roaming charges.

When her uncle didn't reply, she assumed he was busy working. Ed Lucas was returning to the UK the following day so in all likelihood her uncle was in the midst of top-level security briefings. She wondered if he'd had any problems that evening, or if any Russian mafia had been lurking in the crowd.

It was cold in the basement so she put her coat on over her dress. She was glad that she'd insisted on wearing her boots beneath it instead of the uncomfortable shoes with heels the wardrobe woman had tried to press upon her.

Hopping up, she wandered over to Leonardo's masterpiece. It would be good to see the original close up, without having to peer at it between jostling tourists.

The guard was thrilled to have someone to chat to. He removed the cloth reverently.

'Great piktcha,' he said in heavily accented English. 'You like? Leonardo a very great genius. Thees one of his best walks. *Works.*'

'It's beautiful,' agreed Laura, not altogether sincerely. The painting hadn't grown on her with time. It was a masterful piece of art, but . . .

The thought froze in her brain. Her eye had come to rest on the flower. There was a tiny smear on the blue petal. But no, that couldn't be, because this was the original painting.

She stared at it intently. Her brain must be deceiving her. But the harder she stared, the more obvious the smear became. She couldn't believe that the guard hadn't noticed it. It was like staring at someone with a giant red nose and not mentioning it.

'You like?' he asked again.

'Umm, yes, amazing. Thank you,' Laura said distractedly. As she walked away, leaving the guard frowning behind her, she shoved her hands into the pockets of her coat. She didn't want him to notice them shaking.

'Everything all right, love?' asked Luc, the chief hair stylist, who was packing up his driers and potions. 'You look a bit peaky.'

Laura forced a smile. 'I'm good. It's been a great night, but I think I'm ready for bed.'

'I hear you.'

Laura sat down at the table and took a swallow of her lukewarm hot chocolate. If this painting was the copy, the original must have been the picture used in the filming. Since it hadn't been damaged, it wasn't a big deal, unless . . .

The mug began to shake in her hand. Unless the pictures had been swapped deliberately in order to give someone the opportunity to steal Leonardo's version.

But no, that was ludicrous.

Laura picked up Tariq's phone and checked to see if there was a free Wi-Fi signal. There was, but it was faint. As she waited for a search engine to load, a jumble of images poured into her head.

She remembered how, on her first visit to the Hermitage, Igor, seemingly frail and senile and barely able to carry his mop, had saved the boisterous toddler from falling. His hand had shot out with the speed of a cobra strike.

He arrived on the wind, Vladimir had said, *and he may leave the same way.*

'*Who will come out on top?*' Ed Lucas had asked Tariq. '*The good guys or the bad guys?*'

She thought of the Joker on the hotel bed on the first night – the card she'd dismissed once she'd decided that it was a mere coincidence.

Laura's hands were trembling so much that her fingers were clumsy on the phone's miniature keyboard. Twice, she misspelled the name she was after, hit enter too soon and had to start again. She debated whether or not to call her uncle, but he hadn't replied to her text, which meant he was working. Anyway, it was hard to know what to say. Her uncle's faith in her was touching, but even he would find it hard to credit if she called to say that the Hermitage might have been the target of one of the biggest art heists in history, only she was the only person who'd noticed.

She tried the search engine again, but the page refused to load. The signal in the basement was too weak. There was nothing for it but to take the lift to the first floor and return to the scene of the shoot. That way, she could see for herself if there was anything amiss. If the original was still there – and there was no reason that it shouldn't be – she could simply take Brett or Kay aside and tell them that the painting had been swapped by accident and that they should correct the situation before someone got into trouble.

The hair stylist was making himself a cup of tea when she approached him.

'Luc, if Tariq and Kay come looking for me, would you mind telling them that I'll be back shortly? I'm nipping upstairs to fetch something from the Leonardo da Vinci Room.'

'Sure thing, hon.'

There was no one in the corridor. As the service lift rose with a jerk, Laura's heart slammed painfully against her chest. She checked the phone. Still no signal. No reply from her uncle either.

The lift rocked to a halt and the doors shuddered open. The main lights were off and the corridors and salons were illuminated only by cat's eye lights situated at intervals. It was hard not to feel spooked and Laura had to summon every ounce of courage in order to continue. She considered going back to get Tariq or ask Kay's advice, but that would take five or ten minutes. If someone were intent on stealing the painting, every second counted.

Heart thumping, she set off in the direction of the Leonardo da Vinci Room. The ghosts of the dead Tsars and the eyes in the paintings seemed to follow her. For one horrible moment, she envisioned the film company leaving the Hermitage without her. She'd be trapped in the vast, echoing museum, running from room to room, unable to find a way out.

But again that was ridiculous. She was letting her nerves get the better of her. There were exit signs everywhere and dozens of guards in the Hermitage, and the hotel was only five minutes walk from the front door. Besides, even though it was nearly midnight the sun had only just set.

She took a deep breath and focused. The Leonardo da Vinci Room was in the middle section of the wing overlooking the river. Along the way she surprised a dozing guard. He loomed out of the shadows, frightening her half to death, but didn't challenge her explanation that she'd forgotten something in one of the galleries. Gabbling something in Russian, he let her go.

The moment she was out of view, Laura started to run. It couldn't wait any longer. She had to know if she was right or wrong.

The door of the Leonardo Room was shut. She opened it cautiously and slipped inside. The gallery, illuminated by the street and city lights outside, had been restored to its usual immaculate state. By the look of things, every painting was back where it belonged – except the 'Benois Madonna'.

For a moment, Laura's heart seemed to stop entirely.

The masterpiece was gone. She stared around wildly. Perhaps it had been moved. Perhaps the museum curator had failed to realise that the original was the original and was even now trying to give it to Ricardo, thinking that it was his copy. The artist would explain that it wasn't and all would be well.

She sucked in a breath. There had to be an innocent explanation. If the painting had been stolen, surely the alarm would have gone off? If someone had pulled off a real life art heist in one of the greatest museums on earth, surely somebody, somewhere, would have noticed?

Tariq's phone beeped. The signal was back. She glanced down at it. There was another missed call from the unknown number. She clicked the search button again and the Internet symbol swirled. In answer to her question, the Wikipedia page for Deputy Prime Minister Ed Lucas uploaded. She clicked on the link and his biography unfurled, including the information she was looking for: his full name. Edward Ambrose Lucas.

It didn't really help. Lots of people had names beginning with A.

She continued reading. Under the section entitled Early Life, it detailed how Ed Lucas had been given up for adoption by his mother when he was just six months old and had been brought up by the Lucas family, who changed his first and last names, allowing him to keep only his middle name. They thought it might give him a fresh start. The name on his birth certificate was Anthony Ambrose Allington.

Anthony Ambrose Allington. Straight As.

There was a soft noise behind her. She turned in slow motion, the phone falling from her nerveless fingers. It hit the floor with a clatter.

'Good evening, Laura.'

'It's evening, but I wouldn't describe it as a good one. Hello, Mr A.'

~ 18 ~

ED LUCAS GAVE a mirthless laugh that sent chills through her. 'What I like most about you, Laura Marlin, is that you never disappoint me.'

He glanced into the shadows and Laura saw that he had an accomplice – one of his bodyguards. 'Didn't I tell you, Slither, that if anyone could crack our meticulously planned operation and ruin nearly two years of work, it would be this slip of a girl?'

'Yes, sir, boss, you did.'

'Against the advice of Slither here, and even against my own judgement, we waited for you, Laura Marlin. I was sure you'd come. Do you know that over the past few months, as you and your little friend and your meddling uncle have cost the Straight As tens of millions, the thing that has kept me sane is the notion that the best and most worthy adversary I've ever encountered is an eleven-year-old orphan? There's something almost poetic about it. I can't tell you how much I've looked forward to meeting you.'

Laura was so weak with terror she could barely stand, but she knew that her only hope of survival was to stay cool and play for time in the hope that a guard would burst in and rescue her. 'Well, it isn't mutual,' she snapped.

'Really? You strike me as one of the most honest girls who's ever breathed – as honest as Calvin Redfern, and that's saying something – but I don't believe you. All good detectives are infinitely interested in the workings of the criminal mind. Tell me that you're not at least a little bit curious about how we pulled this off?'

'I do have one question.'

'Fire away. Don't worry, we have two guards in our pay keeping an eye on things. No one will disturb us. Besides, the museum director was quite happy for me to have some private time up here.'

Laura's heart sank at the news that no one would be bursting in, but she did her best not to show it. 'Which came first – were you planning to steal the painting and the movie happened by coincidence, or did you happen to hear that there was a film being made about an art theft?'

'The film. About six months ago, a Hollywood business associate of mine heard about *The Aristocratic Thief* on the grapevine. He mentioned it to me because he found the story amusing and thought that we could do something along the same lines ourselves, only in real life. I suggested we go one step further and buy the film studio, Tiger Pictures. That would allow us to use the film shoot as a way of controlling access to the museum and, crucially, getting the alarm turned off.

'In the end it was easy. We bankrupted Tiger Productions, stepped in as fairy godfathers willing to finance both the company and their new movie, and the rest will soon be history.'

Laura did not bother to hide her disgust. 'I take it that Igor was your inside man.'

'He was. To me, it's important to have a sense of humour in crime, and we have had many laughs about Igor. As you can imagine, Igor is not his real name. In the Straight As, he is known as the Warrior – with good reason. He is a legendary kung fu fighter and a supreme athlete, who also happens to be rather good at acting. In real life, he is not yet thirty so the poor man had to endure an entire year of putting prosthetics – a false nose and wrinkled skin – on his face every single day. He was a good sport about it, figured it was worth it for his five million dollar cut.'

'Did he abseil from the window the way the thief does in the movie?'

'Nothing so dramatic. He simply walked unchallenged out of the gallery with Leonardo's "Benois Madonna" in a poster roll under his coat. We dismantled the frame and he tucked that into a box under his arm, along with a few Egyptian and Oriental antiquities. They'll keep the wolf from the door when we reach our destination.'

As he talked, Laura tried to sneak covert glances around the gallery. There had to be a way to attract attention or escape. She just had to keep him distracted. 'How did you swap the paintings before the shoot?'

'Ah, an unexpected lapse from Britain's youngest detective. You surprise me, Laura Marlin. We knew that once we'd got the paintings side by side, exchanging them in front of all those pampered dolts at the reception would be like taking candy from a baby. It was you I was worried about. I was convinced you'd work it out.'

'I did, but not in time. Let me guess. William Raven is an associate of yours or maybe just a man who owes you a favour. He's also an ex-conjurer. He exchanged the paintings while the waiter created a diversion with the spilled caviar.'

'Correct. He's no art thief, William, but he is a man who owes me a favour or two and he is, as you know, a gifted magician. At first he was reluctant to help and had to be reminded by my best men that he's benefitted quite considerably from my generosity and connections over the years. When we offered the additional carrot of a starring role in the film, he saw reason. When one has an ego the size of William's, fame is always going to be seductive.'

Laura glared at him. 'You're never going to get away with this, you know. Once he finds out who you are, my uncle will hunt you to the ends of the earth.'

Ed Lucas chuckled. 'Oh please. The funniest part of this whole Russia trip has been having Calvin Redfern, my nemesis, in charge of my security. A couple of months back, we planted a seed or two at MI5 about the Russian mafia having plans to assassinate me. It's been hilarious watching your uncle run himself ragged over the past week trying to protect me. As we speak, he is probably hard at work on plotting my safe return to London tomorrow. Another pointless exercise.'

'You're not going back?'

'Right again. Which brings me to the urgent matter of our departure. Slither, how are things looking on our exit route?'

A white light flared and Laura saw that Slither, who had greasily gelled hair and reminded her of Dracula, was holding a mini iPad. It showed the museum CCTV on a series of black and white screens.

'The passage is clear now. We should go, boss.'

'Agreed. A brief word of advice, Laura. A busy mind like yours will be considering all options for escape. Trust me when I say that it's not a good idea. If you scream, or set off an alarm, or look anything other than happy and placid if we have the ill-fortune to pass anyone on the way out, I have men in place poised to eliminate your uncle and your little boyfriend before you have time to blink. Am I making myself clear?'

Ed Lucas' strange electricity enveloped Laura so effectively that she felt powerless to struggle. Every hair on her body stood on end. But she knew his magnetism now for what it was: pure evil. She also knew that her chances of getting away from the Straight As would shrink to zero if they managed to get her out of the Hermitage unseen.

Slither grabbed her arm. 'Come on, little Miss Sunshine.

There's no time to waste. We're running late, thanks to you.'

'Wait!' cried Laura, forgetting to lower her voice.

The Deputy PM gave her a dangerous stare. 'I thought we had an agreement.'

'We did. We do. But where are you taking me? Can't you tell me that?'

He didn't answer, but he did nod to Slither, who let go of her arm. They walked on either side of her and slightly behind her, propelling her forward. Within seconds they were out of the gallery and moving silently down an emergency staircase. At the bottom, a guard saluted and unlocked a door. On the other side was a dark tunnel and the stench of damp and rotting fish.

The bodyguard turned on a torch and gave Laura a shove that almost sent her sprawling.

'Play nice, Slither,' warned Ed Lucas.

Disoriented, Laura tried to work out which way they were going. Were they heading towards Palace Square or the river? Judging by the smell, it was the latter. She didn't have to wait long to find out. As they rounded a bend, a powerful figure in black was removing a heavy iron grille.

'Recognise him?' Ed Lucas asked.

'No, but I'm guessing it's Igor.'

The Warrior's rough hands reached into the darkness and plucked her from the storm drain, as if she weighed less than the painting he carried in the cardboard roll beneath his coat.

They were on a jetty beside the river, screened by the riverbank from the nearby road. The black water gleamed like oil. A speedboat was tied to the dock, but nobody made a move towards it.

Laura felt nauseous with dread. 'Where are we going? Why are you doing this to me? If you let me go, I'll try to persuade my uncle to treat you leniently. I'll say that you can't be totally wicked if you were prepared to release me.'

Ed Lucas sighed. 'Laura, we've already been through this. You're coming with us and that's all there is to it. Don't worry, you'll enjoy it. It'll be a huge adventure and you do love adventures. In moments, we'll be on our way to a friendly South American country. We're retiring, you see. The Straight As, I mean. I have a theory that it's good to quit while you're ahead. Besides, the British Government might take a dim view of tonight's activities.'

There was a humming sound and the water in front of Laura began to churn as if a monster was rising from the deep. The speedboat bounced on the waves. Laura's hands, tucked deep in her pockets, shook uncontrollably.

'As for you, Laura, you needn't be afraid. You're going to have a great life. Four of our men have brought their wives and children with them, so you'll have plenty of friends to play with. We've bought a ranch in the middle of nowhere. You'll be able to ride horses in the sunshine. Isn't that the sort of thing you like to do? And if we ever do decide to come out of retirement, we can run our plans by you and you can tell us if we've made any mistakes. However, that isn't why we're taking you with us.'

Slither laughed unpleasantly. 'No, it isn't. What this is really about is payback against your dear Uncle Calvin. We reckon that snatching his precious niece would cause him prolonged pain, whereas if we shoot him it would be over in seconds.'

Ed Lucas grinned. 'So you see, Laura Marlin, Mr Avery was wrong. While everybody loves a hero at the cinema, in reality the bad guys mostly win.'

'Aren't you forgetting something?' said Laura.

The Deputy Prime Minister frowned. 'What's that?'

'You haven't won yet.'

The black water churned and gurgled and the hum grew louder. The monster surfaced, gradually taking the shape of a submarine. It bumped gently against the jetty. There was a hiss of air and a door popped open.

Ed Lucas gestured gallantly towards the submarine. 'After you, Laura Marlin,' he said pleasantly.

~ 19 ~

SKYE SHREDDED THE final page of the *St Petersburg Times* and sat on his haunches to admire a job well done. It looked as if there'd been a snowstorm on the carpet of the hotel room – snow that featured advertisements and headlines and was also speckled with crumbs from a raid on the mini bar. In addition, there was a lace from Tariq's boots and some soft, but unpleasantly fragrant, powder the husky had found in the bathroom.

It had been fun but now, once again, he was bored.

Footsteps drummed a muffled rhythm in the corridor. Skye rushed to the door, hoping it was Laura, but they continued past without stopping. Whining, he returned to the snowdrift of newsprint and flopped down. It was most unlike his mistress to be gone so long. It made him anxious.

In another minute, he was up again. This time he tried clawing at the balcony doors with his good left paw. Nothing happened at first, but then he felt something give. He clawed harder. There was a click and night air full of exciting smells flooded into the room. Skye stepped out onto the balcony and put his nose through the railings. The street was a long way below and the canal too far to break his fall.

He was about to retreat when he spotted a ledge. If he squeezed through the gap between the wall and the railings, he could probably reach it. His ears pricked. If Laura wouldn't come home to him, he'd go to her. Without so much as a glance at the chaotic room he was leaving behind, he jumped.

Meanwhile, at the Hermitage, the movie and museum directors were having words. Brett Avery was begging for time for just one more take.

'One more measly take. It'll take twenty minutes, tops.'

'That's what you said an hour ago, Mr Avery. My staff are exhausted. Your staff are exhausted. You are not being fair.'

'*I'm* not being fair? It was *your* idiot employee who unplugged our power supply in the middle of the last scene. And before that, another numbskull . . .'

'This could take a while,' Kay whispered to Tariq. 'Why don't you go check on Laura? I'll be down as soon as I can. Believe me, I'm as eager to get to bed as I'm sure you both are. But don't worry, tomorrow we get to have a long lie-in.'

Tariq took the service lift down to the basement room. It was almost empty apart from a couple of make-up artists, two extras, the bored guard still keeping watch beside the painting, and the roadies whose job it was to move the heavy equipment cases.

Tariq felt the first flutter of unease.

'Has anyone seen Laura?'

'Haven't seen her for a while,' said Gloria. 'She was looking at the painting and then she went out. She's probably in the bathroom, hon. Help yourself to a hot chocolate.'

Tariq thanked her and sat down to wait. As the minutes ticked by, he grew increasingly anxious. It was possible that Laura had been offered a lift back to the hotel, but it wasn't remotely probable that she would have accepted it without telling Kay. But maybe she'd decided that she didn't want to see the shoot after all and had gone up the stairs just as he was coming down in the lift. Kay would tell her where he was. Any minute now, she'd walk through the door.

To distract himself, he went over to the corner, where the guard seemed to have momentarily lost interest in protecting Leonardo's painting. His eyes were shut. But as Tariq approached, he sprang to life and lifted the cloth before the boy said anything.

'Great piktcha. Your friend, she like very much.'

Tariq smiled. 'I'm sure she did.'

He studied the picture. Tariq had spent years working his fingers to the bone creating tapestries for slave-masters both in Bangladesh and Cornwall, but it had never lessened his love of art. When he looked at a picture he tried to imagine how the artist had mixed his colours or achieved particular effects.

Now, however, he saw something different. Something that made the blood run cold in his veins. He saw the tiny smear on the blue flower.

His heart started to pound. For a moment he wondered if he'd somehow misunderstood and that the guard was well aware that this was Ricardo's copy and not Leonardo's original, but if that was true he wouldn't be watching over it.

Luc tapped Tariq on the shoulder, almost giving him a heart attack.

'I hear you were looking for Laura. She told me to let you know that she was nipping upstairs to fetch something.'

'Did she say where?'

'No, but I'm sure she won't be long.'

Thanking him and the guard, Tariq smiled and made his way casually across the room and out into the corridor, which was crowded with equipment cases. The basement was chilly but he'd started to sweat. He knew his best friend almost better than he knew himself. If she'd examined the picture and realised it was a fake, she'd have gone directly to the Leonardo Room to check if the original was still there. If it wasn't then it had either been stolen or was about to be.

As he walked along the corridor, trying not to attract

undue attention, he nearly tripped over a flat case marked Joker Productions. He stopped a man wheeling a trolley-load of lighting gear.

'Excuse me, who or what is Joker Productions?'

The roadie snorted. 'You're an extra, aren't you? They're the people who pay your wages, kid.'

Tariq's head swam. 'But I thought . . . I thought the name of the film company was Tiger Pictures.'

'It is. But after Tiger went bankrupt, Joker Productions stepped in with bailout money and agreed to finance this movie. They're silent partners. Their role is to take care of the bills, but they're not supposed to interfere in the making of the film. They only had one condition – that Brett and Kay cast William Raven in the starring role.'

'Any idea why?'

The man glanced over his shoulder and lowered his voice. 'Friend of mine told me that William was – how should I put it? – *obligated* to one of the head honchos at Joker. That's how he got the gig. Anyway, what's it to you? Tiger, Joker, what difference does it make as long as we get paid, right?'

'Right.'

The blood in Tariq's ears was roaring like an approaching tsunami. It was so far-fetched that it had to be a coincidence. Tiger Pictures, a successful film company, goes bankrupt almost overnight. Joker Productions – a company named after the Straight As favourite calling card – steps in to finance *The Aristocratic Thief*, using the film's storyline of an art heist as a smokescreen to set up a real life theft. But what if it wasn't a coincidence? What if it was, in fact, a deadly game? And where was Laura?

But he was jumping the gun. The Leonardo painting might be hanging in its rightful place in the Leonardo Room and Laura might be sitting happily with Kay, waiting for him.

As the lift hoisted him up to the first floor, he thought how strange it was that everything and everyone was continuing as normal when some sixth sense told him his world and theirs was about to explode.

On the first floor, all was silent. Outside the windows it was finally dark and he could see the masts of the tall ship that had been turned into a restaurant on the far side of the river. He moved silently along the dimly lit corridors, hoping to pass by unseen but feeling watched by the statues and paintings that lined the walls.

Ahead of him, a door burst open. Two of Ed Lucas' bodyguards emerged looking worried. Since the Deputy Prime Minister had supposedly left the museum at least an hour earlier, Tariq was surprised to see them. A guard stepped from behind a pillar and went towards them. The three talked briefly and the bodyguards rushed away in a different direction. Tariq used the opportunity to bypass the guard and get to the Leonardo Room via a different door.

The first thing he saw as he entered the gallery was the blank space on the wall where the painting had hung. The second was something glinting on the floor. He hurried over and picked it up. It was the back of his mobile phone. He recognised it because he'd scratched his initials on the side of it in case it was ever stolen at school. There was no sign of the rest of it.

Fear paralysed Tariq. Whoever had taken the painting had taken Laura, he was absolutely certain of it. The thought that it might be the Straight As made him feel sick to his stomach. He loved Laura more than anything on earth. She was his best friend and the best person he'd ever known. If anything were to happen to her . . .

But no, it wouldn't. He wouldn't allow it. He had to get help.

He thought of the scene they'd filmed earlier that evening. In it, the boy had touched a painting in order to set off an alarm. Maybe he should do that. Maybe that would be the quickest way to get help.

He dashed over to a picture, but before he could touch it he was seized by powerful arms. A hand was clapped over his mouth.

'Don't make a sound, Tariq,' whispered Calvin Redfern. 'The last thing we want to do is set off any alarms. Laura's life may depend on it.'

20

TARIQ HAD NEVER been so relieved to see anyone in his life. 'Sir, somebody has kidnapped Laura. I think it's the Straight As. They've taken a Leonardo da Vinci painting too.'

Calvin Redfern looked exhausted. His suit was wrinkled from travelling, his hair was sticking up on end and he'd lost his tie. 'Tariq, listen to me carefully. Ed Lucas is the boss of the Straight As. He's the man I've been hunting for my entire career – the kingpin of their whole evil empire.'

'The Deputy PM of Britain is Mr A? Are you sure? Isn't that the most catastrophic intelligence failure in history?'

'It would be right up there, yes. It might bring down the

347

Government. I only wish I'd figured it out sooner. My first clue was when Laura told me that he asked you who was likely to win – the good guys or the bad guys. It's not the sort of thing a politician would say to a child and it made me suspicious that Mr Lucas was not merely corrupt but was involved in a criminal conspiracy.

'Things started to fall into place. I began to do some investigation into his connections, both here and in Russia. What I found horrified me. Then I thought about the subject of the film – how a masterpiece is stolen by an aristocrat. It struck me as the kind of audacious stunt the Straight A gang loves to pull. When the pieces finally clicked into place, it suddenly occurred to me that you and Laura would be in grave danger at the reception. I jumped in a car and raced straight to Heathrow airport. Along the way, I tried desperately to get a message to one of you, but Laura's phone was switched off, Kay wouldn't return my calls, and you weren't answering.

'I arrived in Moscow about an hour and a half ago, but the traffic getting to the Hermitage was a nightmare. Meantime, I'd told Lucas' bodyguards not to let him out of their sight for a second, although I didn't reveal my suspicion that the Deputy PM was Mr A, which was just as well because one of those agents has vanished. Unless he, too, has been kidnapped, I think we can safely assume that he's a member of the Straight A's.'

'Laura was going to text you,' Tariq said urgently. 'Did she do that?'

'I had a text from her around forty minutes ago, using your phone, to say that the evening had gone without a hitch and she was looking forward to some sleep. That temporarily reassured me. But as I pulled up outside the museum in a taxi, Jason, one of our loyal agents, called to say Ed Lucas had given them the slip.'

The door at the far end of the gallery opened and one of Ed Lucas' former bodyguards came in. Tariq recognised him from the film set. 'Sir, we've had a sighting. We think they're headed for the river.'

'Great.' Calvin Redfern put a hand on the boy's shoulder. 'Tariq, you more than anyone know how violent and deadly the Straight As are. If we are to save Laura, my men and I need to do this alone. The best thing you can do to help is to return to the basement crew room and pretend that nothing is going on. If an alarm goes off and people start panicking, we'll have no chance of catching the Straight As.'

'But can't I come with you? She's my best friend. I can help. I won't be in the way, I promise.'

'Tariq, the only promise I want you to make is that you'll go directly to the basement. I don't want you being taken hostage too. I wish I could take you myself, but every second counts. Here, have my phone. In an emergency, call Jason's number. I've got to run. Remember, not a word to anyone.'

Tariq made his way back through the silent galleries, taking a detour to avoid two whispering guards. He felt utterly miserable. Laura had been snatched by one of the most evil men alive and it was all his fault. If he'd stayed with her, if he hadn't insisted on seeing an extra few minutes of filming, he might have been able to save her. If something had happened to her, he'd never forgive himself.

The lift pinged open on the basement floor. The room where the crew had been was empty except for Gloria and one of the wardrobe girls, who were poring over a catalogue. The guard was slumped beside Ricardo's painting, bleary-eyed with tiredness, oblivious to the fact that the real masterpiece was long gone.

Gloria glanced up. 'Boy, are you in trouble. Have you seen Kay? She's hunting high and low for you and Laura. Thinks you've been kidnapped by the Russian mafia. I told her that she's been working in Hollywood for too long.'

Tariq attempted a smile. 'Sorry, we were held up. I'll try to find Kay now. If I miss her, tell her that we're fine and she shouldn't worry about a thing.'

He went out into the corridor and looked at the fire exit at the far end. The crew had used it as an access door for loading and unloading equipment, which meant that it was likely to open onto the road or the river. If he went outside and kept to the shadows, he might spot something useful.

He'd given Calvin Redfern his word that he'd return to the basement, but he hadn't said anything about staying there.

A minute later, Tariq was standing on the riverbank under a blue-black sky. On the other side of the Neva, platinum light rose like steam from the dark silhouette of the Peter and Paul Fortress.

He tried to put himself in the shoes of the Straight A gang. They were audacious. They prided themselves on being the most elite criminals on earth and loved to shock and awe people with their terrible deeds. He could imagine them delighting in the planning of a robbery where art imitated life. The clue to catching them lay in discovering where life had not imitated art.

Could they, for instance, have abseiled out of the window of the gallery? Possibly, because if anyone challenged them they could explain that they were filming *The Aristocratic Thief*. On the other hand, would they have risked being captured on CCTV or being spotted by a policeman?

Unlikely. That meant they must have used one or two insiders to exchange the paintings and carry the masterpiece out of the museum. Who would they have used? William Raven? No, too self-involved. Ana María Tyler? No, who would risk antagonising her mother. Jeffrey, the horrid production manager? No, too stupid. One of the crew? A member of the museum staff?

Oh, it was hopeless. It could have been anyone or everyone, and all the while the Straight As might be spiriting Laura further and further away.

Tariq was furious with himself. He wished he had a mind like Laura's, which seemed designed to solve mysteries. He was reasonably strong and brave, but not nearly as gifted as his best friend when it came to understanding the psychology of criminals.

Think. He had to think. If they had to get away in a hurry with the painting, which way would they go? Palace Square was too exposed and a car waiting even momentarily on the river road would be noticed. By boat then? But where would they moor it and how would they get to it? A tunnel? A storm drain? Where would those things come out?

He hurried along the riverbank. A thought came to him. Kay had mentioned that a submarine was being used in the shoot the next day. If the Straight As were behind the making of the film, they might have used Ed Lucas' political or mafia connections to organise a real submarine – not some old relic that had been hired purely for the film, but a sophisticated one that could whisk them away to Mexico or wherever criminals went to lie low these days.

Tariq began to run. Kay had said that the submarine was docked on the river outside the Hermitage. If it was still there, he must be very close to it. Now that he knew what he was looking for, he spotted it almost immediately. It was moored in the dense, deep dark beneath the bridge, its panther-like hull almost invisible.

Gradually, his eyes adjusted. Three or four figures were milling around it. As one moved forward, there was a shimmer of light. A fraction of a second later, the blackness obscured it, but it was long enough for Tariq to guess it was Laura's blonde hair. They were putting her on board. If the doors shut, she'd be gone for ever.

He sprinted for the bridge. With any luck, the Straight As would be so focused on their task they wouldn't look up. What he was going to do when he got there, he didn't know. All he cared about was getting to Laura before the submarine vanished below the waters, never to be seen again.

So intent was he on his mission that he never saw a

cloaked figure step from behind a bridge support until he slammed into him. For the second time that night, strong arms gripped him and a salty hand covered his mouth.

'You're too late, Tariq,' said William Raven. 'Regrettably, your courage won't help you this time. You're going to have to let her go.'

Tariq bit his palm so hard that the actor snatched it away with a curse, wiping away blood.

'And what about you? Are you only able to stand up and be a man when the camera is on you, is that it?' Tariq said furiously. 'Are you a coward in real life? Or is it the money? Are they giving you a cut of whatever they make on the painting? It was you who swapped the pictures, wasn't it? You used your conjuring skills.'

The faint glow of a far streetlamp revealed William's features. He looked tortured. 'I might be a coward, but if you knew Ambrose Lucas – that's his real name, you know – you wouldn't blame me. He's a monster. A truly evil man. The stories of what has become of people who've crossed him are legendary. I had no choice. I had to help him or finish up dead or in the Hollywood gutter, my career over.'

'So you did it for the glory,' Tariq said scathingly. 'And now you're going to stand here and allow them to kidnap Laura and do nothing to stop them. I don't care about the stupid painting. It may be a masterpiece but it's nothing compared to Laura's life. Well, I hope you enjoy winning an Oscar and smiling on the red carpet knowing that you've stood by and allowed her to be snatched from the people who love her. You're pathetic. Now will you let go of me? I'm going to try to help her. I have the guts to do it even if you don't.'

He wrenched from William's grasp, but the actor grabbed his arm before he could move away. 'Tariq, don't do it. They'll only kidnap or kill you and what use will you be to Laura then?'

'At least I'll have tried to save her – unlike you. When I stopped the runaway carriage and saved you a trip to the hospital or morgue, you said you owed me. You said you always paid your debts. I guess you lied about that as well.'

The actor's eyes, usually so cold, lit up with rage and emotion. 'No, I didn't. I meant every word and I'll prove it to you now. On one condition.'

'What's that?'

'That you allow me to do it on my own. I'll try to help Laura, but if you get into trouble I won't be able to save you both.'

Tariq stared at him. 'You're serious?'

'Deadly.'

'OK. But hurry.'

William started to move away, then stopped. 'I'm sorry, Tariq. It should never have come to this. For what it's worth, if I could go back in time and do things differently I would.'

Despite the circumstances, Tariq felt compassion for the man. 'Just do what you can to fix things, Mr Raven.'

William ran to the river's concrete edge and looked down. 'Ambrose!' he yelled. 'Ambrose, wait!'

Without waiting for a response, he ran down some narrow steps and jumped onto the wood. All Tariq saw was his black cloak billowing like a parachute, followed by the sound of him crash-landing on a wooden jetty.

Tariq lay flat on the cold concrete so he could see what was happening without being observed. William had fallen hard and appeared to have sprained an ankle. He was attempting to struggle to his knees. In the yellow light of the open submarine door, he looked grey with pain.

'Don't do this, Ambrose. Take your painting and go, but release the girl. Run away to South America or wherever it is you're heading. I wish you all the best. But leave Laura with me. I'll take care of her.'

Ed Lucas had Laura by the arm and was advancing on him with an expression that would have shocked to the core anyone who'd ever voted for him or been charmed by him. He radiated malevolence.

'You pitiful fool,' he said. 'I ought to cut you down right here just for using my name, but I have a better idea. I'll take you with us on our claustrophobic journey to the bottom of the ocean. We can see how you like it down there.'

Without looking round, he said, 'Slither, come and get this ungrateful waste of space.'

'Freeze!' yelled a voice. 'This is Chief Inspector Redfern. Drop your weapons and put your hands in the air.'

There was a loud hiss and the door of the submarine slammed shut, sealing the Deputy Prime Minister outside, along with Slither and Laura. The water boiled as the great vessel began to submerge.

Ed Lucas swore, but he didn't waste time trying to appeal to the other gang members to let him in. Using

Laura as a human shield, he drew a revolver. 'If anyone tries to stop me, I will kill her. And don't make the mistake of thinking I won't do it. She's quite something, your niece, ex-Chief Inspector Redfern. A better detective than you ever were. But she's also trouble with a capital T and enough's enough.'

In one fluid move, he was in the speedboat, pulling Laura after him. She stumbled and fell against the boards, but he hauled her upright so it was impossible to shoot him without hitting her.

'Slither, untie the boat,' ordered Ed Lucas. 'Good, now come and join us. Adios, Detective Inspector Redfern. See you in hell, William.'

The speedboat motor roared to life and it surged away from the dock. Spray cascaded over Calvin Redfern and the two agents as they ran down to the water's edge. On the dock, William Raven was in despair. Up on the bank, Tariq was frantic. 'Laura!' he yelled. 'Laura!'

The speedboat bucked on the waves generated by the submarine. It veered dangerously against the river wall. There was a joyous bark and Skye came flying out of the darkness.

'Skye!' screamed Laura. 'Help me.'

And the husky leapt.

21

LAURA MARLIN LAY on the warm rocks beside the ocean and gazed up at the sky. It was the vivid blue of a brand new car, as if it had been buffed and waxed and finished off with a sprinkling of glitter. It looked inviting, good enough to dive into.

'It's weird, isn't it?' she said.

'What's weird?' asked Tariq. He was stretched out on one side of her, watching the ocean, while Skye, his fur standing up in wet spikes, was on the other. The husky had his eye on the picnic they'd laid out beside the rock pool. There was Cornish cheese, home-baked bread, tapas from the Porthmeor Beach cafe and chocolate brownies baked for them by Rowenna. Naturally, there was also ginger beer.

'It's weird that it's only two weeks since I was almost abducted in a Russian submarine and yet it feels as if it's something that happened to someone else in another lifetime. It feels surreal, like a dream.'

'I know what you mean. It feels like a movie.'

'It's going to be a movie, only we won't be starring in it. Well, Skye will but we won't and boy am I glad about that.'

Tariq propped himself up on one elbow and gave her a sly grin. 'You mean you don't want to be a famous actress any more?'

Laura sat up and opened a bottle of ginger beer. 'Tariq, if I ever express any interest in being any kind of actress ever again, you have my full permission to beat me over the head with a large mallet.'

'Oh, I wouldn't do that. A pillow maybe, but not a mallet. Besides, I think most people agree you make a pretty good detective. I mean, if you can stop Mr A, you could probably stop anyone.'

'I didn't stop Mr A. It was a team effort. Skye stopped him when he jumped in the boat and savaged him and that revolting man, Slither. You stopped him by persuading William Raven to do the decent thing. William's intervention caused Ed Lucas to step out of the submarine and bring me with him, and Uncle Calvin and the agents were brilliant once Mr A and his crime buddy ended up floundering in the river.

'The Russians were fantastic too. Thanks to the lightning reaction of their navy, the submarine was intercepted before it left Russian waters. Mr A and the other Straight A members will be brought back to the UK to stand trial at some point, but not until they've spent a few years reflecting on their actions in some awful Russian prison. They're called Gulags apparently.'

Tariq laughed. 'No wonder Brett and Kay changed their minds and decided to make a documentary about the making of *The Aristocratic Thief* rather than continue with the film itself. Truth is definitely stranger than fiction.'

Laura took a swig of ginger beer and shielded her eyes from the sun. A seal was bobbing in the waves.

'I can't wait to see what they come up with. Kay says that they're going to recreate the submarine escape scene, as well as the part where you stopped the runaway carriage. She emailed earlier to ask if we wanted them to cast actors who look like us, but Uncle Calvin says that for security reasons they can't. So you'll probably end up being a cute blond boy and I'll have flaming red hair or something.'

'Presumably they're going to keep Skye as Skye?'

'They have to, I guess. He's unique. We'll be able to go to see him at the cinema and he'll get lots of glory, but nobody can ever know any of the things that happened to us. For the rest of our lives, we'll have to keep it a secret.'

'That's okay,' Tariq responded. 'I've decided I like being someone hardly anyone ever notices. It makes it easier to observe them. Besides, I know already that I want to work with animals when I grow up. I'd choose being an unknown vet over a famous actor any day of the week.'

'Good choice,' Laura said. 'Our neighbour, Mrs Crabtree, came round this morning and she put it best.

Her theory is that fame is like a bubble. It looks gorgeous on the outside, as if it's been painted with pretty colours, but when you pop it there's nothing there. She said that life, love and friendship are what matters, and that what you do is more important than what you show. My uncle agrees. He says everyone loves a hero.'

She lay back down again and tried not to smile, but every time she remembered leaning over the handcuffed, dripping, woebegone leader of the Straight As, Edward Ambrose Lucas, and telling him, 'This time the good guys won,' she wanted to laugh. Stretching out a hand, she rubbed Skye's downy soft ears.

Tariq poked her in the ribs. 'Laura Marlin, I know that look. What are you planning?'

'I'm thinking,' Laura said, 'that we have the whole summer ahead of us, like a blank page with nothing written on it. I'm thinking that anything might happen – and it probably will.'

Collect all of Lauren St John's books:

The Laura Marlin Mysteries

DEAD MAN'S COVE

~~

KIDNAP IN THE CARIBBEAN

~~

KENTUCKY THRILLER

~~

RENDEZVOUS IN RUSSIA

The White Giraffe Quartet

The White Giraffe

Dolphin Song

The Last Leopard

The Elephant's Tale

The One Dollar Horse Trilogy

THE ONE DOLLAR HORSE

RACE THE WIND

FIRE STORM

the
orion star

★ ★ ★